SECOND CHANCE AT THE SEASIDE

BEACHFRONT BILLIONAIRES
BOOK 1

ELIZABETH MADDREY

JoNa TiMa

Cover design by Lynnette Bonner

Published in the United States of America by Elizabeth Maddrey.
www.ElizabethMaddrey.com

1

BENNETT

I glanced up at the knock on my office door and watched my cousin Travis push it open. "Come on in, Trav."

"Thanks, I will." He flashed a grin as he closed the door behind him and dropped into the chair in front of my desk. "Angela said you were free and that I could come on in."

I frowned slightly. Not because I minded Angela saying that, but because she was also supposed to buzz me and let me know I had a visitor. "What's up?"

"I just got a call from a new client hoping to find either a long-term rental or a small place to buy."

"Given that you're in real estate, this doesn't really feel like news. If you came over every time you had a client, you'd never have time to actually serve those clients." I leaned back in my chair. "So what makes today special, other than getting a new client your first day back after the new year?"

Travis started to sing, "Joshua fit the battle of—"

I held up a hand, cringing. "Please stop. Singing is not your gift and you know that."

"Jericho." Travis finished the line and leaned forward, grinning expectantly.

I waited, but he didn't seem inclined to keep talking. "Did Angela also mention that I do have a client of my own coming in after lunch?"

"No." Travis shook his head and sang again, "Jericho."

"I really don't know what you're getting at, unless you're trying to tell me your new client wants to build some kind of huge wall. By the way, the Island Council will never approve that so you should talk them out of that idea fast." Should I reach out to Dad and let him know that the Council might need a heads up? Loring Island wasn't huge, but we seemed to get more than our share of loonies looking to move here on a permanent basis. Usually the Council was able to get them to reconsider.

Travis laughed and shook his head. "I can't decide if you're really this dense or if you're playing dumb. My client? Is Jericho. Jericho Craig."

I blinked and tried to wrap my mind around what he was saying. "Jericho is moving here?"

"That's what she said when I talked to her."

"Why?" Her family hadn't even vacationed here since the summer after my senior year of high school. And Jericho hadn't bothered to come along that final year anyway. I'd written a few times. But she hadn't replied.

Travis's grin took on a gloating edge. "Apparently, she's our new town librarian."

Mrs. Sanderson had announced her retirement at the September council meeting, and the news had spread through our small community before the minutes were published the next morning. Dad had mentioned that the council was gathering resumes and looking at candidates, but he hadn't said a word about Jericho applying.

Or being hired.

My thoughts might be a jumble, but I wasn't going to let Travis see that. My cousin was known for his propensity to tease relentlessly if he sensed a weak spot. It was, usually, in good fun. But it could get old. Most of us had learned not to give him an opening. "I'm glad they found someone so quickly."

"That's it?" Travis cocked his head to the side.

I shrugged. "Yeah. What were you hoping for?"

"I don't know." He scowled. "More than that reaction, honestly. I thought she was the great love of your life. Didn't you spend that whole summer after high school moping around the beach because she wasn't there?"

"No." I drew the word out. "I spent the summer after high school working at the golf course like I did every summer as soon as I was old enough to be hired."

Travis groaned. "Fine, Mr. Lawyer, go ahead and be that way. I just thought you might be interested to know."

"Sure. I always like knowing when we get a new year-round resident. Do you think Mr. and Mrs. Sanderson will head to the mainland like they keep threatening?"

"Probably. She's already sent me a couple of emails talking about the upgrades they're considering. She wanted to know if I thought they were worthwhile and would increase the property value. Sounds like prepping to sell to me."

I nodded. That made sense. They'd wanted to be closer to their grandchildren for years, but the council kept begging her to delay her retirement until they had a replacement. "Couldn't Jericho just buy their house? It could be the librarian home."

Travis snickered. "That sounds like an assisted living situation."

I laughed. "I didn't mean it that way."

"I know. And it's not a terrible idea, except that it's way more house than she said she wants. And it's in town. She wants to be near the beach."

Of course she did. The problem with that, and Travis knew it so I wasn't going to bother saying it aloud, was that those houses were either short-term rentals or occupied year-round. And people didn't tend to get rid of them. Even if they moved off the island, they just converted their cottages and houses into rentals. Loring Island was a popular vacation destination from mid-March through the end of September. Owning a rental here was never a bad idea. "Are you going to be able to find anything for her?"

"There are a handful that are on the outskirts of town that are available. And maybe one or two coming if the rumors I hear are accurate." Travis shrugged. "I have some short-terms I could consider transitioning into a long-term. I'd have to run the numbers, but it's not outside the realm of possibility."

"You'd do that?"

"Yeah. Why not? If the numbers work, it doesn't matter to me. And honestly, I'd save on cleaning fees and wear and tear."

I nodded slowly. I didn't own the number of rentals that Travis did—well, between Travis and his dad. Uncle Rob had started Island Realty forty years ago. Now it was about the only game on the island—as well as across the bridge in Bennett, the town named after the same ancestor as I was.

"What are you thinking? I know that face." Travis pointed at me. "You're mulling."

"You know me well."

"Of course. I'm your favorite cousin."

I laughed. "Right."

"So? I can probably dig up a penny if you need me to."

"Haven't you heard about inflation? It's at least a quarter these days." I leaned back in my chair, grinning. "But keep your money. I was just thinking, if you didn't want to do that with yours—or if your dad wasn't on board—I'd be okay switching Heron Cottage over."

"Heron? Really?" Travis's eyebrows shot up. "It's not already fully booked for the season?"

"Nope. Apparently, a disgruntled client did some digging, realized it was mine, and review bombed the listing on all the sites. My rating got so low, two of them removed it pending an investigation. I've been meaning to get it all untangled, but I've been busy here." I shrugged. "You know I don't love property management. I only bought it because you said it was a good investment, and I agreed with everyone that we couldn't let that corporation buy it."

"How did I not know that was going on?"

"I only found out two weeks ago. I didn't want to spoil Christmas. And I figured I had time to straighten it out and still get the bookings. You know we always have people calling looking for cancellations." Now, though? Maybe this was God. He had a way of setting up situations that I didn't always understand. Or necessarily appreciate.

"Is there legal recourse?"

I sighed. "There could be, but why? I'm not going to make his bad situation worse just because he took out his frustration on my property. If he'd listened to me, he wouldn't have been disgruntled. I told him from the start that what he wanted was never going to happen. He didn't believe me until the judge banged her gavel. By then, he'd irritated the other party so much, there was no chance for a reasonable compromise between them."

"I couldn't do what you do."

"Right back at you." I grinned. "It's a good thing, though. Anyway, if you think she'd want Heron—and if you can figure out rent that makes sense—let me know. I'll just pull the listing down everywhere and not bother trying to unravel the review mess."

"Can you go ahead and pause whatever listings are still live so you don't get reservations in the mean time? I'm pretty sure she's going to want to take you up on that. When she listed out the things she was looking for, she might as well have been reading the description of that cottage. She's coming out this weekend to look at whatever I can show her, so it wouldn't be off of the rental listings for long if she ends up going a different direction."

I scribbled a note on the yellow legal pad that I always kept out on my desk. "Yeah. I'll do that after my next client. Do you have to tell her I own it?"

Travis's eyebrows lifted. "I guess not. You're running everything through Dad, right?"

"Yeah."

"It should be fine to keep it like that. You know she's going to find out though, right? Everyone knows you bought Heron. Three, maybe four conversations once she starts at the library and she'll know." Travis cleared his throat and lowered his voice, mimicking the deep, slow drawl of Artie Feldman, one of the three octogenarians who took up residence at their table in the diner every weekday morning from opening until noon. "Well, now, I hear y'all're out in Heron Cottage. Good thing that young Bennett did, buying it. Even if he is a lawyer, his folks raised him right."

I couldn't help but laugh. "You've always been able to nail an impression of Artie. But you're not wrong. I'm not asking you to hide the information. Just maybe don't volunteer it?"

"Yeah, okay." Travis stood. "I'll let you get back to all your important lawyer stuff."

"And you can get back to the fascinating and delightful world of real estate."

Travis made finger guns and pointed them at me. "You know it. Later."

"Say hi to Caroline, and let Grady know I bought a new Lego set I'm going to need his help with."

"Another one? You realize the kid could swim in the Lego we have at home, right?"

"Yeah, but I need to make sure I'm still his favorite uncle. Now that he's eight, I figure the rest of the guys are going to start trying to hook him into their hobbies." I grinned at Travis before he left my office, pulling the door closed behind him. Maybe keeping the Lego at my house instead of theirs would make Travis's wife smile. That was something that was becoming rarer and rarer in the last few months.

And Travis wasn't talking about it.

We'd all tried to get him to open up, but he could be a vault when he wanted.

Since I was thinking about it, I took a minute to pray. God knew what was going on. I might want the details—I was a lawyer; details were my bread and butter—but I didn't need them in order to know that God had it under control.

The intercom buzzed.

I pressed the button to answer it. "Yes?"

"Your appointment is here. Should I send her back?"

"Yes, please. Thanks, Angela." I hit the button again to turn the intercom off and stood, moved around my desk and crossed to open the door.

That afternoon passed quickly enough. I'd had only the one in-person client, but several calls and the inevitable paperwork kept me busy until the end of the day. But it was finally here, and I was glad to shut down my computer, lock up my files, and head out.

Angela had left early, so I double-checked that the lights were off throughout the office on my way out.

When I finished locking up, I stood a moment on the side-walk and breathed in. The scent of the sea was always in the air here, and something about it smoothed the rough edges of the day. The sun was low in the sky, burning away the day in orange and gold and pink. It'd be completely set by the time I arrived home, but that was how winter worked. The tradeoff was the long summer evenings when the sun hung in the sky until nearly nine.

I zipped up my coat as the breeze picked up, intensifying the chill, then strode quickly to where I'd parked my motorcycle. I slung my messenger bag diagonally across my chest and pushed the bulk to the back so it wouldn't be in my way as I drove. I reached for my helmet, put it on and threw a leg over the bike to kick the engine on. The muffled roar made me grin. There wasn't a lot of traffic on the island, but I did a quick check before making a tight turn and heading out of the main commercial area and out toward the far side of the island. I drove past the more tightly packed homes in the grid of streets leading to the public beach, past the country club and golf course, toward the lighthouse.

It was a short ride—in nicer weather, I often rode my bicycle—and before I had too much time to get lost in the thrill of the world zipping past, I was slowing, then turning into the short driveway that led to my house. I pulled the motorcycle into its spot in the garage that made up the ground floor and killed the engine.

I patted the hood of my car as I passed it on my way back out to the stairs that took me up to the front door. I unlocked it and went in, pausing to toe off my shoes and hang up my bag as I bumped the door with my hip to close it behind me. I dug my phone and travel mug out of the bag and headed to the kitchen.

With a sigh, I rinsed the mug at the sink and set it on the drying rack for tomorrow. I opened the fridge, but just stared at the contents. For good or for ill, there was nothing keeping me distracted.

Jericho was coming back to Loring Island.

I squeezed my eyes closed and shut the fridge door.

"Why, God?" I rested my forehead on the cool stainless steel. It might have been sixteen years, but the ache in my heart was still there. Oh, sure, it didn't throb like it had. I no longer wondered why people couldn't see my soul bleeding. But it was there.

I dug my phone out of my pocket and tapped the contact for my brother Christian. He was the middle of the three of us, although third in line when we counted our cousins, which we usually did. We'd all grown up in one another's pockets. Our houses had sandwiched Grammie and Gramps's on the north end of the island.

But for some things, a brother trumped cousin.

"I wondered when I'd be hearing from you." Christian answered the phone, as he usually did, without any sort of greeting.

"You heard, I take it?"

He snorted. "Travis didn't get the reaction he was hoping for when he dropped by the office, so he came to the clinic to tell me. Maybe we should round up the guys and play poker this weekend. Apparently, you've been practicing schooling your expressions and could actually win."

"You're a laugh riot, you know that?" I scowled, crossed the small space to my living room, and flopped onto the sofa.

"Middle child. I have to get attention somehow. I chose comedy. Or maybe comedy chose me."

"Right. Don't quit your day job."

Christian chuckled. "I've worked too hard to get here, so no worries on that front. Seriously though, do you need me to come over?"

Need? No. Want? I kept my voice dry. "If it's not interrupting your busy schedule."

"I mean, we could have some kind of emergency that doesn't warrant a trip across the bridge to the hospital. Then I'd have to go. But otherwise? I'd been planning to put on the TV and zone out. You have food?"

"I think I can throw together some burgers." I vaguely remembered seeing ground beef in the fridge.

"Nice. I'll bring a bag of chips."

"I can always count on you." I shook my head. Christian didn't cook. And despite being a nurse, he probably had the worst eating habits of all of us.

"You want me to see what Evan's up to?"

Did I want my youngest brother to come? He'd only been fourteen the summer Jericho broke me, so it was unlikely he remembered much. But he could have interesting insights when he wanted. "Yeah, why not?"

"I'll be sure to pass along your enthusiasm when I call him."

"Whatever. See you twerps soon." I ended the call and tossed my phone on the coffee table. I sat for another couple of minutes before dragging myself off the sofa and back to the kitchen to start prepping the burgers.

I'd just finished washing the burger mixture off my hands when the loud banging on the front door signaled my brothers' arrival. I dried my hands as I crossed the room to let them in.

"We need keys. Both of us." Evan wiggled his thumb between himself and Christian.

"Not happening. Mom has a just-in-case spare and she's promised, on Gramps's life, to never share it with you." I spun the dishtowel between my hands and flicked it at my youngest brother. "I also will point out that I don't have a key to your places."

Christian shrugged. "What you just said? Same goes."

Evan rolled his eyes and kicked off his shoes. "Yeah, whatever. I guess that tracks." He sniffed the air. "Why don't I smell cooking meat?"

"Because it takes you two what, ten minutes to walk over

here? I just finished getting them ready." I glanced at Christian who held up the bag of Doritos. "Are we dumping those in a bowl or eating out of the bag like savages?"

Evan shook his head and took the bag out of Christian's hands. He opened it and reached in. "Savages. Obviously. Unless you invited Mom and Dad."

Christian laughed. "Like he would. Technically, he didn't even invite us. I invited us."

"That's not..." I paused and thought through our phone conversation. "...completely false."

Evan pointed to the kitchen. "Go cook food. I'm hungry."

"Knowing how you eat, I went ahead and used two pounds of beef. Each burger is a half-pound. Think that'll suffice?"

Evan either hadn't caught the sarcasm or he chose to ignore it. "I might need that second one."

I shook my head and stepped out onto the deck that ran across the back of my house and looked out over my stretch of beach to the ocean. There was a full deck like this on both stories of the house, providing a nice cover for the first-floor area. I'd started preheating the grill before I made the burgers, and the app had signaled that it had reached the proper temperature while I was chatting with my brothers. I lifted the lid and carefully transferred the burgers from the plate to the grate. I took a moment to push a temperature gauge into one of the fat patties before lowering the lid.

In the summer, we'd hang out on the deck, but the January wind off the water made that a less appealing prospect. The weatherman said we'd dip into the forties overnight. Given the current feel of things, it might be one of the rare times he was right.

I stepped back into the house and moved to put the plate into the kitchen sink. I glanced toward the living room. Christian and Evan were sprawled on the sofa.

"Make yourselves at home."

"Thanks. We did." Evan grinned over. "Are we eating tonight in honor of the pinnacle of truth and beauty returning to the island to take over the library?"

I raised my eyebrows. I'd written a few sappy poems to Jericho the summer we fell in love like only seventeen-year-olds can. And I might have used the phrase "pinnacle of truth and beauty," but my little brother shouldn't know that.

Christan punched Evan's shoulder.

"Ow." Evan scowled at Christian. "What was that for?"

"Probably because you just let me know that you *were* sneaking into my room and reading my personal things." I crossed my arms and strode to the living room and pinned Evan with a glare. "But I recall you protesting your innocence and me getting in trouble for not following the law of innocent until proven guilty."

"Excuse me, counselor." Christian held up a hand. "What's the statute of limitations on brotherly snooping?"

I shifted to include Christian in my glare. "There isn't one."

He winced. "I was afraid of that."

"Come on. I was like fourteen. You ignored me all summer because of a girl. What was I supposed to do?" Evan held out his hands. "Besides, Mom declared me innocent. Pretty sure that double jeopardy thing applies here. For me at least."

Evan sent Christian a toothy smile. "Not sure about you, since you weren't involved in the initial trial."

"Because then, as now, I deny all involvement in the crime." Christian scooted away from Evan, as if separation on the sofa would prove his innocence.

"In this instance, I renounce the law and invoke older brother vigilante justice. You won't know where. You won't know when. But it's coming for you."

Evan and Christian exchanged a guilty look.

Christian cleared his throat. “So. Jericho returns. How does that make you feel?”

Evan snorted. “Glad you could join us, Dr. Freud.”

“Shut up, loser.” Christian looked at me. “Why is he here?”

I pointed at him. “Your idea.”

“Oh. Right.” Christian sighed. “It’s still a good question.”

I settled in the recliner that sort of faced the sofa but still allowed for good TV viewing. It also happened to be the only other seat in the room. “I don’t honestly know.”

2

JERICHO

As soon as I made it across the bridge, I headed for the marina parking lot and parked into the first space I saw. I took my shaking hands off the wheel and flexed my fingers to alleviate some of the strain from having white-knuckled it for the last two miles. Maybe I should be glad that the bridge connecting Loring Island to the mainland wasn't one that had commercial ocean traffic passing under it, so it wasn't high in addition to long.

Yeah, I couldn't quite get there.

When we'd come out to the island for the summer growing up, Dad never seemed to mind the bridge. Mom would studiously read—although, on road trips she tended to be reading most of the time, so maybe that wasn't bridge related. My sisters always seemed oblivious. I did a lot of praying. With my eyes shut tight.

Somehow, it had seemed like keeping my eyes open while I was driving was a better idea. There'd still been an awful lot of praying—even if most of it was along the lines of, "Oh help me, Jesus." I figured He'd understand.

After five minutes, my hands were finally steady and the

rolling nausea in my stomach had settled into gentle queasiness. Or was it hunger? A glance at the clock on my dashboard suggested the latter might actually be the culprit.

I wasn't supposed to meet the real estate agent until one thirty. That gave me time to have a leisurely lunch. Maybe even drive around the town to reacquaint myself. I'd steer clear of the library for now. I didn't want Mrs. Sanderson to think I was there for her orientation. She'd been precise about that starting on Monday at nine sharp. So that was when I'd show up.

But there was plenty else to see around town.

I glanced around, looking for some kind of sign that would tell me if I could leave my car here, or if I had to be on marina business. I didn't see anything. Would it be better to beg forgiveness?

I wrinkled my nose.

Probably not. Starting off my time as a new resident rather than one of the "summer people" with a parking ticket seemed like a bad idea.

I took one more deep, calming breath, and backed out of the space. My memories of the town held plenty of street parking. So I'd find something closer to a café and park there. Hopefully God's mercies would extend to a space that didn't require parallel parking.

The fifteen mile an hour speed limit was just as I remembered it. Most of the buildings looked familiar as well. But many of the business names had changed. It made sense. It wasn't as if Loring Island was Brigadoon or some enchanted island that only rose out of the mists of time when conditions were right. It had been here the whole time. People lived here. Tourists came and went. And I'd avoided it studiously.

Now, because God had a sense of humor, I was back.

I cut off that train of thought as I spotted two open spots on the curb up ahead. Two meant I could pull in. Score! I turned on my turn signal and did just that. Now all I needed to do was find someplace to eat and pass the time until my appointment.

I shut off the engine and got my cell phone out of my purse. I opened the map app and typed "food near me" in the search bar at the top. The available options populated the map and I zoomed in some to see what options I had to choose from. Hmm. Books & Bites sounded promising. Plus, it was only a couple of blocks up the same road I was on. Less wandering around on foot sounded like a great plan. I needed to get the lay of the land, sure, but I'd just as soon do a drive through or two before committing to going on foot.

I grabbed my purse and glanced around my car. Did I need anything else? My gaze landed on my laptop bag. Should I take it, too? Mom and Dad had always considered Loring the safest place on the planet. Small town charm surrounded by the ocean. But that was years ago. Things had changed—maybe that was different now, too.

Ugh. I really didn't want to lug it around.

Fine. I'd leave it. Lock the car. And hope for the best.

I checked for traffic—there wasn't any—then pushed open my door and got out of the car. I hooked my purse over my head so it draped diagonally across my torso, hit the lock on the door, and closed it. After a moment's look around to get my bearings, I double-checked the map on my phone, and started off in the direction of what I hoped would be a place I frequented a lot.

The nearly constant breeze had more of a bite to it in the winter than the summer. My cheeks stung as I passed the shops. Most had a handful of people in them. Others just one bored-looking employee sitting behind a counter. Loring Island might not be Brigadoon, but it still had that feeling of waiting for something hovering over it. I couldn't help but compare the walk to the strolls with my family in the carefree summers of my childhood. We'd had to dodge other families and groups of teens or college students who giggled and licked ice cream cones as they strolled through town—a break from hours of basking in the sun on the beach. Today, I might have been the only person walking around town.

After crossing a street, I finally saw a sign shaped like an open book swinging from a bar above a door. Around the store name, someone had painted lines that looked like text on the pages of the book and added a cup and saucer, as if whomever had been reading left their snack to step away for a moment but would be back any time.

I couldn't help but smile.

I looked in the windows before grabbing the knob and turning, then pulling the door open and stepping inside. Cheerful bells jingled against the door. I paused and inhaled the heady scent of warm bread, coffee, and sugar that seemed to swirl around the place, all with an undercurrent of the paper-and-ink smell I had always associated with books. Mom had said my habit of sniffing books was bad for me. But if I could spend my days wrapped in that smell? I'd be a happy woman. Why else would I have become a librarian?

The bookshelves were all on the shorter side, giving a clear view of the store and revealing the café tucked in the back corner. I headed in that direction, absently noting a small seating area tucked out of the foot traffic. The proprietor seemed to be happy to have people stay a while. That was good.

The café had four small tables, each with two chairs. Two of the four had occupants engrossed in their phones while they ate.

"Hi. Can I help you?" The woman behind the counter smiled at me as she wiped her hands on a towel, then tossed it over her shoulder.

I studied the chalkboard menu on the wall behind her. It

was simple, which I didn't mind, and it ran to more than pastries, which made me happy. "What's the soup of the day?"

"Did I forget to write that?" The woman turned to look then shook her head. "I knew I forgot something. It's chicken tortellini. Kind of like chicken noodle, but yummier. And no carrots."

"That sounds perfect." I scanned the pastries behind the glass in the counter. "And maybe that half-baguette?"

"Sure. Did you want butter or jam? And I can toast it if you want." The woman was already sliding open the case and reaching for the bread with tongs that had appeared out of nowhere. At least from my perspective.

"Plain is good. I plan to dip it in the soup." I fought a cringe. She didn't need that information. She couldn't possibly care. Or, if she did care, with my luck it would be because she was adamantly opposed to soup dipping.

"Always a good idea." She grinned and set the bread on a plate before turning to the back counter where a large, bright green kettle rested. She took a generously sized bowl from a stack, flipped open the kettle's lid, and ladled soup into the bowl. The rich scent of the broth made my mouth water. "Anything to drink?"

There was an entirely separate chalkboard menu of coffee and hot chocolate options, but I wasn't in the mood for either of those. "Just a soda?"

"Sure. There are bottles in the fridge over there." She set the soup on the plate next to the bread and nodded to the wall.

I hadn't noticed the fridge. I crossed to it and, after a short debate, opened the door and took out a Coke. I held it up for her to see.

"Great." She moved to the register and punched some buttons. "That's seven dollars and fifty-two cents. Cash or card?"

"Oh. You know what? I probably have cash." I unzipped the

top of my purse and pulled out my wallet. There was a single, lonely ten inside. I plucked it out and offered it.

More pokes at the register and she was counting change into my hand. "You're pretty brave to visit the island in the winter. It happens, but it's not like the summer."

I added the change to my wallet and tucked it back into my purse. "It's worse than that. I'm moving here."

The woman's eyebrows lifted. "You must be the new librarian."

"That's me. Jericho Craig." I extended a hand, pleased when she shook it. "Nice to meet you."

"Sara Farrell. Chief cook and bottlewasher, as well as book slinger, here at Books and Bites." She grinned wider—which I hadn't thought possible. "Welcome to Loring Island."

"Thanks." I tucked the soda bottle under my arm and picked up the plate holding my bowl of soup and the baguette, then headed to the table farthest away. It wasn't that I was antisocial. I liked people well enough. You had to as a librarian. It wasn't all hiding in the stacks, surrounded by books—there was a lot of customer service involved in running a library. But right now, I could see the questions starting to form in Sara's expression and I wasn't up for an inquisition. Maybe after I'd been on the island more than a few minutes.

I settled in my seat and, after a quick prayer for the food, dipped my spoon in the aromatic broth. It tasted even better than it smelled. Pleased with my choice, I tucked into the food in earnest. It didn't take long to finish the entire meal. I pushed the dishes away from the edge of the table and cracked the seal of my soda bottle, leaning back before taking a sip.

Much better.

I checked the time on my phone. Still about an hour before I had to meet the real estate guy. Was his name Travis? That sounded right. I stood and collected my dishes, then carried them over to the trash bin that also had a bucket to return plates, bowls, and silverware. I returned to the table and picked up my soda, screwing the lid back on before I wandered out into the bookshelves.

I'd always loved books. I could remember Mom hyping me up for our annual trip to the beach when I was probably six with the words, "Two whole weeks with nothing to do but read!" It wasn't what most kids wanted to spend their time at the ocean doing, but it had worked for me. Every year—except one—I'd read at least ten books while we were here. Often, I finished up the stack I brought along and started through the collection that most of the vacation rentals stocked. They might not have always been age appropriate, but I was happy and not causing trouble, so my parents let it slide.

My little trip down memory lane wanted to veer off into thoughts about the one summer I hadn't read a single complete book. The summer my parents decided to spend a whole month at the beach instead of our usual two weeks. The summer I got to know a boy who shared a name with the town across the bridge because his family had founded it, as well as the island.

The summer I fell in love.

I swallowed and pushed the thoughts firmly back into the locked chest where I'd been successfully keeping them for sixteen years. I was absolutely not delving into that when I was standing in a bookstore, surrounded by opportunities for my imagination to take flight into a story with a guaranteed happy ending.

Because that was just one more reason I became a librarian. I liked knowing that, by and large, my surroundings were filled with stories that ended well. No one could guarantee that for the real world, but fiction? It rarely let you down.

I skimmed the titles in front of me and purposefully moved to another set of shelves. I might be up for a happy ending, but I wasn't ready for one that took place between the covers of a book whose whole purpose was to tell you about people falling in love. I was not in the right headspace for a romance novel. My steps slowed and I looked at the books in front of me and nodded. SciFi. Much better. Maybe a romantic thread here or there, but saving the world or exploring new planets would take up the bulk of the plot. Setting off on a grand adventure sounded like the perfect thing to encourage me on my own journey. Loring Island might not be a different planet, but it was definitely a different world.

It took some time to narrow my choice between four titles. In the end, I couldn't decide between two of them and decided I might as well get both. It wasn't as if there was such a thing as too many books.

Of course, in the back of my head, I heard my mom's voice explaining in clear detail that yes, there was. Particularly when I was paying to have them moved across the state. But I wouldn't have to pay to move *these* books. They were already here. Take that, Mom's voice.

I carried them to the register closer to the door and set them on the counter.

"I'll be right there." Sara's voice came from...somewhere.

I looked around but didn't spot her. She wasn't in the café. I ought to be able to see her if she was in the bookshelves. But where...?

Her head popped out of the wall. Which, obviously wasn't a wall, but a door that I'd missed when I was looking around. That made sense. Everyone needed an office.

"Sorry about that." Sara hurried over to the register and slipped behind the counter.

"Don't worry about it. Everyone deserves a minute to themselves."

"Ha. If only." Sara rolled her eyes. "Paperwork makes the world go round. I try hard to get it done here, though. I don't like taking work home."

I nodded. "I can understand that. I don't like taking the paperwork home, but I'll always take books home."

Sara chuckled. "I don't consider that work."

She reached for the first book and scanned it. "I hope you'll let me know how this is. I've been meaning to read it but, well, I get distracted by other things I keep meaning to read."

I grinned. "Can do. I plan to have a shelf of recommendations at the library with short reviews. I'm hoping to get resident participation."

"Good luck with that." Sara scanned the second book and put it in a bag with the other. "I liked this one a lot. Good twist at the end."

Hm. I wasn't sure I wanted a twisty ending right now. Maybe I'd start with the other one. I desperately wanted to know why she'd wished me luck, too, but I wasn't going to ask. I'd figure it out. Or, hopefully, I wouldn't need to know because the islanders would jump at the chance to share what they were reading with one another. It was a small town. Weren't small towns supposed to thrive on friendliness and shared experiences?

I tapped my credit card on the card reader. It beeped and moments later the receipt printed. Sara tore it off and offered it.

"Thanks for dropping in. I hope I'll see lots of you."

"I'm sure you will. Sometimes you have to own the book, not just check it out." I glanced over my shoulder at the mostly empty shop. "I have a little more time to kill. Is it all right if I sit and read until my appointment?"

"Of course. Make yourself at home."

I bobbed my head in thanks and carried my things over to the comfy looking chairs that were tucked in among the books. I settled in and pulled out the book Sara had said she hadn't read yet. I opened the cover and let myself sink into another world.

"Jericho?"

I glanced up, startled. "Yes?"

"Hi. I'm Travis. You probably don't remember me. I'm Bennett's cousin."

I stood and offered my hand. "And my real estate agent. Am I late?"

"Not at all." He shook my hand. "Sara called to tell me you were here waiting. I was available early, so I headed over this way."

"Oh." I tried to think through the brief exchanges I'd had with Sara. Had I mentioned meeting Travis? Or house hunting? Maybe she assumed. Or had been talking with him. For all I knew, my coming was the talk of the town. "Well, great. I'm ready to get started if you are."

Travis tucked his hands in his pockets. "Sure. Like I told you on the phone, we don't get a lot of turnover, so there aren't hundreds of options. Do you want to go back to the office and look at the listings, or just hop in the car and drive around?"

"I'd rather see things in person when I can."

"Sounds good." He nodded toward the door. "I'm parked reasonably close, if you don't mind a little walk."

"I like to walk." I tucked my book back into the bag with the other and slid my now empty soda bottle in with them. "Lead the way."

Travis held the door open for me and I passed in front of him, then paused, unsure which way to go. He pointed to the right and I fell into step beside him.

"So. What made you want to be a librarian?"

I chuckled. It was probably the number one question people

asked me and I was never sure what they expected to hear. "I love books. Being surrounded by books seemed like a great way to spend my life."

He nodded. "I'll admit to not being a big reader. But I do appreciate that we have a library here on the island. Driving over to Bennett every time I needed to do research for a school project would have been awful. Especially before I could drive myself."

"True. Although, I imagine the school has a library, too."

"Sure. But that's on the mainland as well. Plus, you can't check out reference books. Or has that changed?"

"No. That's pretty constant." I cleared my throat. "I guess I forgot you have to bus across the bridge to school from here."

"Yep. K through twelve are all in Bennett. We don't tend to get tons of young families who want to live here year-round. Those who do are usually the ones who grew up here themselves. Even then, that urge to get out of the small town where you grew up? That seems to hit harder when the small town was also on an island." He shrugged and his steps slowed as we approached a black Jeep. "This is me."

He clicked the key fob and the lights blinked as the car beeped a welcome. He grabbed the passenger door and pulled it open for me.

"Thanks." I climbed in and reached for the door to tug it closed, then felt around for the seatbelt.

Travis rounded the car and got in behind the wheel. "I know you said you want to rent for a year first. Are you open to purchasing at all?"

I bit back a sigh. I'd love nothing more than to buy a house and make it fully and completely my own home. But... "Right now, I only have a one-year contract. The island council wants to make sure I'm a good fit. I got the feeling they're worried that I'm too young and will decide island life isn't for me."

"Ah." Travis nodded. "Well, the three I have to show you are all open to renting, but two of the three would love to sell. So keep that in mind. Maybe we could work out a situation where your first year's rent comes off the sale price if you go ahead and buy when your contract is extended."

I laughed. "When?"

"Power of positive thinking." Travis grinned over at me. "I know a number of people are excited you're here."

I tipped my head to the side and considered his words. I wasn't sure I believed him. And I also wasn't going to ask him to elaborate. He probably just meant that the town was excited to have someone younger coming in. Even if they were wary about my age meaning I couldn't, or wouldn't, stick long term. That must be what he meant...right?

There wasn't time for a lot of conversation before he pulled into the driveway of a large house on the edge of town. It was painted a cheerful, sunny yellow with bright blue trim. The paint looked fresh, as did the plantings in the front flower beds.

Travis cut the engine. "I know this doesn't really meet much of what you asked for, but we don't have a ton of options right now. This is the Sanderson place, and since you're taking over for her at the library, she hoped you'd at least also consider her house."

"Oh." I bit my lip. It really wasn't what I wanted at all. And I was getting the feeling that nothing I wanted was available, given how frequently Travis kept mentioning their low inventory. I really didn't want to live across the bridge and drive over every day. If anything was going to convince me to look for another job? It was probably having to cross the bridge twice a day. "Well. Let's take a look."

After two hours, Travis pulled his Jeep alongside my car. "Take some time to think about it. If you want to see one of them again, just give me a call. I'll keep my ears open for more listings. Do you want me to expand the search into Bennett? You might have more luck finding something on the beach there."

I winced. "I guess. But it would have to be perfect to get me over that bridge twice a day."

Travis laughed, then he sobered. "You're serious?"

"Uh. Yeah. That bridge is a menace."

"Hm."

My hand froze on the handle of the car door. "What does that mean?"

"Just that it might be a challenge to live on Loring if you're not willing to head to Bennett for things. You've seen our supermarket, right?"

Not recently, but I had memories of zipping in during our time here in the summer to restock. Although, now that he pointed it out, I also remembered that we stopped at the store in Bennett before we came over for the big shop. "I'm sure it's fine."

"Okay. Like I said, call me if you want another walk through."

"There's really nothing on the beach? Or at least in an easy walking distance?"

He sighed. "There's one. It's usually short-term, but the owner mentioned he'd potentially be willing to go long-term."

"Why didn't we look at it?" I crossed my arms. The whole reason I looked up an agent was so I didn't have to do a ton of calling around to figure it out on my own.

He shrugged. "We can go now, if you want."

"I do want. I'm sure the Loring Inn is a great place to stay, but I really want to get settled as soon as I can."

"Right. Of course." Travis shifted back into Drive. "Let's go."

This time, the drive was what I'd been hoping for. We left town and hit the big road that went out toward the lighthouse. There were several streets that turned off into the beachfront neighborhoods, and Travis finally flicked on his turn signal so that we could head that way.

I smiled as we got closer and closer to the beach. Why had he shown me any of the other options? I wanted this one. It could be filled with cat hair and mold and I'd still want it.

Finally, he turned into a driveway and parked.

I turned to look behind me, grinning as I saw the public beach just across the street. "Sold."

"You haven't seen inside yet." Travis pushed open his door.

I followed suit. "Don't care. Unless it's falling down around my ears—and maybe even if it is—this is what I want."

I glanced in the semi-enclosed area under the house. It would be fine for parking my car and storing a bicycle. Maybe a kayak. Then I headed up the full flight of stairs to the front door. A copper statue of a heron stood in the corner of the porch, the angle of its beak drawing my eyes to the huge window that looked in to the living area.

Travis unlocked the door and pushed it open, then stepped aside.

I went in, glanced around, then turned back at him and grinned. "Done. Sold. I'll even buy it if the owner doesn't want a long-term rental."

Travis laughed. "Pretty sure it's not for sale, but the rental I can work. You don't want to look around and be sure?"

"I'm sure. But I'll still look around." I crossed the living room, admiring the soft whites and blues that made the outside view of the ocean feel as though it extended right into the house. The kitchen was small, but workable. More importantly, it was open to the living room and, therefore, the ocean. There was a small island that held the stovetop and had an overhang and two chairs where I could eat. A door in the back of the room opened to a small mudroom type space that held a washer and dryer and another door out onto a deck with stairs down to a small fenced yard.

I crossed back through the kitchen and turned down the hall. There was a full bathroom on the right, across from a bedroom that looked like it had a queen bed in it. There was scarcely room for more than the bed, a dresser, and a chair, but hopefully it wasn't the primary bedroom. I kept walking the last few steps and through a doorway into what was obviously the main suite.

The bed looked to be about the same size, but at least it wasn't crowded in with barely enough room to get around either side. It also had a huge window looking out at the ocean. Floor to ceiling drapes hung on either side of the glass. I wandered over to see if they could close and found the cord to do just that. On the opposite side of the room, sharing a wall with the door from the hall, another doorway led to a full bath. No tub in this one, but a large shower that looked like it had all the fancy fixtures I could dream of.

I glanced over and noticed Travis in the doorway. "It's perfect."

"All right. I'll let the owner know and get a contract worked up. You're not even asking what the rent will be." Travis frowned. "You know it's going to be more than any of the places closer to town, right?"

I nodded. "I do. Unless it turns out to be triple, I should be all right."

"Okay." He paused as if he was going to say more, then shook his head slightly. "Let me drop you back at your car. Do you want to leave it furnished?"

I bit my lip and looked around again. That might be easier. I'd never gotten around to investing in furniture that I cared about, so most of what was currently in my moving pod waiting for me to call and get delivered had come from Ikea or something similar. "Can I?"

"I don't know why not. If you needed it out, he'd have to find a place to store it." Travis shrugged. "I'll write it into the contract and see how it goes."

"All right. Thanks." I scooted past him and started toward the front door. "As soon as I can move in, I'm ready."

"I'll let him know."

3

BENNETT

"Aren't you freezing?"

I tore my gaze away from the last dregs of the sunrise over the waves at Travis's voice and shook my head. "Come on in."

"We aren't in." Travis pulled the door from my kitchen closed as he stepped fully out onto my deck. "And you didn't answer my question."

"Not really." I gestured to the hoodie and sweatpants I was wearing. "It's what, fifty? It's not exactly Maine here."

Travis shrugged and plopped into a chair beside me. "You clearly have thicker blood than I do."

"Clearly." I took the final sip of my coffee and stood. "Let's go inside so you don't die. I'd hate for Aunt Deb to lose her eldest to the elements."

"If I wasn't desperate for warmth, and maybe some of that coffee, I'd come up with a scathing retort that you'd never recover from." Travis rubbed his hands together as he stood.

He followed me inside and once again closed the door.

I crossed to the coffee pot, paused to grab another mug out

of the cabinet, and then filled them both up. "What brings you over early on a Saturday?"

"She's in love with Heron Cottage."

I nodded. That wasn't surprising. I'd honestly been expecting Travis to call me last night about it. "I'll need a few days to get the furnishings out."

"She wants it as is."

I paused in the act of dumping sugar into Travis's mug. "Really?"

"Yup." Travis took a seat at the island. "She made those girly noises as she walked through. Apparently, you have style. Who knew?"

I snorted and carried the coffee over to the island. I put Travis's in front of him and sipped mine, leaning one hip against the counter. "That would be my mom. Not me."

"Aunt Linda decorated it?" Travis frowned. "How did I not know that?"

"Dunno. But when I bought it, what, five years ago? Mom was in the process of deciding if she was going to retire from the law firm. But she wanted some kind of hobby to keep her active. So she gave interior decorating a try. I let her have full rein in the cottage. I think it's the only project she did."

"Huh." Travis sipped his coffee and smiled. "If you were a girl, and not my cousin—and if I wasn't already married—I'd marry you for your coffee."

I batted my eyelashes at him. "What makes you think I'd say yes?" Travis punched my arm, causing coffee to slosh over the rim of my mug onto my hand. "Ouch."

"Maybe you are a girl. There's no way that hurt."

"Not your weak punch, loser. The coffee is hot." I wiped the liquid off on my sweats. "Did you bring a lease over for me to look at?"

"I emailed you a draft, but you never did tell me what you wanted to charge, so I couldn't finish it."

"Ah." Right. We'd discussed that briefly. I was supposed to have texted him a number. "Sorry."

Travis shrugged. "She didn't seem to care. Heron's better than any of the other options available right now. Especially when you take what she was hoping for into consideration."

I pulled my phone out of my pocket and opened the calculator app. I punched in my usual summer rate and multiplied it by a hundred, then did the same for my off-season rate. I added them and divided by fifty-two and flipped it around for Travis. "Does that seem reasonable?"

"I'd probably bump it up another three hundred, but yeah. As it is, it's in line with one of the in-town places. She's right on the beach in Heron. That's a premium."

"She's the town librarian." I listened to my dad talk about council meetings enough that I knew they were paying Jericho the bare minimum they could get away with. "It's still more than I'd make when you factor in off-season rentals."

"That's a point." Travis studied my face. "How much of that is the ex-girlfriend discount?"

I sighed. "I wondered how long it'd take for you to bring that up."

He just sat, silently sipping coffee.

I set my mug on the counter and stuffed my hands in my pockets. "I told you before, it was a long time ago. She probably doesn't even remember me. Or if she does, it's in that nostalgia for teenage life way."

"And you? How do you remember her?"

As the only woman I'd ever loved.

But I sure wasn't telling Travis that.

"Same. We had a fun summer. Then she left and I never saw her again." I brushed my hands together. "End of story."

Travis sent me another long look, then shrugged. "All right. Will you at least bump this another hundred?"

"Will it get you to shut up if I do?"

"About the rent? Yes. In general? Come on, you know me better than that. My words and thoughts are gifts I give to those closest to me."

I laughed. "True enough. Fine, bump it a hundred."

"Cool. If you get your laptop out, I could modify the draft I sent you, print it here, and get you to sign it. Then I could send it over to her to look over. Do you have a move-in date in mind?"

"It's just sitting there. It should be clean—maybe a little dusty. Do you think Caroline would have time to zip over and do a quick spit and polish?" Travis's wife didn't work consistently, but she did house cleaning on the side for people she liked or when she wanted a little extra spending cash. Or just a reason to get out of the house and have Travis watch Grady.

"Probably. We don't have anything planned. Why don't you give her a call while I tweak the lease?"

"All right." I crossed to the living room and unplugged my laptop and carried it over to the island. I set it down, flipped up the lid, and logged in. I opened my email program and scrolled to Travis's message and clicked. "You can take it from here, I imagine?"

"If I get confused, I'll let you know." Travis's tone was dry as he took the mouse and slid the computer over so it was in front of him.

I picked up my phone and tapped on Caroline in my contacts.

"Hey, Bennett. What's up?" She sounded wary. And tired.

I frowned. Maybe this was a bad idea. "You can say no if you want."

Caroline's sharp, mirthless laugh made me hold the phone

away from my ear for a second. "You know nothing good starts like that, right? What do you need?"

"I'm renting Heron to the new librarian. I had Harriet and her team through after my last short-term renters left, but that was before Christmas. I wondered if you'd be able to swing by and just do a quick touch up. Dust. Make sure there aren't toilet rings. That kind of thing. I don't imagine it'd take you more than an hour. Maybe two?"

"Yeah, I can do that if Travis can come watch Grady. Trav said something about this lady wanting to move in as soon as she could?"

"That's what he said. She seems excited to get settled." I paused and glanced at my cousin, who was working steadily on my laptop, seemingly oblivious to my conversation. "Tell you what, if you're willing to do it this morning, why don't you just drop Grady here on your way to Heron? He can hang with me and Travis for the day."

"The day?" She perked up. "Not just while I'm cleaning?"

I covered the end of the phone with one hand and lowered it to my side. I kept my voice low. "Trav. Can she take the whole day?"

A flash of annoyed frustration flitted over his face so fast I second-guessed myself about what I'd seen when Travis's usual smile took its place. "Of course. We'll have a man day."

I put the phone back to my ear. "We're on for man day here."

"Excellent. I'll be by in twenty with Grady. Fifteen if I can get him moving faster. Thanks, Bennett."

"You're—" I stopped talking once I realized she'd already ended the call.

"Grady and I will get out of your hair once I'm done with this lease." Travis didn't even look over.

"Nah, man. I like Grady. We're buds. Plus I have that Lego set if nothing else seems interesting. In fact, if you want to go with Caroline and have a date day, I'm fine with that."

Now he did look over, scowling. "She wouldn't appreciate that."

I opened my mouth, then shut it. I should probably say something, but I had no idea what.

Travis went back to the lease.

"Offer stands. Either way, why don't you plan to hang here? It's breezy enough, we could probably get some kites up." Grady loved kites. The kid was a natural with them. "After that, maybe find some new shells for his collection."

Travis leaned back and closed his eyes. "Thanks, man. That sounds perfect. We could go into town for lunch at the diner. I could drop the lease off with Jericho then."

"Sure." I'd have to figure out a way for me and Grady to get out of that portion of the program. Maybe the ruse of needing to make sure we got a good booth? Or I could see if Travis would let me take Grady in on the bike. He was usually up for a ride on the motorcycle—what kid wasn't?

All I really knew was that I wasn't ready to see Jericho yet. Living in a small town on an island, it was inevitable that we'd bump into each other, but the longer I could put that off, the better. No sense in rushing into an awkward interaction.

"I'm almost ready to print. It's all hooked up?" Travis glanced over at me to confirm.

"Yeah." I pointed to where a printer sat in the corner of the living room. My house had three bedrooms, but I'd never bothered converting one into an office. When I brought work home, I did it on the couch. Or at the island, like Travis was right now. I had an office in town. Having one at home seemed like a gateway drug to workaholism. "I guess I'm going to go throw on actual clothes if we're going into town."

Travis smirked. "Can't have the town attorney showing up at the diner in sweats, can we?"

I scowled. I'd been into town—and the diner—in sweats plenty of times. And Travis knew it. "What's going on with you?"

Travis ran a hand through his hair. "Sorry. I'm sorry. That was uncalled for. Just...had a big fight with Caroline first thing this morning and...you don't want to hear about this."

I pulled out the chair next to Travis and sat. "Yeah, actually, I do. Spill it."

He turned back to the laptop and, after a moment, the printer whirred quietly to life. He pushed the machine away and sighed. "I don't know what's going on. She's unhappy being at home all day. So I said great, you could get a job if you wanted. Or go back to school. Or start a club. Honestly, I don't care. You know we don't need the money, so she could do whatever she wanted to fill her time. When we got married and Grady came along, what she said she wanted was to be home with him. So she is."

I nodded, although I'd overheard Mom and my aunt talking in those early days and it hadn't sounded as if Caroline actually was home very much. She was big on dropping Grady off with Aunt Deb and disappearing for hours at a time. Aunt Deb never minded, but it had worried her. Apparently, she hadn't shared those worries with Travis. Did he know about all the drop offs?

Travis shrugged. "Now that Grady is in school, there's no reason she can't find something to do that makes her happy. She doesn't want to cook and clean, since she wouldn't get paid for it, so we have people who do it for us. But she's also not content to sit on her couch and scroll on her phone."

"Well, I mean, who would be?"

He gave a short laugh. "There's that. I don't know man, she complains and I try to empathize and suggest ideas of how to fix the problem and then she gets mad and says I don't understand. I really don't know what to do. When I was putting him to bed last night, Grady asked me why his mom didn't like him."

"Whoa."

"Yeah." Everything about Travis seemed to sag. "I tried to assure him that of course she did, but how bad does it have to be when I'm not around for him to ask me that?"

"She wouldn't hurt him, would she?"

He took a moment, then shook his head. "I don't think so. I don't think she pays enough attention to him for that."

I winced. In some ways, that seemed worse. Neglect caused trauma the same way physical abuse did. I patted his shoulder. "I'll pray for you guys. Maybe...do you think she'd go talk to the pastor with you?"

Travis snorted. "Please. I have a hard enough time convincing her to come to church with us every Sunday."

"I thought she liked church?"

"I thought that too, until about six months ago when she started pressuring me to start looking at churches on the mainland. Not even the ones in Bennett—it's still too small-town, according to her."

"You're supposed to drive more than an hour each way for a bigger church every Sunday?"

"I guess." Travis pushed away from the island and stood, then strode to the printer and pulled off the pages of the lease. "I shut it down. And I keep shutting it down. But she twists it all into this whole thing about trapping her on an island, surrounded by my family."

"Trapping *her*? That's rich."

Travis glared. "Come on, man."

I held up my hands. "Sorry. I'm sorry. That was uncalled for."

He shoved the papers in front of me and pointed to several

lines. "You need to sign here and here, and initial here, here, and here."

I patted my chest, looking for the pen that generally lived in a pocket when I was dressed for work, then stood and crossed the kitchen to the corner of the counter where I kept a notepad and the decoupaged juice can turned pen holder. It had been a gift from Grady. He'd made it in kindergarten and every time he visited, he searched it out, beaming when he saw it was in its proper spot.

I was never getting rid of it.

I grabbed a pen and went back to my seat beside Travis. "I really am sorry."

"It's fine." He sighed. "Maybe you're right. Maybe you always have been. But even if Grady's the result of a baby trap, I wouldn't change it for the world."

I glanced up from the lease and met his gaze. "None of us would. He's the best."

A ghost of a smile flickered on Travis's face.

I made short work of reading, signing, and initialing the lease, then slid it back to my cousin. "Done and done. Thanks for handling this."

"Any time. Seriously. Because if you even consider using a different property manager or real estate agent? I'll tell your parents who really broke the stained-glass window in the church."

"Dude. Really?"

Travis shrugged. "Do the crime, do the time."

"Pretty sure there's a statute of limitations that's long expired here."

"Please. You think your parents—or mine—believe in those when it comes to their kids?"

I winced. Probably not. "I'm going to go throw on jeans."

It didn't take me long to go back to my bedroom and change

my sweats for jeans. I even paused to flip the covers of my bed up. That was as close to "making the bed" as I got these days. Mom would roll her eyes, but it was at least better than leaving everything in a tangle. Wasn't it?

I was on my way down the hall when the doorbell rang. I got to the living area as Travis pulled open the door and Grady barreled in, followed by Squirtle, their eight-month-old chocolate lab who had wrenched his leash free from Caroline's hand and was leaping and barking with joy at the chaos.

I grinned.

Grady spotted me and flew across the room, ramming into me full speed before throwing his arms around me. "Uncle Bennett! Mom said we could bring Squirtle and I have three new Transformers in my backpack and maybe we can play Minecraft this afternoon because I get to spend the whole day with you and Dad, isn't that great?"

I squeezed him. Hard. "It *is* great."

Caroline dropped Grady's Star Wars backpack on the floor by my couch. She didn't look like someone who was planning on cleaning a beach house. Diamonds glittered at her ears and on her ring finger. The delicate, pale pink sweater was probably cashmere and I was reasonably certain her cream slacks were wool. And who cleaned a house in heels?

My eyebrows lifted.

Caroline must have caught my expression because she rolled her eyes. "I called Shalene. She's always looking for extra cash. I paid her, so you can settle up with Travis."

"I thought—" Travis bit off whatever he'd been about to say.

"What's the difference?" Caroline propped her hands on her hips and glared at her husband. "Bennett gets his house cleaned and I get my day off. Shalene gets money. Everyone wins."

"Of course." Travis's smile was visibly stiff and obviously forced. If Caroline noticed, she didn't comment on it. Given her mood, I would've put money on her saying something if she had. "Have fun. I thought we could grill those New York strips for dinner and do up some fancy potatoes."

"Fancy potatoes!" Grady yelled exuberantly and began to wave his hands above his head as he chanted, "Fancy fancy plancy" before it devolved into the repetition of sounds that he found fun.

Caroline shot a look of disgust toward her son. Thankfully, he didn't seem to notice. She turned her gaze back to Travis. "I'm not sure when I'll be back. Don't wait to eat."

"Of course."

I didn't know if Travis realized he was repeating himself. I also couldn't tell if Caroline recognized the hurt her words caused her husband and how he deflated. It wasn't obvious, but I'd known him my whole life. Shouldn't she know him well enough to see it, too?

Maybe she just didn't care.

The thought was sobering, and my heart bled a little for my cousin.

I deliberately turned away and hooked my arm around Grady's shoulders. "What do you say we go out to the beach and fly kites?"

"Shells!" Grady scrambled toward the kitchen door.

"Hold it." Travis's voice brought Grady to a skidding stop. "Say goodbye to Mom."

"Bye!" Grady didn't even turn.

I snagged Squirtle's leash and unwound it from between the puppy's legs. "We'll be on the beach, Trav. Thanks for bringing them by on your way to town, Caroline."

I reached around Grady to pull open the door and the three of us poured out onto the deck. Grady ran down the stairs. Squirtle and I followed a little more sedately, though the puppy tugged at his leash trying to keep up with his boy. By the time we reached the ground, Grady had already flung open the storage closet in the garage and selected his favorite kite from the collection I kept there. Grady's near-constant sing-song of nonsense sounds continued as he raced toward the beach, kite in hand.

I briefly considered a kite of my own, but between helping Grady and keeping Squirtle from tripping us all up? Probably not the best idea.

4

JERICHO

I shuffled down to the breakfast room at five minutes to ten. The innkeeper had been emphatic that breakfast was over at ten when I checked in last night. I hadn't had the heart to tell her I wasn't big on eating in the morning. There was a coffee maker in my room—a nice perk I hadn't expected—and I'd spent the morning in bed instead of rushing down here for that oh-so-needed jolt of caffeine.

"Good morning." The innkeeper's smile seemed strained. "I was just going to start cleaning up."

"Sorry." I fought the urge to check my phone for the time. I was reasonably certain I was still before ten, but maybe she wasn't a stickler for punctuality. Or, maybe she figured if I hadn't been down yet, I wasn't coming. I scanned the offerings quickly. "I'll just grab a muffin and more coffee and get out of your hair."

"It's no problem. Did you sleep well?"

"I did. Thank you. You have very comfortable rooms." I hadn't been sure what to expect. My family had always booked cottages when we came. Mom and Dad liked to cook—and I imagine when all was said and done, it saved them money to do it that way, too. Plus, we weren't all crammed into one room when it was bedtime.

"I'm glad. Do you have plans for today? We don't have much going on in town during the winter, but some of the shops are open."

I picked up a plate, then slid down the serving table to the small stack of muffins and plucked the top one off the pile. "I'm hoping I'll get a lease for the house I'm renting and can start moving in."

She nodded. "Just let me know if you decide to check out early. We don't have penalties in the off-season."

"I appreciate that." I moved to the gleaming silver urn and held a mug under the spigot before pushing down on the tap to start the flow of coffee. "I was honestly surprised you were open at all."

She chuckled. "Well, now. We do get visitors to the science station up at the north end of the island. Dr. Loring always keeps a trickle of folks coming through. Sometimes she'll take on assistants for college credit, and most of the time we work out a long-term rate that benefits everyone."

I nodded. "I'd forgotten about the science station."

"Most do. I think Dr. Loring prefers it that way, honestly. She has the elementary school kids out in the spring for field trips and does programs for homeschoolers occasionally, but she likes her quiet. Now that her nephew Evan is helping her, she doesn't seem to need as many longer term helpers. Although, I hear rumblings that he's going to start a lot of programs when he takes over completely." She shrugged. "I guess we'll see. None of us are going to mind extra folks coming out in low season, so long as they stay on the island and don't try to commute from Bennett every day."

"Will they be able to find housing? They won't all want to

stay here, I imagine." I sipped the coffee before taking a seat at the nearest table.

She waved the concern away. "Lots of the summer rentals stay empty all winter. I don't think the owners are going to mind getting them cleaned and earning a little extra with a few weeks of extended use. And if they do, well, I've got twelve rooms here. We can make it work."

I peeled the wrapper away from the muffin and twisted off the top, then I took a bite. Juicy blueberries exploded on my tongue. I chewed and chased the bite with a sip of coffee. "This is delicious."

"Glad you like it. I like to freeze fresh berries in the summer and save them for the winter months. I know I could buy them frozen, but they just aren't the same to me."

"I'm going to have to agree." I smiled and took another bite.

"I'll leave you to your breakfast. If you don't mind, would you just pop your plate and mug on the counter in the kitchen when you're done?"

"Sure thing." I leaned back in my chair and reached for the coffee again. The innkeeper hefted a tray in each hand from the buffet and used her hip to push open the swinging door that bore a sign declaring "KITCHEN" on it.

She was in and out a few more times while I sat in the dining room. I'd snuck over to top off my coffee before she cleared the urn away. I wasn't in a hurry this morning. Mrs. Sanderson would probably have a kitten if I wandered into the library against her direct orders. I'd yet to see anything from Travis about my lease. And I didn't really want to go wander around town. It might be sunny out there, but the sky had that clear blue that told me it was going to be crisp. And I could already hear the wind gusting between the buildings.

My phone chimed with a text. I tapped to read it and grinned.

Travis wanted to bring the lease by on his way to lunch with his son, did I mind? No. I did not mind in the slightest. I tapped back a quick affirmative and glanced down at my clothing. I'd basically thrown a sweatshirt on over my pajama top. And while I might not mind heading down to the breakfast room of an inn in sweats, it wasn't really the overall look I was going for generally.

I drained the rest of my coffee, then stood. I grabbed the plate and crossed the room to the kitchen door. I gave a brisk knock and when I didn't hear anything, pushed cautiously. There were still dishes lined up by the sink, but the innkeeper had obviously been called away in the middle of handling them. I took my plate and mug over to the counter and set them down, then hurried back out and headed up the gorgeous old staircase at the front of the building to my room.

It didn't take long to swap out the sweats for jeans and a thick sweater. I considered my hair and opted for a headband. The problem with short hair was that I couldn't throw it into a bun or ponytail and call it a day. Of course, my propensity to do just that was what had convinced me to cut it all off in the first place. But short hair had a mind of its own. At least mine did.

I gave it one more pass with my hairbrush before sliding a headband in place. I wrinkled my nose at my reflection. It wasn't perfect, but I wasn't trying to impress Travis. I just wanted to look presentable. So. Mission accomplished. Out of habit more than anything, I pushed the French hooks of my brightly colored book-shaped earrings through my ears and gave a nod.

Good enough.

I took a few minutes to tidy up the room. I hadn't unpacked last night. I'd been hoping that the cottage would be available and had the vague notion that acting like the inn was temporary would help it along. I didn't go in for the whole manifestation thing—it really wasn't in line with loving Jesus—but I was working on having a more positive outlook.

I zipped my bag shut and set it near the door. I wouldn't move anything out of the hotel room on the off-chance Travis had a lease but said I couldn't move in right away. Ugh. Could he do that? Of course he could. Hopefully he wouldn't.

I stuck my phone in the back pocket of my jeans, grabbed the room key and pushed it into a front pocket, then I headed back out into the hall, pausing to check that the door had latched behind me.

I spotted Travis when I got half-way down the stairs. "Sorry. Did I keep you waiting?"

"Nope. Just got here. I was about to text and see where you wanted to meet."

I pointed to the left. "There's a nice sitting room right there. Does that work?"

"Of course." Travis headed into the inn's casual lounge, and I hurried down the remainder of the steps and joined him.

I sat in one of the armchairs and had to fight the urge to bounce. "I really appreciate you getting the landlord to agree to a year-long lease."

"It wasn't hard. Hopefully, once you look this over, you'll be okay with the rent." Travis sat, opened his backpack, and drew out a manila folder. He offered it.

I took it and flipped it open, then frowned slightly. "I thought you said you were eating with your son. You didn't leave him in the car alone, did you?"

Travis laughed. "No. Although, he's eight so I could. And have. He's on his way to the diner with his uncle. They're making sure we get a booth."

I nodded. That made sense. "I imagine it gets busy on weekends."

"Off and on season." Travis confirmed.

I turned my attention to the lease and began to read. I fought a wince when I hit the rent, but it wasn't unexpected. I'd insisted on beachfront, and I'd known when I did that, I'd have to pay for it. If it was even available. This was doable on the salary the island had offered me, but only just.

I flipped to the next page and paused when I saw the signature and the typed name underneath.

Bennett Thomas.

I bit my lip and looked up at Travis. "He knows it's me?"

"He does."

I wasn't sure how to feel about the fact that Travis didn't even pretend to need an explanation or clarification. Or about how nonchalant his tone had been. I'd spent six weeks agonizing over the decision to even apply for the librarian job on Loring Island because of Bennett. But God had been busy closing doors until this was the only one that was open to me. Even with that, I'd done a lot of praying for Him to slam this one shut, too, and find me a different beach town to work in.

No such luck.

I cleared my throat. "Do you have a pen?"

"Of course." Travis tugged a pen from the placket of his polo and offered it.

I took it and signed the lease above my typed name before I could talk myself out of it. The important thing was beachfront living. Not who owned the house. It wasn't like Bennett would be handling any landlord interactions himself. He kept busy with his family's law firm. And his big, tight-knit family.

Not that I'd been keeping tabs on him.

I just happened to look him up now and then. Curiosity wasn't illegal.

"Done." I flipped the folder closed and offered it back to Travis.

"There's a copy in there for you." Travis took the folder, opened it, and flipped to the back before pulling out the extra pages I'd missed. He offered them to me.

My face heated as I took them. Of course there was a copy for me. I'd seen the papers, just hadn't keyed in that it was a repeat. I flipped to the end and saw Bennett's signature. "Great. Um. When can I move in? Did I miss that?"

"He has a cleaner in there today, so tomorrow." Travis paused and held up a finger. He stood and dug into his pocket, drawing out a ring with two keys on it. "These are yours."

I took the keys and closed my fist around them. "I couldn't stay there tonight?"

Travis's eyebrows raised. "I'm not sure how long the cleaner will be there. She's just one woman and, between you and me, she's not the most focused person."

Okay. The cottage wasn't that big though. "How long can it take? I didn't see that there was all that much to be done."

"Tell you what, I'm guessing Shalene will let Bennett know when she's finished. If it's not super late, I'll let you know. But it might be too late to avoid paying for the night here."

"That's fine. I'd be paying to stay here either way, right?" I shrugged. I had savings to cover the gap between when my paycheck from the library picked up and moving onto the island. It wasn't a huge pile of money, but it could cover two nights at the inn. Especially since the innkeeper had been generous with the off-season discount.

"That's true. I'll keep you posted." He stood and extended a hand. "Welcome to Loring Island."

I stood and shook his hand. "Thanks."

Travis headed toward the front door of the inn, pausing to chat briefly with the innkeeper before tossing a wave in my direction.

"Moving out?" The innkeeper smiled.

"Not sure. I guess we'll see how long it takes the cleaning lady to finish."

"Travis said Bennett got Shalene out there." She shook her

head. "That girl's the definition of flighty, but it ought to just be a quick buff up, so she oughta be able to get it done. You end up not spending the night, I won't charge you."

"Oh. You don't have to do that. I don't want you to lose out because I'm impatient."

She waved my words away. "It's nothing. And maybe you look the other way a couple times if I end up with an overdue fine. It'll all come even in the end."

I chuckled. "I feel like I'm getting the better end of that deal, but I appreciate it."

"You don't know how bad I am about returning my books." She grinned. "Now. You should get outside and get some fresh air. Take a walk around. I can get you some dried corn and you can head over to the marina and feed the ducks."

"Don't you feed ducks bread?" I frowned. That had certainly been what we always did.

"Apparently that's bad for them. I don't know if it's true, but I had a guest from the science center give me a lecture about it, so I've started buying dried corn. Says on the bag it's for squirrels and such, but it's corn. I don't see why a duck wouldn't be able to eat it, too."

I wasn't sure about feeding ducks, and I sure wasn't keen on being out in the winter wind, but I also didn't want to be rude. She was trying to be helpful, and I was new on the island. I wanted to make a good impression. Make friends. The year-round population was a tight-knit group—I'd noticed that when we'd visited in the summer. I was one of them now. I wanted them to see me that way.

"All right. That sounds like a plan." I wasn't going to lie and say fun, but that's probably what she expected. "Thanks."

"You're welcome. I'll put a little bag of the corn on the table by the front door. You run on upstairs and get your windbreaker.

You probably don't have a resistance to the winter weather here yet."

I nodded. I needed to take my new lease upstairs anyway. I didn't want to carry it around with me. I should probably change to sneakers, too, not the suede slippers I was wearing for schlepping around the inn.

With a wave, I headed upstairs to my room.

Inside, I lingered over changing my shoes and digging my jacket out of my suitcase. Why had I packed it? Maybe it had been some kind of latent wish for spring. Ha. That was a pipe dream for sure. By the time we hit spring on the island, I would hopefully be well-settled.

Finally, unable to find any other ways to dawdle longer than the half hour I'd managed, I headed back downstairs. The innkeeper had indeed left a brown paper sack on the table by the door. A quick peek inside confirmed cracked corn like my dad had loved putting out for squirrels. Could ducks really eat that?

I was tempted to do a quick internet search, but what was I going to do if it said no? I wasn't going to follow in the footsteps of whatever scientist had given her what for. Maybe said scientist had gone as far as to recommend the corn anyway.

With a sigh, I snagged the sack. I pulled open the inn's front door and stepped out onto the porch. I regretted it almost immediately as the wind gusted in my face, seeming to laugh at my pathetic attempt at a jacket.

I could do this. I lived here now. I was a local who would spend winters on the island.

My little lecture didn't actually help, but I forced myself to walk to the steps and then down off the porch. Once I got going, it was easier to keep on, and the sun definitely offset the chill. The wind wasn't constant. Or the buildings blocked it.

Maybe both.

Regardless, by the time I'd walked the three blocks to the marina, I was contemplating unzipping my jacket.

The marina was busy. Saturday sailors didn't stop during winter here, apparently. I hadn't expected that. Fish probably didn't care about the season above the water. If this was where they lived, then they'd be out there swimming. And if they were out there swimming, those who were so inclined were probably going to be on a boat trying to catch them.

Since I enjoyed partaking in the results of their efforts, I couldn't say it was dumb, but I was also glad that I wasn't the one who had to catch the food I wanted to eat.

I scanned the parking lot and the grassy areas closer to the docks and spotted a little...pod? Gaggle? They weren't geese, so probably not gaggle. What were groups of ducks called? Flocks? Probably flocks. I winced inwardly at my initial thought of pod, but promptly blamed it on my prior musing about fish. Although, that would be school, wouldn't it?

I sighed.

None of that mattered.

I crossed closer and studied the birds. They seemed content as they picked at the dead grass and waddled here and there before slipping down into the water and paddling around. I didn't know what kind of duck they were. I could spot a mallard, and maybe that's what these were, but they didn't look exactly like I expected.

Then again, how long had it been since I'd paid attention to a duck?

I edged closer. Most of the birds were in the water now, probably scared of me. Did they think I was going to fight them for whatever they were getting out of the grass?

I reached into the paper bag and got a small handful of the corn, then tossed it out into the water.

The ducks went insane.

In spite of myself, I started to laugh as I watched them swarm and dive for the kernels. I dug into the bag for more and tossed it in a different direction, hoping to spread them out some. I had plenty, they didn't need to fight. It helped a little, but some of them seemed to thrive on trying to get the same kernel another one was going after.

How long was I supposed to do this?

I peeked in the bag. There was a lot of corn still there; was I really meant to feed them all of it? That seemed excessive. Standing out here in the chilly wind also seemed excessive.

I tossed out another handful and glanced at my watch. I'd left the inn thirty minutes ago. It'd take a little bit to walk back. I didn't even have to go back to the inn. I could go to the bookstore and get a hot drink. Sit there and spend some time reading. Why hadn't I thought of that before?

I hunched my shoulders. The innkeeper had told me to go feed the ducks, and because I was used to doing as I was told, feed the ducks I did. But I was going to change that. I certainly hadn't been told to take a librarian job on Loring Island. In fact, I'd been told—rather forcefully—to stay put and work through whatever problems I was having.

Well, I wasn't doing that. And I didn't have to stay here and feed these dumb ducks in the cold any more than I wanted to. I tossed out one final handful of corn, then rolled up the bag and stuffed it into the pocket of my coat before turning around and starting back into town.

All I had to do now was remember where the bookstore was.

5

BENNETT

I walked beside Grady, ready to grab Squirtle's leash if he pulled too hard, but so far, my nephew—Technically, I was pretty sure he was a second cousin, but who was going to say that all the time? Not me.—was handling things fine. Concentrating on that situation was better than listening to Travis yammer on about Jericho. She'd signed the lease and my banking app had notified me that I had a move-in deposit working its way into my bank account. That was all I needed to know.

"Are you even listening?" Travis poked my arm.

"Ow. Are you ten?" I rubbed where he'd jabbed me and scowled.

"Deflection. So no. You're not listening."

I sighed. "Fine. Not really. I don't care. Okay? She's renting a house I happen to own, and that's the only interactions we need to have."

Travis shook his head. "You're going to stop going to the library?"

I shrugged. "I've been meaning to get one of those e-readers.

Maybe this will finally get me to dive into that newfangled technology."

"Oh yes. Super new. They've only been around, what, twenty years at least?"

"Just about enough time for them to work out the kinks." My footsteps slowed as we neared the little bookstore. "Or, I could go back to buying everything I want to read here. I'm sure Sara would appreciate the business and it's not like I don't have the money."

Travis paused in front of the window. "Who wants a hot chocolate?"

Grady spun around, tangling himself in Squirtle's leash. "Me! Me! Me!"

Squirtle joined in with a chorus of excited barks.

I laughed as Travis tried to calm the dog and untangle his son while being jumped all over by an overexcited puppy.

"I'm good. Really. No need to help at all." Travis shot a glare at me over his shoulder as he squatted to help Grady step out of a loop of leash. Squirtle took the opportunity to bathe Travis's face with slobbery kisses and his attempts to get away sent Travis to the pavement with an "oof!"

Still laughing, I grabbed Squirtle's collar. "Drop the leash, Grady. I've got him."

But Grady was too wound up now to listen. Maybe even to hear. He was squealing—I wasn't completely sure if it was with excitement or something else—and was covering his ears with his hands. I reached over and carefully pried the hand that had the leash looped around it off Grady's ear just long enough to slip the handle over his wrist. I dropped the leash, then grabbed the end that connected to the collar and gently tugged. Between my efforts and Travis's, we got Squirtle unwound from Grady. I took the dog several steps down the pavement. With a little space, he stopped barking, though his whole body still wagged with joy.

Grady was still squealing. Freed from the leash, he'd curled into himself and sort of oozed into a ball on the ground. His eyes were screwed shut and his hands still covered his ears as he lay there in the fetal position.

I bit my lip. I never knew how to help in this situation.

Travis sighed and reached out to rub Grady's arm. "Shh."

I cleared my throat.

Travis glanced over. "I should take him home. Once this starts, I never know how long it's going to last."

"I'm sorry."

"It's not your fault." Travis stood, then bent down and lifted Grady up. The boy stiffened at first, then shifted to cling to his dad. Travis adjusted his hold on his son, then held out one hand. "I can take Squirtle's leash."

"You sure? I can walk back to the car with you. I don't really need a book or anything."

"Nah. You should enjoy your Saturday afternoon."

I frowned, but I went ahead and hooked the excited dog's leash over Travis's wrist. "My offer to grill for dinner stands."

"Appreciate it." Travis brushed a kiss over Grady's hair. The boy had quieted some, but was still in the throes of his meltdown. "I'll let you know."

"All right." I watched as Travis turned and began retracing his steps toward the diner. With a sigh, I shifted to look at the bookstore door. I didn't really need another book. And if I was going to start reading on my yet-to-be-purchased e-reader, I should probably avoid buying more paperbacks anyway. Or, and this really was the more reasonable option, I could get over myself and just keep using the library. It wasn't as if I'd been in the habit of long conversations with Mrs. Sanderson. So why would that change just because we had a new librarian?

I snorted quietly. I couldn't delude myself even in my thoughts. It might have been sixteen years since Jericho ghosted me, but I wasn't over it. No matter how much I tried to convince everyone—myself included—that I was.

I pulled open the bookstore door and went in. The mix of scents from the café and the subtle undertones of paper and ink were instantly soothing. I wasn't a fan of hot chocolate, but a latte with a ton of whipped cream on top, maybe a cookie to go with it? That would make browsing the shelves just a little better.

I skirted along the edge of the shelves to the café in the back of the shop. I'd learned the hard way that once I started getting into the books—even a casual walk through—I'd be there too long.

"Morning, Bennett." Sara grinned at me as she came out of the small kitchenette behind the café counter. "What can I get you?"

"How about a latte, don't be skimpy with the whipped cream, and—" I paused and scanned the display. "Ooh. One of those brownies."

"Nice choice." Sara punched the order into the register. "You know Macey?"

"Everyone knows Macey." I chuckled and dug my wallet out of my pocket, then tapped my credit card to the reader. Everyone pretty much knew everyone else if they were a year-rounder on Loring.

"True. She's starting up a cake shed. Probably seasonal, because there really isn't going to be enough demand year-round for that kind of thing. But I told her she could test out her products here while she put her ideas together. Honestly? I might just stop using the supplier from the mainland and let her handle it. Because these brownies are to die for." Sara ripped the receipt off the printer and offered it to me before moving to a stack of plates. "You're eating in?"

I nodded and put my card back in my wallet, then stuffed it and the receipt into my pocket. "Thought I'd see what new books needed to come home with me."

"It's always a good day when you stop by." Sara used tongs to transfer one of the huge squares of chocolate to a plate before setting it on the top of the display. "Although, the new librarian seems like she might give you a run for your money."

I froze for an instant in the process of reaching for the treat. I ignored my racing heart and tried to keep my voice casual. "Oh?"

Sara shifted to the coffee machine as she spoke, which hopefully meant she hadn't noticed my reaction. "Yeah. She was in yesterday when she was waiting for her appointment with your cousin and she's back again today. The two of you should get to know each other—you have the same taste in snacks."

The noise of the milk frother meant I had a moment to collect myself. Sara wouldn't have heard anything I tried to say over the hiss of the steam.

I wasn't sure what to say, anyway.

Sara was a solid ten years younger than me, so she probably didn't know the history I had with Jericho. What seven-year-old pays attention to a high school romance? I couldn't imagine that her parents would have said anything about it, either. My family might be descended from the original settlers on the island, but it wasn't as if we strutted around reminding people about it. Of all of us, I was the one who got the most questions since my mother, bless her, had decided to name me after that original ancestor. The one who, by all accounts, had been arrogant enough to insist the town on the mainland also shared his name. At least Grammie and Gramps had only had girls, so Mom and Aunt Deb ended up with different last names when they got married. I didn't think I'd enjoy walking around as Bennett Loring, suspected pirate. Or, as family lore preferred, privateer.

"That enough whipped cream?" Sara set a large mug with a towering spiral of fluff on top.

I laughed. "I think it'll do. Thanks."

"No problem. Don't get the merchandise sticky." She pointed a finger at me.

I shook my head. "One time."

"Yeah, well. I figure it bears repeating."

I carried my treats over to one of the tables and set them down. Her reminder of the one time I'd gotten absorbed in scanning titles while also drinking coffee and ended up missing the edge of the shelf I'd been trying to set my mug on, resulting in coffee on quite a few of the books had me reconsidering my initial plan to browse and snack at the same time.

I was half-way through the brownie, and considering asking for a bag to take the rest home, when a woman stepped up to the counter with a plate and mug. She set them in the dish return tray. The clinking brought Sara out from wherever she'd wandered off to.

"Thanks. Oh! There's someone you should meet." Sara gestured for her to follow and crossed to my table. "Bennett Thomas, meet our new librarian, Jericho Craig. Jericho, meet Bennett. He can handle any of your legal needs—he and his parents have a law firm here on Loring, although his folks are mostly retired."

Inbred manners had me standing and extending my hand before I really stopped to think about what I was doing.

Jericho tipped her head to the side, her expression neutral. She took my hand.

I'd been braced for it, but the spark of electricity that zinged up my arm at the contact was stronger than I expected. Or wanted. The small sliver of hope that I could continue on pretending that it was no big deal died. I cleared my throat. "Welcome to Loring Island."

One corner of Jericho's mouth twisted up. "Thanks."

I quickly retrieved my hand from hers.

"I should probably get going." Jericho stepped back and pushed her hands into her pockets.

Sara frowned. "I thought you said you had time to kill until your rental was ready? You really should chat with Bennett some. In addition to being an attorney, he's probably the biggest on-island patron of the library. Mrs. Sanderson even has a display shelf near the check-out desk of his recommendations. I suspect the town will want you to keep that going. I know I do. I get a huge influx of sales on days the display changes out."

"You do?" I resumed my seat. "I'm glad to hear that. Mrs. Sanderson and I were both a little worried that the library made it harder for you to stay afloat."

"Nope." Sara shook her head. "I see us as a symbiotic relationship. Not everyone can afford to buy every book they want to read. I get that. At the same time, sometimes you just have to have your very own copy of something you love. I do okay."

"Good. That's good. The town is better off for you being here." I glanced down at the brownie and bit back a sigh. I definitely wasn't going to finish it. "Could I get a little box or a bag? I'm not going to be able to finish this."

"Absolutely." Sara pointed at Jericho. "Sit. Seriously. Bennett is someone you should know."

I waited until Sara had, hopefully, moved out of earshot. "You might as well sit a minute. She's not going to let it go."

"So gracious."

My eyebrows lifted.

"Sorry." Jericho closed her eyes and took a deep breath. "I'm sorry. This isn't how I'd planned to see you again."

"Oh?" I left it at that. Would she go on and fill me in with what her plan had been? Because I'd definitely love to hear that. How did one plan to breeze back into someone's life after ghosting them for sixteen years?

Jericho swallowed and pulled out the chair. She sat.

Sara bustled back to the table and put a little box down beside my plate. She beamed at Jericho. "This is good. I'm around if y'all need anything."

I took advantage of Sara's departure and Jericho's seeming unwillingness to speak to slide the half-brownie into the box. I picked up my coffee and sipped.

"Look. There's a lot you don't know."

I snorted.

Jericho bit her lip. "Should I tell the town I've changed my mind? I thought…I guess I thought it had been long enough and that the island was big enough that it would be okay for me to be here."

"I don't own the island."

Her head bobbed from side to side. "You kind of do."

I fought to keep my voice neutral, calling on all my lawyer skills to do so. "No. I don't. I own my house. I own a lot up near Gramps's house. And I own a couple of rentals. That's it. Loring Island is a public island and part of the state of North Carolina. Therefore, it's part of a free country. Which means you get to do what you want."

"I don't want to make things hard for you."

"That ship left the harbor so long ago it's probably a wreck on the ocean floor by now."

Jericho winced. "I'm sorry."

I nodded. It shouldn't matter. Not after sixteen years. But her words helped. I drained my coffee and stood, then picked up the box. "Me, too. See you around."

I didn't wait for her to respond. Instead, I carried the mug over to the dish return and set it inside, then headed for the front door.

Sara poked her head around the shelves she was sitting in front of. "You're leaving?"

"Yeah. Forgot I had something I needed to work on this afternoon."

Sara frowned. "I thought—"

"Sorry. I've gotta go. I don't like being late." None of that was untrue. Oh, it definitely gave the wrong impression, but technically, I didn't like being late. Ever. And given the situation with Jericho? I definitely had to go.

I strode rapidly out of the bookstore and turned toward the diner. I'd go retrieve my motorcycle and then...what? I wasn't going to head home and go crazy thinking about how good Jericho looked, or how nice it had been to have her hand in mine again. I definitely wasn't going to obsess about the fact that she didn't wear any jewelry on her left hand.

She'd signed the lease as a single resident, so there'd been no reason to expect that she was married. But engaged was still a possibility. Seriously dating probably couldn't be ruled out even now.

And none of that mattered. It wasn't like the two of us were going to get back together. We'd had a summer fling. If I'd gone off the deep end and imagined it was meant to be more than that, well, that was my problem. Jericho obviously hadn't meant the same thing I did when she said "I love you."

So. Nothing had changed.

Nothing beyond the fact that now I knew where she was and that she was doing just fine without me.

Too bad I couldn't say the same thing about myself.

6

JERICHO

At nine a.m. on the nose, I pulled open the door of the Loring Island library and stepped inside. The building was smaller than I remembered it from my summers here.

Mrs. Sanderson looked up from the computer monitor at the desk straight ahead and nodded once. "Good. You're prompt. That's important for a librarian."

It was important for anyone, honestly, but I got the distinct feeling that any sort of comment along those lines would be considered impertinent.

"Are you ready to get started?"

"Yes." I crossed the space between the front door and the desk. "I appreciate you taking the time to show me around."

"Of course. I saw your resume." Mrs. Sanderson sniffed lightly. "You've never been completely in charge of a whole library."

"No, ma'am." I paused. Should I add more? I believed I was fully qualified for this position. It wasn't as if we were in a major metropolitan area. The building was just over four thousand square feet and, if I recalled the data sheet the council had included with the job offer, the collection was under twenty thousand items. "I appreciate the opportunity."

"As you should. It's not every day a young person gets to be the head librarian for a town. We may be small, but we're a vital part of this community. The island council is responsible for setting the open hours, and I've found the current times very conducive to having a fulfilling job as well as a life outside of work. Everyone needs a life outside of work." She pinned me with her gaze.

"Yes, ma'am." It seemed to be the expected response.

Mrs. Sanderson nodded again. "Good. If I can be bold, you should find yourself a man and settle down. Loring Island is a wonderful place to raise a family. I wish the school wasn't over on the mainland, but you can't have it all. Do you want children?"

"Oh. I...haven't given it much thought." That was a lie. But it was also none of Mrs. Sanderson's business. Still, because I didn't prefer prevarication, I tagged on, "Lately."

"Hmm." She sighed. "Well, maybe it's time you did. The years zip away before you realize it."

I nodded, not trusting myself to speak. She was beginning to sound like my mother. In this case, that was not a good thing.

"Anyway, come on behind the desk and I'll walk you through the computer system. We have an hour yet before we're open to the public, and I don't think we'll need time beyond that. I figured you could shadow me today. Then tomorrow, I'll shadow you. After that? Well I guess we'll see what we see."

I would have liked to object. I had actually been working—consistently—in libraries since I finished my degree. Sure, not as head—or in this case, only—librarian. But I knew what I was doing. On the other hand, I got the feeling it would be a good thing for Mrs. Sanderson to be confident leaving me as her replacement. She'd been here a long time and could probably convince the council they needed to get back to the drawing board if she decided I wasn't a good fit.

"All right. That sounds great."

By the time six p.m. rolled around, I felt comfortable with my ability to handle the library on my own. I'd been slightly surprised that there wasn't even one part-timer to come in and help with any of the routine tasks during the week. Thankfully, I'd kept that to myself. Mrs. Sanderson had very strong feelings about the ability of anyone without the appropriate degrees working in the library. Even as a volunteer.

I didn't share them. Volunteering in the library as a teen had been the start of my decision to study library science. So many of my best memories centered around the time spent at the library. And when everything began to fall apart, it had been my refuge.

I shied away from that line of thinking. Nothing good or productive could come from it. The past was the past. I only looked forward.

"I think you'll do." Mrs. Sanderson gathered her tote bag and purse, then gestured for me to precede her through the door. When she joined me on the front step, she drew a keyring from her pocket and locked the library behind her. She gave the door a good push, then tucked the key away. "Most days, I only show up about fifteen minutes before opening. Tomorrow, why don't we say thirty just to be safe?"

"Okay." I flashed a smile. "Thanks again, Mrs. Sanderson."

"You're welcome, dear. I'll see you tomorrow."

I watched her walk toward the parking spot reserved for the town librarian. It had its own sign and everything. I'd ended up parking down the street near the diner. I tugged my jacket closed and zipped it against the chilly breeze, then headed that way. Living on the beach meant I was going to have to drive—or get a bicycle maybe for nicer weather. The island wasn't huge, but it was still large enough that walking from the beach into town wasn't a quick undertaking.

My gaze drifted to the diner as I approached my car. As if on cue, my stomach rumbled. The sandwich I packed for lunch and ate in the office with Mrs. Sanderson felt like years ago. I bit my lip. I had food at home. And it would still be there tomorrow. I'd live on the edge and eat out—call it celebrating my first day of work, if I needed an excuse.

I bypassed my car and angled across the little parking lot in front of the diner. It didn't look like it had changed since it was built in the 1950s. The big arch over the double-doors leading in was reminiscent of a jukebox and had never failed to make me smile. Today was no exception. I grabbed the door and tugged it open, cheerful music spilling out as I did so.

I crossed the black-and-white checkered tiles to the hostess stand. The young woman standing there blinked. "Can I help you?"

"Table for one?" I glanced at the long counter that ran the length of the diner and separated the dining room from the kitchen. The bright red vinyl of the stools set off the chrome legs. "If you're busy I can sit at the counter, but I'd rather a booth."

"We're never too busy in January. Maybe on Saturdays." The girl gestured to the mostly empty space. "Take your pick."

I hesitated, then turned toward the emptier side of the restaurant and started walking. I didn't want to be right by the door. Enough cold air had followed me in that I didn't imagine that would be a pleasant place to sit. I paused by an empty booth. "Is it okay if I sit here?"

"Sure." The hostess pointed to the miniature jukebox against the wall and the stack of menus propped behind it. "Someone will be by for your order soon."

"Okay." I shrugged out of my coat and dropped it on the

bench. I looked around but didn't see a server bearing down on me, so I headed to the restrooms.

"Jericho?" A chair scraped on the floor, drawing my attention. The older woman stood, hands on her hips. "Jericho Craig! It is you."

"It's me." I managed a weak smile. Why hadn't I gone home and thrown something together? "Hi, Mrs. Thomas."

"Pfft." Mrs. Thomas threw her arms around me in a squeeze that rivaled any species of boa constrictor out there. "I think you can call me Linda at this point. Are you meeting someone?"

"No. I was just going to grab a bite and head home."

"Absolutely not. Come join us. There's nothing worse than eating alone in a restaurant."

I didn't mind it. Never had. "I have a book."

Linda laughed. "Of course you do. But you can read later. Come and sit."

I gestured toward the restrooms.

"Right. Ha. When you're finished. Do you have a coat? You're not walking around out there without a jacket, are you?"

"I left it in my booth. I really don't want to intrude." She kept saying "us" and I couldn't come up with a definition for that phrase that wouldn't be awkward.

"Nonsense. I'll find your coat and bring it over to the table. I'm early. I always beat the guys. So I'll save you the seat next to me."

I opened my mouth to object once more but caught the steely glint in Mrs. Thomas—Linda's—eye and snapped it shut. "If you're sure."

"Completely." She patted my arm and grinned.

I tightened up my smile, hoping it didn't look as sickly as it felt, and headed toward the sanctuary of the restroom. There was no convenient exit to an alleyway that I could use to escape. Besides the fact that I needed my jacket. I only had the one, and while the town paid well enough for me to live, my new salary didn't extend to lots of clothes shopping. I could cover rent, food, my phone plan, a single streaming service, and if I was careful, an occasional meal out.

Besides, that jacket was new.

Ugh.

I stared at myself in the mirror as I washed my hands and muttered, "You moved to a small town. You knew they lived here. You can't avoid the family—they basically own the town."

I closed my eyes. Why on earth had I thought this was a good idea?

I shook the water off my hands and grabbed a paper towel to dry them, then took a deep breath. I could do this. Part of being a librarian was fostering a good relationship with the people I served. And besides, it was just Mrs—well, Linda. Maybe her husband.

I'd always loved Bennett's family. Honestly, they'd been a big part of the draw all those years ago.

I could do this.

I squared my shoulders and pushed open the bathroom door. I strode, determined, toward the table. My steps faltered as I neared and saw that another table had been pushed over, expanding the seating to eight.

So. *Not* just Mr. and Mrs. Thomas.

Please don't be their kids. Please don't be their kids.

Linda turned and grinned. She patted the chair beside her—the one with my coat hanging over the back. "The boys should all be here in a minute. David says he's retired, but he spends a lot of time in the office for someone who isn't working anymore."

I chuckled.

It seemed to be the response she was looking for because her grin widened. "Then again, so do I. The law is too interesting to give up entirely."

I pulled out the chair and sat, then leaned forward to snag a menu from the middle of the table. "It's good to find a career that doesn't feel like work."

"Isn't it?" Linda nodded. "Is that the library for you?"

"Yeah. It definitely is."

She patted my arm. "I'm glad you found what you were looking for."

I glanced over then quickly back down at the menu. What had she meant by that? Was it a dig? That seemed out of character for her, although it had been a long time since I'd basically been adopted as part of their family.

The realization hit me with an almost physical force. I hadn't just ghosted Bennett. I'd abandoned the whole family.

Did they all hate me like he did?

I started to stand. "I should go."

Linda tipped her head to the side and studied me. "How far?"

I frowned. "What do you mean?"

"Where will you go? At some point, if you stay on Loring Island, you're going to end up seeing us all. None of us are likely to give up on reading. Or patronizing the library, although Bennett just got a new e-reader and is giving it a whirl. I don't see that lasting. He likes the smell of books too much." Linda's eyebrows lifted. "So you can go, if that's really what you want. But you're simply delaying the inevitable. Be brave. Rip the bandage off."

I swallowed and sank back into my seat.

"Thatta girl." She smiled and patted my arm again. "I think you'll find it's not as bad as you expect."

"I doubt that very much." I thought about Bennett's cold demeanor and harsh words in the bookstore on Saturday.

Linda's lips quirked up. "Give him some time. You broke his heart."

It hadn't exactly been a picnic for me. Then again, whose fault was it? Mine. Only mine.

I got out of having to come up with a response, because several loud voices filled the diner. I couldn't see the entrance from where I was sitting, but I recognized Bennett's voice and assumed the others were his brothers and father.

The men came around the corner, looking for the world like the tight-knit group I knew they were. It was almost as if the love between them was visible.

"There she is." Mr. Thomas made a beeline for his wife. "Love of my life."

He leaned down and kissed her, not seeming to notice or care that his kids were watching. Or that I was there.

"David." The mild reproof in Linda's voice was betrayed by her laugh.

"What? It's just the boys. I think they've figured out we have something going on." He grinned. Linda inclined her head slightly in my direction, and his eyes followed. "Oh. My apologies. I only had eyes for my wife."

"It's fine." I took a breath, steeling myself for the introduction and subsequent awkwardness.

"Is that Jericho?" Christian, the middle brother who also stood sandwiched between Bennett and their younger brother Evan, started to laugh. He punched Bennett in the arm then moved away from the group and claimed the seat at the end of the table, putting him next to me on the other side of Linda. "I'd heard you were coming, but I didn't realize you were already here. It's good to see you."

"Thanks." I'd forgotten how outgoing and cheerful Christian was. Especially in comparison to Bennett.

"Hey." Evan lifted a hand and scooted around the table to sit by his dad, who had taken the table end next to his wife.

That left Bennett the seat facing me.

He gave me a long look as he hesitated before pulling out a chair and sitting.

"David, you remember Jericho." Linda patted her husband's hand.

"Of course I do." He flashed a smile that was so like Bennett's I had to blink. "I'm glad the Island Council made the decision to hire you. And that you accepted. Where are you staying?"

Startled, I shot a quick look across the table at Bennett, then cleared my throat. "I'm renting a place on the beach."

"I transitioned Heron into a long-term rental." Bennett reached for a menu as he spoke, then disappeared behind it.

David and Linda exchanged a glance that I couldn't interpret. Did they not approve? Was it going to cause friction in the family somehow?

"Well. That makes property management easier, certainly." Linda filled the silence that threatened to take over the whole meal. She shifted to look at me. "How are you liking it?"

"I love it. It's only been two nights—I moved in Saturday, late—but I drank my coffee on the porch looking at the waves both mornings and it's exactly what I hoped for."

"Brr." Linda shook her head. "My guys all try to get me out there on winter mornings and I say a hearty no thank you. You must be made of sturdier stuff than me."

"Nah, Mom. You'd be just fine if you gave it a shot. Next time I'm over, I'm dragging you out. You'll see." Christian flicked Bennett's menu. "What's with the menu, bro? You always get the same thing."

Bennett laid the menu down and scowled at his brother. "I do not."

"You do." Evan shook his head. "Country-fried steak with a side of hashbrowns."

"Extra crisp." Bennet's dad chimed in.

"And a Coke." Linda shook her head. "No matter what time of day."

Bennett frowned.

I reached for my own menu and used it to hide a smile. That had been his go-to when we were an item. Did he seriously still eat that every time he came here? That was a lot of years of country-fried steak.

"Evening y'all." A girl in her teens sashayed toward the table and fluttered her eyelashes at Evan as she spoke. "What can I get you?"

"Hi Geena." David leaned back in his chair and casually took Linda's hand. "How're your folks?"

She shrugged. "Same as always. Mom's trying to convince Dad we need chickens. Who ever heard of raising chickens at the beach?"

"I think the Sandersons did for a while. It's doable in town. No ordinances against it, either." David chuckled. "You do with that information as you will."

"Yes, sir. If it's the same to you, I'll keep it to myself. Mom thinks chickens will teach me responsibility. I told her I thought a cat would do just as well. She reminded me that my brother's allergic, and then I said that's why I wanted one. Then she took my phone away for three days." Geena gave a hearty sigh. "You want a Coke, Mr. Thomas?"

"Not tonight. I think I'll go with iced tea like my lovely bride." He sent Linda a loving glance.

"Yes, sir." She turned to me. "Ma'am?"

I fought a wince. I was back in the South so I'd better get used to it, but I didn't know if I'd ever feel old enough for someone to call me ma'am. "Just water please. With lemon if possible."

"Sure thing. Mr. Christian?"

He flashed her a grin. "Iced tea. Thanks, Geena."

"And a Coke, right?" She turned toward Bennett.

"No. Tonight, I think I'll stick with water. No lemon though." His smile was tight and looked uncomfortable.

Geena's eyebrows lifted as she made a note on her pad. "Mr. Evan?"

"Can I get a Sprite?"

"Of course. Y'all ready to order food, too, or do you need a minute?"

David looked around the table, his gaze stopping on me. "Are you ready, Jericho?"

"I can be." I hurriedly looked down at the menu. The problem with the diner—and diners in general, in my experience, was that they had too many options.

"We'll go ahead and order. I'd like the burger with fries. Medium well. Extra pickles." David glanced at his wife. "Love?"

"Oh. I should be good and get a salad, but I'm not going to. I'll have the chicken and dumplin's, with the collards." Linda leaned back in her seat.

Right. My turn now. "The cobb salad, please. Blue cheese dressing on the side?"

Geena nodded. She looked at Christian. "Usual?"

"You know it." He laughed.

"And you, Mr. Bennett? The usual?"

Bennett put his menu down. "Actually, no. I think I'll have what my mom's having."

"Really?" Linda's face expressed the surprise that seemed to echo around the table. "You're voluntarily eating collards?"

Bennett shrugged. "Past time to do new things, don't you think?"

His gaze bored into me, but I refused to meet it. Even if his family didn't catch the undertones hiding in his words, the arrows had certainly hit home with me. I focused on my breathing and willed my eyes to stay dry and my heart not to race.

I was only moderately successful.

Movement caught my attention and I looked up to see Geena walking away. Since her path took her directly behind Bennett, our eyes met. His were flat.

I looked away.

"Evan, honey, you have to stop letting her flirt with you. She's entirely too young. Or you're too old, take your pick." Linda chastised her youngest.

"She knows that, Mom. I've talked to her. She has her eye on Matt Carter. You remember him?"

Linda shook her head.

"He graduated last year, but is taking a gap year and working the fishing tours with Austin while he tries to save up for college. He got a partial track scholarship, but it wasn't enough to cover everything and his family wasn't going to be able to help."

David shook his head. "How do you keep all of that in your head?"

Evan shrugged. "Just smarter than the rest of y'all, I guess."

"Oh, please." Bennett made a gagging noise as he looked at Linda. "You had to get the baby started on how he's smarter just because he abandoned the family business?"

"Hey! Christian isn't a lawyer either." Evan pushed Bennett's shoulder.

"Yeah, but medicine is a calling. Unlike, what is it you do again?" Christian leaned forward. "Count turtle shells?"

Evan drew in a breath, but Linda's stern voice forestalled whatever he was going to say. "Boys."

Christian's face flamed red. Bennett looked away. Evan crossed his arms, a sulk pulling at his lips.

"You'll have to excuse my children." David sighed. "We don't let them out in public very often, and it shows."

I snickered and tried to turn it into a cough.

David's lips twitched. "Why don't you tell us all about what you've been up to, Jericho? It's been...a while."

Geena's return with a tray of drinks bought me a few minutes to collect my thoughts and figure out just what, exactly, I was going to share.

It was a lot harder than figuring what I needed to keep to myself.

7

BENNETT

"Would anyone like dessert?" Geena stacked empty dishes and lifted them.

"None for me." Jericho patted her lips with a napkin. "Could I get my check separately from the rest?"

"Of cou—"

Mom cut Geena off. "Nonsense. This is our treat. Consider it a welcome back to the island, if you can't just view it as the first of hopefully many nights out with friends."

I concentrated on the last few bites of food on my plate while peeking to see Jericho's reaction. She was visibly struggling.

Finally, she spoke. "Thank you. You don't need to do that, but I appreciate it."

"It's our pleasure." Dad glanced at Geena. "Do you have apple pie?"

"Yes, sir. Do you want it warmed up with ice cream?"

"I do."

"David." Mom shook her head, then looked at Geena. "Bring an extra fork, if you would."

"I never said I'd share. What if I want it all?" Dad's eyes

sparkled, and I fought a smile. They did this every time Dad got apple pie.

"Well, that's too bad." Mom winked. She turned to Jericho. "Will you have some pie?"

"No. Thank you." She scooted her chair back. "I really need to be going. I appreciate you including me in your family dinner. I'm sure I'll see you around."

I watched her as she stood, collected her jacket off the back of her chair, and lifted her fingers in what was probably meant to be a generic goodbye to everyone at the table. Then she walked off.

I sighed.

"Did anyone else want pie? Or something else?"

I glanced at Geena. What did she think of that whole exchange? She was too young to have any idea about the history between Jericho and me. So she probably didn't think anything about it.

"Can I get a banana split? Strawberry and vanilla for the ice cream and lots of whipped cream?"

"Sure thing." Geena got orders from my brothers, too, and moved off.

Mom looked at me. "You okay, Bennett?"

"Why wouldn't I be?"

"That's your upset dessert."

"I don't have an upset dessert." I frowned. "What does that even mean?"

"Bro." Christian shook his head. "You're constantly trying to say you're smarter than us and yet you can't figure that out? Also, it totally is."

"It is, man. You don't get a banana split unless you're unhappy." Evan shrugged. "Facts are facts."

Fine. It was true. I even recognized it. That didn't mean I

needed my family pointing it out to me. "Maybe I'm changing it up. Now it's my 'everything is perfect' dessert."

Christian snorted.

Dad grinned. "Don't kid a kidder. You know you can't avoid talking to her forever, right? She lives here now."

"I talked to her on Saturday. I talked to her tonight." I crossed my arms. Maybe I hadn't said a lot, but I'd talked. Words came out of my mouth. I wasn't the chatterbox of the family. That distinction belonged to Christian.

Mom waggled a hand from side to side. "You were barely on the right side of polite, my boy."

I shrugged.

As long as I was on the right side of it, I didn't care. I probably hadn't been on Saturday. But I didn't really care about that, either. Mom hadn't seen or heard about it, so I was in the clear. "Can we just let it go? It was a long time ago. I'm over it."

I could tell they didn't believe me, but thankfully, no one challenged my assertion. Maybe if they let it go, I could convince my heart once and for all that it was true. Of course, I'd have to stop seeing her for that to work. Even though we'd had only two interactions since she'd come back, I was already drowning. Would I even be able to keep up with my plan of aloof detachment? Probably not.

Maybe I should quit trying.

"What made you decide to turn Heron into a long-term rental?"

I looked over at my dad and shrugged. "Travis, basically. I told you all about the issue I was having with some of the listing sites. Then Travis mentioned how Jericho was looking for something near the beach and the only real options were in town, so it all kind of worked out."

"God has a way of doing that, doesn't He?" Mom smiled and reached for her iced tea.

"Whether you understand it or not." I shot her a wry smile.

"Speaking of Travis, when did you last chat with him? Because he was supposed to come over and help me move some things at the clinic after church yesterday, and he didn't show." Christian frowned. "For that matter, I didn't see him at church, either."

"We spent Saturday morning together. It was supposed to be all day, but after brunch, Grady had a meltdown and Trav decided to take him home." I hadn't seen him at church yesterday, either. At the time, it hadn't stuck out, but now it did. I looked at Mom and Dad. "Did you see him at church?"

Mom looked at Dad, who shook his head. "No. Neither did I. I found out Deb and Rob snuck off for a weekend on the mainland when I called to invite her and Rob over for dinner nachos. Gramps was in the mood to make his fresh tortillas and fry them up. You know Rob loves those."

"You know who else loves them?" Evan gestured to Christian, himself, and me. "Your children. I didn't get an invite. Did either of you?"

Christian shook his head.

"Nope." I cocked my head to the side. "Why is that?"

Dad laughed. "Maybe Gramps didn't want to make quite that much food?"

"I certainly didn't." Mom chuckled. "Honestly, I'd hoped my handsome boys who are all young, eligible bachelors might have dates."

Geena showed up with dessert, cutting off any retort that my brothers or I would have made.

"I'll leave the check here too, but there's no rush. I can take it when you're ready or you can pay up front when you leave, whatever is easiest."

"Thanks, Geena." Dad grabbed one of the forks that Geena

had set down and stabbed through the melting ice cream into the warm pie. His lips closed around the bite. "Mmm."

I dug out some ice cream, whipped cream, and banana, contemplating while I chewed. "I'm going to text Trav after dinner. Maybe I'll get some pie to go and swing by. Grady always loves apple pie from here, and Caroline has never said no to a milkshake."

"That's a good idea." Mom used her fork to push Dad's out of the way so she could get a bigger chunk of ice cream. "I hope everything's all right."

"Why wouldn't it be?" Dad touched Mom's hand lightly. "Deb would be on our doorstep the minute something bad happened. Or at least on the phone."

Mom nodded.

I had to agree with Dad. Mom and Aunt Deb were the kind of siblings people only dreamed of having. Well, I guess I had that with my brothers, but it was more a nightmare than a dream. They were always in my business.

Maybe there were moments it was nice, but it could also be a real pain.

"If you find anything out from Travis, you let me know." Mom pointed her fork at me. "Actually, even if you don't find anything out, tell me that, too."

"Yes, ma'am."

"Suck up." Christian reached over with his spoon and stole a scoop of whipped cream off my split.

"Hey." I grabbed for his spoon.

Christian started to laugh and pointed.

I turned in time to see Evan popping half of my strawberry ice cream into his mouth.

"Ugh. Mom!"

Mom laughed.

"Why did you have to have more? I'm sure you could have found couples out there who would have been willing to raise these two. Or a pack of wolves somewhere. That seems more their speed." I scooted the bowl closer and wrapped an arm around it.

"Well, honey, sometimes when a man and woman love each other very much—"

"Ew. Mom. Gross." Evan clapped his hands over his ears.

Christian stuck a finger in his mouth and pretended to vomit.

Dad scooped the last bit of pie into his mouth, then scooted back his chair and stood. He held out a hand to Mom. "I believe that's our cue. Shall we?"

"Yes, indeed." Mom rose and blew a kiss to me and each of my brothers. "Don't fight about who's paying too much."

Christian and Evan immediately put a finger on their nose.

I groaned. "Really? How old are you? I keep a spreadsheet, and it's not my turn."

"The nose knows." Christian kept his finger firmly on his face. "Not. It."

"Yep. No spreadsheet can compete with not it." Evan grinned and wiggled his finger without taking it off the tip of his nose.

"Mom?" I looked at her and frowned when I saw the amusement on her face.

"Sorry, baby. On the positive side, as a lawyer, you do earn more than either of your brothers. I know, because I approve the paychecks." She patted my shoulder. "Think of it as being a good landlord for Jericho by taking her to dinner."

I narrowed my eyes at her. "Yeah, right."

"Bye, boys."

I glared at Mom and Dad's retreating backs, then reached for the check. "Put your fingers down, you look like morons."

Christian and Evan both lowered their hands.

I pursed my lips. "Huh. That didn't help at all. You still look like morons."

It was a pretty good parting line, so I stood up and headed to the front with the bill, enjoying listening to my brothers sputter behind me.

Thoughts of my brothers' reactions kept me smiling most of the way to Travis's house. The dirty looks they shot my way as they exited while I was waiting for the takeout didn't hurt. But as I turned into Travis's driveway, I frowned. The garage door was open and Caroline's car wasn't in its usual space. Granted, she could have gone out with friends or to the grocery store. Honestly, there were any number of places she could be. But the reality was, everything Travis had told me—or that I'd observed—suggested she would be home after dinner on a Monday evening.

I pulled up behind Travis's car, cut the engine on the bike, and unhooked my helmet as I studied his house. Every light appeared to be on and the golden glow beat back the deepening darkness of winter evenings. I could just make out the sound of the surf from the beach behind his house. Another sound, higher pitched, pierced through the twilight serenity.

I dismounted the motorcycle, balanced my helmet on the seat, grabbed the takeout bag that I'd slipped into the saddlebag, and crossed the driveway. I took the stairs to the front door two at a time and punched the doorbell. The Westminster Chimes echoed loudly enough that I could hear them perfectly from outside. Even over the shrieking.

I winced. If that was Grady, this might not be the best time to pay a visit to Travis. On the other hand? Maybe he could use a hand.

I waited a full two minutes and considered pushing the doorbell again, then decided against it. I tried the doorknob and my eyebrows lifted when I found it unlocked. Loring Island might be a small-town beach community, but we weren't the kind of place where doors were left open. We had too many visitors to the island for that. I trusted everyone in the year-round population intensely, but even so, good security made good neighbors.

I pushed open the door and called out, "Travis? It's me. Bennett. Can I come in?"

An unearthly shriek preceded the blur of Grady running out from the doorway that led to the kitchen. He barreled into me and wrapped himself around my legs.

"Oof. Hey, Grady." I fought to keep my balance as I reached down and tried to pry his arms away from my legs. I set the takeout bag down so I had both hands free. "Hey, bud. Let me pick you up, okay?"

Grady didn't speak, but he didn't fight me quite as hard this time when I unwound his arms and hefted him up. The minute he was waist high, his arms formed a chokehold around my neck and his legs locked around me. I staggered back a step before I recovered and stepped into the house, shutting the door behind me.

A harried-looking Travis, shirtless, pants covered in what, for the briefest moment, I thought was blood, shuffled out in his son's wake. "Hey."

"Hey." I cocked my head to the side. "Spaghetti night?"

Travis's brief smile somehow managed to convey desperation and exhaustion at the same time. "That was the plan. He's not having it."

"I thought it was his favorite?"

"Yeah, me too." Travis gave a resigned shrug. "Come on back. I either need to keep cleaning or give up and decide marinara is my new color scheme."

I hitched Grady higher—he was really too big to carry like this, but it didn't seem like I was going to be able to set him down anytime soon if his grip on me was an indication—and followed Travis. I paused when I got a look at the kitchen. Spaghetti sauce splattered on nearly every visible surface in big streaks that emanated from what was presumably Grady's stool at the kitchen island.

"Wow. It's like something from CSI."

Travis snorted mirthlessly as he reached into a bucket, sloshed the contents, and pulled out a sponge. He squeezed it out, then began attacking the mess on the counters.

"There's no way you're going to get this all before it stains. Let me call in reinforcements." I shifted Grady's weight and he tightened his grip around my neck.

"No, man. I've got it." Travis glanced up briefly from his scrubbing, misery plain on his face.

I hesitated, torn between a desire to respect his wishes and the knowledge that there was no way he could do this alone. Or even with just me, if I was able to untangle Grady enough to help. I shook my head. "You don't. And that's not what we do in this family."

Travis closed his eyes, his face and shoulders drooping. Finally, he nodded. "You're right."

I grabbed my phone and quickly tapped Mom's contact. It rang twice before she answered.

"Didn't I just get rid of you?" Her voice was full of laughter. "You're not calling to tattle on your brothers, are you? Because if you are, I'm going to have to remind you that you're all over thirty and capable of solving your own differences."

"Ha. Ha." I flashed a tight smile at Travis. "No. I need you and Dad to come to Trav's. See if Aunt Deb and Uncle Rob are free, too."

"What happened? Is someone hurt? Should I get Christian?" All the humor was gone from Mom's voice as she shifted into emergency management mode.

I took a look at the mess and my exhausted cousin before answering. "No one's bleeding, if that's what you're asking. But if the guys can come, we could use all hands on deck."

"Ten minutes." Mom ended the call.

I tucked my phone back in my pocket.

"Did you have to say all hands on deck?" Travis dropped the sponge back into the bucket and sagged against the counter.

It was a family code, of sorts. One that meant there was an emergency that couldn't be explained right then. Kind of like throwing a big Bat Signal into the sky. I stared at him, then nodded. "I did. More than that? You should have."

He sighed and looked away.

"What's going on, Trav?"

"Let's wait until everyone gets here." His voice was resigned. "Why don't you go sit in the living room? I'm going to go take a quick shower and put on clean clothes."

"All right." I stepped back to let Travis scoot past, then made my way into the living room. The massive sectional was a mess. Pillows and cushions were strewn around like they'd been used for a fort that was hit by a tornado. Considering Grady didn't appear to have any intention of loosening his grip, I opted for the recliner in the corner.

"No!" Grady's grip tightened as I tried to sit.

"Hey." I rubbed his back. "I'm not putting you down. I just need to sit a minute. Okay?"

He didn't speak, but I was able to lower us to the chair and shift his legs so they weren't smashed into my back when I did so. I looked around. Where was Squirtle?

Maybe it was a dumb question. If Travis had any sense—and he did—he'd put Squirtle out in the yard when it was clear that spaghetti night was turning into a disaster. An overly enthusiastic puppy in the middle of flying red sauce was more than anyone could be expected to handle.

After about five minutes, there was a knock on the door, then it pushed open. Christan entered, followed closely by Evan, Ryan, and Austin.

Evan tripped over the takeout bag. "What's this?"

"Sorry." I winced. "It's the p-i-e and s-h-a-k-e I brought. Can you stick them in the fridge?"

"Yeah, sure." Evan scooped up the bag and headed into the kitchen. He stopped in the doorway and whistled.

Austin and Christian strode over to look and both jolted.

"What on earth?" Austin glanced back at me.

I just shook my head. "Trav said he'd explain when everyone was here. But he obviously needs help cleaning."

"You think?" Austin shook his head and pushed up his sleeves. "Might as well get started before the moms come or we'll hear about it."

"You're not wrong." Evan glanced back at me. "You going to put him down and help?"

At the word "down," Grady's arms tightened around me and he began to shriek.

I glared at Evan. "What do you think?"

"Sorry." He held up both hands. "I didn't realize you were helping already."

Ryan had started reassembling the sofa cushions. "I'll be there when I get it tidied up in here."

Evan, Christian, and Austin headed into the kitchen and the sounds of cabinets opening and closing, along with good-natured joking created a comforting and familiar backdrop that seemed to help Grady relax a tiny bit.

"You have any idea what's going on?" Ryan tucked a cushion into place and picked up another. He paused to brush cereal off it, then wrinkled his nose. "What do we use to wipe leather?"

"Damp cloth?" It was my best guess. I couldn't imagine that

adding bleach or any kind of cleaning solution would be a good idea.

"Seems legit. Back in a second." He put the cushion down and went into the kitchen. "Whoa."

I chuckled. At least I wasn't the only one having that initial reaction. What was going on?

Travis came down the stairs, his hair still wet, but dressed in clean lounge pants and a long-sleeved t-shirt. "Did I hear someone come already?"

"The guys are getting started in the kitchen." I nodded at Ryan as he came out with a damp paper towel balled up in his hands.

"Hey, man. It's not like you to have a party and not invite us." Ryan grinned and collected the sticky couch cushion so he could attack it with the paper towel.

"Right. I'll keep that in mind." Travis sighed, his whole body seeming to deflate, as he reached for another cushion.

Ryan's mouth opened but he caught my subtle head shake and snapped it shut. As they were putting the last cushion back, the door opened again and Mom, Dad, Aunt Deb, and Uncle Rob came in.

Mom looked around, her gaze landing on me. She tipped her head to the side, her eyebrows lifting.

"The rest of the guys are in the kitchen." I nodded toward the doorway.

"Don't." Travis held up a hand. "Just come sit down. I'll go get them and explain."

Aunt Deb frowned at Travis, then crossed the room to look in the kitchen. The shock on her face would have been comical under just about any other circumstance. "Oh, my."

"What is it?" Mom crossed to where her sister stood and her jaw dropped.

Travis cleared his throat. "Seriously. Just come sit down."

"Oh, honey." Aunt Deb looked at Travis and shook her head. "This is definitely a clean first, explain later situation."

Travis's shoulders slumped.

"Go get your broom and vacuum. Ryan can vacuum the living room. Rob, you can sweep. When you've finished with that, Ryan can mop. Linda and I will help the other boys with the walls. What does the rest of the house look like?" Aunt Deb stood with her hands on her hips.

"Not as bad. Grady's bathroom is a little rough." Travis rubbed the back of his neck. "I'll start on it after I get the broom and vacuum."

"Bennett, why don't you—" A shriek from Grady cut off whatever Aunt Deb was going to say. She frowned at me sympathetically. "You can just stay right there."

Mom smiled at me, then looked at Travis. "Where's Caroline?"

"You said you want explanations after we cleaned." Travis started toward the coat closet. "I'll get the stuff and we can get started. I really appreciate you guys coming to help."

Mom and I exchanged a confused look.

Aunt Deb drew in a breath but Mom shook her head. Aunt Deb frowned but nodded. The two of them went into the kitchen.

Uncle Rob took the broom from Travis and Ryan crossed over to grab the handle of the vacuum cleaner.

Dad moved across the room and clapped Travis on the shoulder. "I got left out of the rotation. Why don't I help you with the bathroom?"

"Yeah, all right. Thanks." Travis started up the stairs with Dad trailing in his wake.

Ryan pulled the cord out of the vacuum cleaner and plugged it in, then switched it on. The noise drowned out the conversations from the kitchen. I'd half expected Grady to react negatively to it—he'd never been a fan of loud sounds—but he just burrowed into my shoulder a little deeper and continued to cling to me.

I rubbed his back and rested my cheek on the top of his head. If Caroline wasn't here—and all signs certainly seemed to point in that direction—where was she?

It took about an hour of everyone working together to get the house put back to rights. Squirtle came bounding in from the kitchen—someone obviously let him in—and leaped onto the couch. Looking worn out, the rest of the family joined Grady and me in the living room, taking seats on the couch or other chairs.

When everyone was settled, all eyes turned to Travis. The house was clean so the family was due an explanation. He seemed to shrink under the attention. He swallowed. "Caroline left me."

8

JERICHO

"I'm going to head home." Mrs. Sanderson set her purse down on the check-out counter and studied me. "I'll admit I had my doubts about the council hiring someone so young, but you're going to do just fine."

I smiled. Praise from Mrs. Sanderson felt like cresting a previously insurmountable summit. The little squeeze of uncertainty that had been tight in my chest all week finally loosened. "Thank you. That means a lot."

She chuckled. "I was hard on you this week. I'm not going to apologize for it, but I will say you exceeded my expectations. And they were pretty high. Now I can retire and know the library is in good hands."

"It is. I promise."

"I'll hold you to it." She picked up her purse and hooked it on her shoulder. "More than likely, Mr. Sanderson and I are going to end up back here for a week or two every year. It's hard to imagine that we're not retiring at the beach after living here the entirety of our married lives."

"Grandkids beat the beach, though." Although I couldn't help thinking that any grandchild would love having grandparents to vacation with at the shore. I wasn't going to say that. I still wasn't willing to risk her changing her mind. Then I'd be out of a job.

"They do." She sighed. "And I don't know where we went wrong that none of our children like the beach. They all settled near Charlotte and refuse to come out even for a week. The ocean's dangerous, apparently."

I fought a smile. "Well, it can be."

Mrs. Sanderson waved a hand. "Of course it can be. But so can crossing the street. Or getting up in the middle of the night. Doesn't matter. We'll come out for some time at the beach, and we'll spend the rest of the time entertaining the grandkids. We found a nice little property about thirty minutes away from the kids—reasonably equidistant—and it has a little bit of land, so we're not stacked up on top of our neighbors."

"Sounds lovely." It really did. It wasn't the beach, but if I had to live near a city, I'd want to be on the outskirts with some land, too. I'd done the whole downtown living thing. It wasn't for me. Never would be. "I know you'll be missed, so I'm glad you plan to come back and visit."

"Couldn't keep me away." She turned and looked around the library, then sighed. "All right now, hon, you take care. Do me proud, you hear?"

"Yes, ma'am." I waved and watched her trail her fingers over the top of the shelves on the way to the door. She left without looking back. Was she worried about turning into a pillar of salt? Maybe that was harsh, but the idea was legit. Looking back wistfully was a waste of time. The past couldn't be changed, so why dwell on it?

The future was much more interesting. And the library on Loring Island was now one-hundred-percent mine. I rubbed my hands together, then turned to finish loading the day's returns onto a cart so I could get them reshelved and ready for the next patron to find.

When the cart was loaded, I pushed it around the counter and started toward the stacks. I glanced over as the door opened and my stomach sank. What had I just been telling myself about leaving the past behind?

It was a lot harder to do when that past could stroll casually into your library whenever he wanted to.

"Good afternoon." I fought the urge to check the time. We closed at two on Friday afternoons, and that had to be soon. Didn't it? Not that I was going to chase patrons out at 1:59, but ugh. Why did it have to be Bennett? And why was he holding the hand of an adorable little boy?

His boy?

Surely not. He would have brought his kid to dinner with his family on Monday. Wouldn't he?

I filtered through the town news—everyone called it news, not gossip—I'd picked up over the week. There'd been no mention of Bennett being married, let alone having a child. His cousin Travis did. There'd been mutters all week about "poor Travis" and "that sweet little boy." Something was going on there, but I hadn't managed to overhear just what. Since I only had a real estate relationship with him—and it was basically done now—I hadn't felt like I could, or should, reach out to ask. Or offer to help somehow.

I grabbed the first book off the cart and slid it into the proper place, then moved down the aisle between the shelves.

"What sort of book do you want for the weekend, Grady?" Bennett's voice carried through the library even though I couldn't see him.

"I don't wanna read. It's hard." The defeated resignation in the boy's—Grady's?—voice caught me off guard.

I set the book I was holding back on the cart and walked out from the stacks. I glanced around, then spotted them in the kids' area. Bennett knelt beside one of the bookcases, a book in each hand. The boy stared up at the ceiling.

"Can I help?"

Bennett glanced over and shrugged. "Grady's teacher says he needs to spend at least thirty minutes a night reading. He's behind. Since reading is one of my favorite things, I told Travis I'd help."

I nodded and joined them by the books. "Hi, Grady. I'm Jericho. What do you like to do?"

"Not read." Grady wouldn't look at me. He kept staring up, though his head turned a little. He wasn't still. His hands balled and flexed. He shifted his weight from side to side.

"That's okay. What do you like doing? Do you swim?"

His gaze flicked to me, then Bennett, then away. "Yeah."

"Pool or ocean?"

Grady shrugged.

I looked at Bennett. His gaze was intense. "Both. They have a nice pool. But the beach is right there."

I nodded. "So it is. Bet the pool is warmer in the fall and spring though."

Bennett chuckled. "Definitely."

"Do you like dinosaurs?" I tried to gauge how old the boy was and if that was, in fact, too old for dinosaurs. Not that I believed that was a thing. Dinosaurs were cool no matter how old you got.

Grady's head tipped to the side. "Ankylosaurs are the best. They're like tanks and they smash with their tails. Everyone likes the T-Rex, even girls, but I don't. Velociraptors are kind of like smaller T-Rexes and they're smarter and faster and better. But the triceratops is cool."

"I'm going to say that's a yes." I grinned and took a few steps along the shelf, squatted, and grabbed three books from the same series. I took them back to Grady.

He'd continued talking about dinosaurs but paused when I held out a book. He frowned. After a minute, he tentatively reached out and took the book. "That's an ankylosaur."

"Yep. His name's Andy."

Bennett snickered.

Grady looked at Bennett and they traded grins.

I'd obviously missed something.

Bennett glanced up at me. "Andy's the name of one of the marina cats. He's a mean, orange tomcat who keeps the mouse population under control."

"I'm not sure this Andy eats mice, but he's not always the nicest dino on the block." I tapped the triceratops in the background of the cover. "Terry though, she's cool."

Grady bit his lip.

"Do you want to look inside? They've got some fun pictures." I had to stop myself from taking the book and showing him. I really wanted Grady to take the initiative. Maybe he'd see that it wasn't scary in there on the pages. I liked these books because they weren't huge walls of text. The reading level might be lower than he needed, but I'd also found that kids who didn't like reading could benefit from a gentler introduction.

"I'd like to, if you don't." Bennett craned his neck like he was trying to peek inside the book Grady held. "It sounds like a cool setup."

That seemed to nudge Grady into action. He flipped open the cover, then turned a couple of pages. His brow knit as he looked at the start of chapter one. His lips moved. After a moment, he turned the page, revealing one of the first full-color pictures.

He laughed and turned the book so Bennett could see.

Bennett grinned. "Uh oh. What happened to Terry?"

Grady shrugged one shoulder.

I looked at Bennett and lowered my voice slightly. "There are ten in the series so far, and I saw an announcement that they're planning to release at least three this year."

"Cool." Bennett pushed to his feet.

The motion brought him closer to me than I'd anticipated and for just a moment, I could feel his warmth drawing me near like a siren song.

I stepped back and pushed the other two books toward Bennett.

He took them—probably more as a reflex to keep the books from jabbing him in the chest than anything else. One corner of his mouth poked up. "It was nice seeing you at dinner on Monday."

I blinked. "No, it wasn't. You were mad that I butted in on your family dinner."

"Mad? No." He shook his head. "I'll give you surprised."

I sighed. "I'll take surprised, if we add irked."

"Hmm." Bennett glanced at Grady, who still stood looking at the book. He'd moved from the first page to the next, but not beyond that. He returned his attention to me. "I hate to refuse a good counter offer, but I can't accept irked. What about mildly discomfited."

Mildly discomfited? I snickered. He'd always had a big vocabulary. It probably came in handy as a lawyer. Probably had learned it from his two lawyer parents. "Is that your final offer?"

He nodded.

"Fine. I accept. But I'm also still apologizing for butting in. Although, your mom didn't really give me a choice."

Bennett laughed. "That sounds like Mom."

It did. She'd always been open and welcoming. Bennett's whole family had been. "It was nice to see everyone. I guess I didn't realize your brothers had stayed on the island."

"We don't tend to roam." Bennett shrugged. "After school, we migrate back. It's hard to say no to the beach."

"It is."

Silence stretched between us. He cleared his throat. "The cottage is working out okay for you?"

"Yeah. Yes. It's perfect."

"Good. That's good." He looked away a moment, then back. "If you have any trouble, just text me. Or call. Whatever."

My eyebrows lifted. "Travis gave me a property manager number."

"Oh. Right. Um." He hugged the books to his chest. "That works, too. Obviously. But maybe you should have my number as well. Just in case."

I blinked. I couldn't imagine why I'd need it. I had the property manager. I had Travis's number. And Bennett's initial reaction to me being on the island hadn't exactly been positive, warm, and welcoming. Or even one of those all on its own.

"Or not." He reached out and touched Grady's arm. "Hey, bud. Let's check these out and we can go. Miss Jericho probably has stuff she should be doing."

"Okay." Grady gave the book back to Bennett.

I was struggling to catch up while avoiding whiplash from Bennett's change of attitude. I moved to the checkout desk on autopilot, then slipped behind.

Bennett set the three dinosaur books on the counter, then tugged his wallet free from his hip pocket. He pulled out a library card and offered it.

I scanned the card, glancing at the computer to make sure the account was in good standing. "This is your card. Grady doesn't have his own?"

"I don't think so." He glanced down at Grady. "Do you have a library card?"

Grady shook his head.

"Do you want one?" Bennett started to reach for the form that stood in a clear plastic holder to the side of the counter.

Grady shook his head again.

Bennett went ahead and took a form, folding it in half. "I'll tell Travis to look into it. It's okay if they're on my account though, right?"

"Sure. Of course." I smiled. "But you'll be responsible for any fines."

"I can handle that."

I scanned the three books, grabbed a bookmark from the pile nearby and tucked it into the cover of the top book, then slid them across the counter. "Enjoy your books, Grady. Maybe when you bring them back, you can tell me who your favorite is."

Grady took the books then turned his serious expression my way. After a moment of thought, he nodded.

"Have a good weekend." I lifted a hand to wave.

"You, too." Bennett rested his hand on Grady's shoulder. "Maybe we'll see you at church."

I didn't respond. Staying silent was the safest option, since I had no intention of getting into why I didn't go to a physical church anymore. Not with Bennett. Or anyone.

Bennett cocked his head to the side and looked like he was going to say more. I steeled myself for whatever was coming. In the end, though, he didn't speak to me. "Let's go, bud. Miss Jericho's probably ready to close up and start her weekend."

"I'm not in a rush." I fought a wince as the words escaped. They were leaving. Wasn't that exactly what I wanted them to do?

Bennett just smiled and shook his head before steering Grady toward the door. When it closed behind them, I picked up the handset of the phone and pressed the key sequence that turned it into the intercom for the space. "The library will be closing in five minutes. Please bring your books to the desk to check out or return them."

I was pretty sure there wasn't actually anyone in here, but Mrs. Sanderson had been adamant that this was a necessary step in the closing process. I set the handset back on the cradle and waited, fighting the urge to check my watch every few seconds.

When two o'clock came, I hurried over to the door and flipped the lock. At least that way, no last-minute patrons would come running in looking for the book they just had to have for the weekend. Or to print something fast. Or any number of things that tended to happen at closing time. I'd seen them all at the other library where I'd worked. Up to and including a final trip to the restroom for members of the homeless population.

I did a quick walkthrough of the entire library, checking to be sure no one was hunkered down with a book and earbuds in. I knocked on both bathroom doors, then pushed them open. "Closing time!"

I didn't see feet under the stalls, so I flipped off the lights and continued my check. The building was small enough that it hadn't taken long. And I had nothing pressing for my Friday night. So I went back to the cart of books to reshelve and continued the methodical and soothing process of restoring order to the library.

Unfortunately, methodical also meant I had entirely too much time to think. And my brain—no matter what I tried to distract it with—would not veer off the subject of Bennett Thomas.

Why did he have to look so good? Couldn't he have had premature balding or a ton of wrinkles from too much time in the sun? Maybe a little paunch because he spent his days behind a desk?

No. Of course not. He looked like the grown-up version of

the boy I'd loved—somewhere between the dignified handsomeness of his father that I'd admired as a teen and that gangly teenager.

What did I look like to him?

"No. Stop that line of thought immediately." I closed my eyes and took a deep breath. I'd considered all the angles before applying for the job here. I'd prayed about it relentlessly. I'd tried every other possibility I could find, but those doors kept slamming in my face.

This one opened.

I sighed and glanced down at the cart. Last book.

I picked it up and walked down the shelves several steps until I found where it went. I slid it in place, then returned to the now empty cart and pushed it back toward the front desk. I took my time tidying everything up, shutting down the computers, and turning off lights. Then I grabbed my purse and lunch bag out of the locked drawer where I stored them, hooked my keys around a finger, and strode to the front door.

I clicked each switch on the bank of light switches one at a time, smiling slightly as the room darkened from back to front, though winter afternoon light still shone through the windows, keeping it from complete darkness.

I let myself out, then relocked the door and double-checked it like Mrs. Sanderson insisted, even though she wasn't standing here over my shoulder anymore. She'd been right about the catch being tricky occasionally, and while I couldn't fathom that anyone would break into the library after hours, it wasn't impossible. There was a little petty cash, some easily sellable technology. Desperation could make people do all kinds of things.

I made my way down the steps and breathed in deeply. Would I get used to the salty tang in the air and come to take it for granted? Hopefully not. Even as the breeze picked up and brought hints of iciness with it, I smiled. This was where I was meant to be. Why? That wasn't something I'd figured out completely as yet.

It definitely didn't have to do with Bennett Thomas, though.

Couldn't.

Shouldn't.

Wouldn't.

Annoyed, I zipped my coat and hurried to my car. Time to go home, change into comfier clothes, and maybe take a walk on the beach. To my landlubber nose, it smelled like rain—well, that and I'd checked the weather app this morning. If I was going walking, I should get to it sooner rather than later.

Maybe on the way home, I'd come up with a way to keep my thoughts from drifting to Bennett for the entirety of my stroll.

9

BENNETT

"Thanks, man." Travis flopped onto my couch looking like he'd been running marathons all day.

"It was fun. We had a good afternoon, right, Grady?" I glanced over at my nephew, who was building Lego in a corner of the living room.

He didn't look up, just shrugged.

I chuckled. "I had fun, anyway."

"A shrug is honestly pretty high praise." Travis sighed. "What are we going to do, Bennett?"

I winced. I had no idea. I wasn't even positive Travis was really asking. He might have just been saying the words as some kind of rhetorical expulsion of emotion. "You still haven't heard from her?"

He shook his head.

"Maybe that's a good sign."

Travis scoffed. "How would that possibly be good?"

"Let me preface with reminding you that I don't handle a lot of divorces, because I hate doing them. That said, there's no requirement for a legal separation agreement here, but with Grady in the mix, you need one. And she hasn't had someone contact you about that." I didn't add—because I didn't have to—that it hadn't even been a full week yet. So any sort of legal paperwork was unlikely to have arrived. But it could. Any time now.

"That's kind of scraping the bottom of the barrel in terms of good signs."

I chuckled awkwardly. "I know. I'm sorry. You know I'm going to help you—we all are—however we can."

"I don't want this. I thought we were happy." Travis frowned. "Everyone probably says that. We had little bumps. And lately she'd been struggling a lot with Grady. But I honestly just thought it was a hurdle we'd get over together."

I glanced over at Grady. He appeared absorbed in his building, but what if he wasn't? I stood and jerked my head toward the kitchen. "Why don't you two stay for dinner? Let's go see what I have on hand that might work."

"Oh. Well, Squirtle—"

"Will be fine. You were home at lunch." I cocked my head to the side. "Or are you making a dig about my cooking? We can always go out. I'd even cross the bridge if you wanted to find a chain restaurant instead of the diner or the bookstore café."

"You forgot pizza." Travis stood and glanced at Grady. "We've been eating a lot of that."

I nodded. The little mom and pop Italian place in town made great pizza and they had a son in high school who was always willing to do delivery if you asked nicely. "I figured. That's why I didn't mention it."

"I did switch it up and get ravioli the other day." Travis jammed his hands in his pockets. "That ended up being a bad plan."

"Not a fan?"

Travis shook his head. "Nope."

Grady could be a picky eater. He wasn't a dino nugget only

kid, but there were definite preferences that were easy to spot. "Let's see if I have anything that'll work. If nothing else, I'm pretty sure I have a couple blue boxes of mac and cheese."

"That always works." He leaned against the counter. "We could do that for him and something else for us. I wouldn't mind not eating kid food, but fixing two meals has been more than I've been able to even contemplate. Especially after the whole spaghetti situation on Monday."

"I'm surprised your mom—and mine, for that matter—haven't been showing up with food." I opened the fridge and looked in.

"I told them no."

I glanced over my shoulder at him. "Why would you do that?"

He shrugged. "This is my problem."

I grabbed the package of ground beef from the meat drawer and closed the fridge. "First, that's not a thing in our family. You know this. We share the burden. Second, taco salads?"

"Taco salad sounds great." He sighed.

"And the other?"

"I know you're right. I just...it's the whole thing with Grady. Caroline's adamant that there's nothing wrong with him. And she was absolutely firm on the fact that we weren't sharing any of the struggle with the family. Not even when the school started pressuring us about testing."

That was news to me. I got a pan out of the cabinet and set it on the stove. "When was that?"

"Start of the school year."

My eyebrows lifted. I opened the ground beef and dropped it in the pan, then took the packaging to the trash before washing my hands. "That's been a minute."

"I know. I've been trying to get her to see that the meltdowns aren't what every kid does. And you got those books for him at the library, but he's so behind there. I'm reasonably sure he has dyslexia, too. The internet says it can be common for dyslexia to co-occur with autism and ADHD." Travis blew out a breath. "Not that we have an official diagnosis for any of that, because Caroline refuses to acknowledge that we should check it out."

I filled a pot with water and set it on the back burner so it could boil for Grady's mac and cheese, then started breaking up the ground beef with a wooden spoon. "Well, maybe here's the bright side."

"Oh, goody." Travis's voice was resigned.

I smiled slightly. "Seriously. You want an evaluation, right?"

"I don't know about wanting one. But I think we need one."

"Okay. And she's not here to stop it." I turned to face my cousin. "So seize the day, man. You know your mom and dad would have tried to help you convince Caroline if you'd asked them to."

"Yeah, but that's part of the problem."

I lowered the heat on the meat and thought about Travis's words. "Because we're a close family?"

"She didn't phrase it that way, but yeah."

I nodded. Occasionally, when I'd let myself wonder what went wrong between Jericho and me, I'd questioned if the family was part of it. Her family had seemed pretty typical—close, but not the kind of family who were all going to end up living in the same town. And that's what we were.

Mom and Dad had never required us to stay on Loring Island. They hadn't even really suggested it. They'd always supported whatever we wanted to do. Aunt Deb and Uncle Rob always came across the same way. Grammie and Gramps, too, for that matter. They were all proud of our family heritage and its connection to the island, but if I'd wanted to move to some big city and join an enormous law firm, they would have wished me well.

"I'm sorry she doesn't really understand our family dynamic."

Travis blew out a breath. "That's exactly it. I joined Dad's company after college because it was what I wanted to do, not because I didn't have other options or was too scared to strike out on my own. I think, at some level, Caroline expected me to want to move across the country and only fly back for Christmas."

"Yikes." I gave the meat another stir before crossing to the pantry to get a packet of taco seasoning and the box of mac and cheese. "Although, I guess seeing how she's been with her family, I'm less surprised."

"They definitely set the standard in her mind. I think she talks to her mom once a quarter. Maybe. They've only met Grady twice. Even if I didn't love how close our family is, I would never want that kind of relationship." Travis reached for the mac and cheese. "Let me get that."

I gave him the box and turned my attention to the taco meat, adding the packet of spices and then some water. I stirred it around, then turned off the heat under the pan. It would stay hot enough to finish cooking the sauce and it let me get out of Travis's way. "I guess the way you two got married meant you didn't find most of that out beforehand."

"Yeah. And I never would have thought it mattered. Maybe if I was better at communicating it wouldn't have come to matter as much as it has."

I frowned at him before turning to the fridge to get the rest of the fixings for our dinner. "I'm not going to say you were perfect, but it takes two people to make a marriage. Did she communicate with you?"

"No." Travis stirred the noodles in the boiling water then turned to lean against the counter again. "I guess I know that, here," he touched his head, "but right now, I'm looking for something—anything—to make sense of what my life has become."

I set the head of lettuce and container of cherry tomatoes on the counter. "You're going to be all right."

"Promise?" Travis flashed a sardonic smile.

"Ultimately? Yeah. But I can also pretty much promise that until you get there, it's probably going to suck. I've been ghosted before, don't forget. I know—at least a little—what you're dealing with."

Travis studied me a moment before nodding once.

Our conversation drifted to other topics as we finished getting supper ready and loading up plates. It took a good bit of cajoling to get Grady to join us at the table, but he finally did, he attacked the mac and cheese with gusto.

After dinner, Travis stood and started to clear the table.

"I can get that. Don't worry about it." I stood and picked up my own plate.

"Can I go build more Lego?" Grady dropped his spoon into his bowl from high enough that it made a loud crash.

"Sorry, bud. We need to get home. Squirtle will want some yard time and his dinner. And we should start on one of those cool dinosaur books Uncle Bennett helped you choose, since you're going to go back to school on Monday."

Grady's lower lip poked out. "I don't want to go back to school."

"I know. And yet." Travis rubbed his son's shoulder. "Come on, let's head home."

Moving more slowly than I'd thought possible, Grady pushed his chair back and stood. He cast a longing glance at the Lego in the corner.

"I'll keep them right there for you, so next time you come over you can pick up right where you left off. Okay?" I squeezed

Grady in a half-hug. "Thanks for hanging out with me this afternoon. Don't forget your books."

Grady scooped up the books from the little table by the front door.

"Thanks again, Bennett."

"Any time. Seriously." I pointed a finger at my cousin. "You're not alone."

Travis nodded and held the door for Grady to go out, then pulled it shut behind them.

I sighed and turned to look around. There'd been a big part of me that had hoped they'd hang out for the evening. I'd forgotten about Squirtle. Maybe I should have suggested they go get him and come back, but I hadn't gotten the feeling from Travis that he was up for that. He looked worn out. I hadn't asked outright because I didn't want to set Grady up for another meltdown if Travis said no. Or yes. Apparently, things with Grady had hit a point that either answer might have set him off, depending on whether or not it was what he wanted.

I gathered the dishes that were still on the table and carried them to the sink. It only took a few minutes to get them into the dishwasher and tidy up the counters.

Now what?

I could call my brothers and see what they were up to. Or my other cousins. Chances were high that I could swing by Mom and Dad's and they'd let me crash on their couch to join them for whatever movie they'd put in. That was their usual Friday night activity and had been for as long as I could remember.

Family movie night.

I'd always thought it was a tradition I'd continue with my own family.

Restless, I checked my pockets for my keys and phone, grabbed my coat, and stepped out the back door. I'd go for a walk on the beach. If nothing else, maybe that would put me in the mood to sit still and watch a movie on my own.

I deliberately turned in the opposite direction of my family's homes. The lighthouse shone in the distance. Between its strobe and the full-ish moon in the mostly clear sky overhead, I didn't need a flashlight.

The wind off the water stung my cheeks and ruffled my hair, bringing with it the scent of sea that, to me, had always signaled home.

I let my thoughts wander as I walked.

In some ways, I understood Travis's reluctance to share his troubles with the family. Especially if Caroline was so against it. In other ways though? I just didn't.

Family helped.

Not just blood family, either. One of the big, recurring themes in the sermons from our small, island church's pastor was on unity of the family of God. How God created us for community and we were commanded to be there for one another.

Our little island wasn't always perfect, but even though there were occasional spats, we'd all rally around anyone who needed help. Church member or not. Loring family descendant or not. How had Caroline missed that? Why had Travis let her?

Maybe it wasn't a matter of letting her. It wasn't as if I'd "let" Jericho disappear all those years ago. I certainly hadn't wanted it. I'd sent her letters. Email. I'd even tried calling a few times. No response.

Ultimately, Dad had sat me down and asked me to consider if I was getting close to the "stalker" line. I hadn't wanted to even consider the question, but the takeaway was the same: I'd had to let her go and try to figure out how to move on.

I was still working on that last part all these years later.

A bright flash from overhead revealed I'd walked farther

than anticipated. I was at the lighthouse, and a glance up at the sky revealed that the deepening darkness wasn't just because of the hour. Thick clouds were moving in rapidly across the sky, glowing briefly as lightning flickered inside.

I jogged to the awning that covered the entrance to the lighthouse. Another flash lit the sky, this time followed by the crack of thunder after only a couple of seconds. I dismissed the thought of making a dash for home. I certainly wasn't going to run home back the way I'd come along the beach.

Maybe I could just wait it out here. Storms like this weren't always long affairs. I dragged my phone out of my pocket and pulled up the weather app. I frowned. The forecasters didn't always get things right, so there was the small possibility that the storm wouldn't last for the next four hours, but I also wasn't excited about testing that theory from the dubious safety of this overhang.

Now what?

I shifted my gaze toward the public beach and the houses that stood just across the road from it. Heron Cottage—my cottage—was right there. The yellow glow of the porch light a warm beacon in the distance. Fortunately, or maybe unfortunately, it wasn't empty. A week ago, I could have dashed over, let myself in, and just hunkered down there until the storm passed. Now?

What kind of reception would I get from Jericho?

She'd been friendly-ish today at the library. And at dinner on Monday. If I was being fair, she'd been better to me in all of our encounters than I'd been to her.

I winced.

For years, I'd been telling myself, my family, and God that I'd forgiven her and was over it. But her return to the island had shown me just how empty and untrue that was.

Another flash and an almost immediate boom was followed

by the rush of water as the clouds opened and began dumping rain in thick sheets. The wind picked up, slinging the hard droplets sideways in stinging missiles. I might be under cover from above, but I was also now completely soaked.

I couldn't stay here.

I took a deep breath and let it out slowly. I had two options. I could call a family member and ask them to come out in this to pick me up and take me home. Or I could run to Heron and throw myself at the mercy of Jericho.

I looked down at my phone, then back out at the hammering rain.

I couldn't ask someone to go out in this.

I shoved my phone into the scant protection of my jacket pocket, popped the collar and hitched my coat up to provide a little more cover to my head, and fixed my gaze on the glowing beacon of Heron Cottage's porch light.

Then I ran.

10

JERICHO

I clicked the TV off and set aside my giant mug of cocoa. The storm had started in earnest and the satellite signal that had been iffy all evening completely cut out. I couldn't bring myself to mind. I hadn't been able to focus on any of the shows I'd tried to watch. My lack of focus was why I was watching TV in the first place. I would much rather have been reading, but tonight was one of the rare nights that didn't seem to be working either.

The windows of my cottage rattled with another crash of thunder. I hunched my shoulders. I wasn't afraid of storms, really, but it had been a while since I'd been around one this violent.

I stood and crossed to the picture window that faced the ocean. It was dark, but I could make out the froth of white on the edges of the waves that the wind whipped up. Another flash of light brought the scene into almost daytime clarity and the boom that followed quickly on its heels almost disguised the sound of banging at my door.

I angled my head to try to see who was there—if it was a person. Maybe it was simply trash getting blown up onto the porch and against the walls. Except it was definitely too rhythmic for that. I could just make out the silhouette of someone standing, fist raised to knock again.

In the back of my mind, I could hear both of my parents scolding me for being too trusting. Too naïve. Too…everything. I grabbed my cell phone off the table beside my mug, unlocked it and dialed nine and then one. I kept my finger poised over the next one as I moved to the door and nudged aside the thin curtain covering the sidelight window.

Frowning, I clicked off my phone, shoved it in my pocket, and hurried to unlock the door.

"Bennett?" I stepped back and gestured for him to come in. "What on earth are you doing out in this?"

He stepped in, shivering and dripping on the little rug in the foyer.

I closed the door and relocked it. "Let me get you a towel."

"Thanks." Bennett stepped out of his shoes and nudged them to the side, then unzipped his jacket.

I hurried down the hall to the guest bath and grabbed both towels that hung on the bar. Returning to the main room, I offered them to Bennett.

He'd shed his jacket and socks in the short time it took me to fetch the towels. He took them with a look of gratitude and shook one open before scrubbing it over his face and hair.

I propped my hands on my hips. "You're going to catch your death."

He snickered as he wrapped one towel around his shoulders and shook the second one open. "You sound like Grammie."

"She was a sensible woman." I shook my head. "That's not going to do you any good. Go in the hall bathroom and take a hot shower. I probably have sweatpants or something that will be better than wet jeans."

His eyebrows lifted. "Are you sure? I don't want to put you out."

I tilted my head to the side and just looked at him.

He hunched his shoulders slightly. "Any more than I already am?"

"It's fine. I'll see what I can dig up that has a chance of fitting and leave them outside the door. When you're warmed up and dry, bring your wet clothes to the kitchen and we can put them in the dryer." I turned and headed back down the hall, this time continuing to my bedroom. It was probably a good thing I liked baggy clothes for weekends and schlepping around the house, but even with that, nothing I had was going to be long enough to be anything other than ridiculous on Bennett.

It was still probably better than cold and wet though.

I pulled out a dresser drawer and rooted through for black sweats. From another drawer, I grabbed my most oversized hoodie. Finally, after a moment's thought, I dug out a pair of thick socks. Those would probably be the worst fit, but even if the heel was closer to the arch of his foot, they'd keep his toes warmer than being barefoot.

I paused at the door to my bedroom and listened. I could just make out the sound of the shower—ever so slightly different from the pounding rain outside.

Good. He'd followed my instructions. Suggestion? He could have chosen to stay wet and cold. He would've been stupider than I ever thought possible if he had, but it was still a choice. I strode down the hall and dropped the clothes on the floor by the bathroom door, then knocked once.

"I'm heading to the kitchen. Clothes are here. There are more towels in the linen closet in there. Which you probably know, since this is your place. Anyway. Take your time." I didn't wait for an answer before going the rest of the way down the hall, through the living room, and into the kitchen.

I filled the kettle at the tap and put it back on the stove, then cranked up the heat. Did he still prefer tea to cocoa? Even if he did, was there any tea in the cottage? I certainly hadn't stocked any. I'd never understood the point of tea. Bennett had teased me about it when we'd been together. Just like I'd given him grief about not appreciating the finer points of smooth hot cocoa piled high with whipped cream.

At least we'd both agreed that mornings called for coffee.

I crossed to the little pantry and opened it, looking at the shelves other than the one I'd used to store boxes of protein bars and cans of green beans. I'd never claimed to be the world's best cook, but I did try to focus on getting the nutrition that responsible adults needed. Jumping, I peeked at the top shelf.

Hm.

I dragged one of the tall chairs from the kitchen island over and climbed up. Success! In the far back corner of the top shelf there was a box of tea bags. I grabbed it, wrinkling my nose at the layer of dust.

Could tea go bad?

I hopped down and dragged the chair back to where it belonged, then flipped open the box and sniffed.

It smelled like tea to me. Would I even be able to tell if it was stale—or whatever the tea equivalent of stale was? Probably not. On the positive side, it didn't actively smell bad. So it was probably fine. I'd ask Bennett when he got out of his shower.

I got a mug down from the cabinet where they were stored, then I grabbed the sugar bowl and a spoon. Did he add milk to his tea? That little detail appeared to be lost to the sands of time. If he did, the fridge was right there.

I covered my face and groaned. Why was I worrying about this? It was tea. For all I knew, he'd stopped drinking tea and would want coffee. Or cocoa. Or...anything else. Coke? That's what the server yesterday had assumed he'd want. But I didn't have that, anyway. Water was still an option.

And I was still obsessing about offering Bennett a drink.

Stop. Just stop.

I crossed into the living room to retrieve my cocoa, doing my best to avoid any glances down the hallway. Not that I'd see anything more than a pile of clothes and a closed door. Or a closed door and no pile of clothes. Except the water was still running—I cocked my head to the side and listened—yeah, definitely still running. So pile of clothes.

Oh. My. Word.

"Get a grip, Jericho." I muttered under my breath as I carried my mug back to the kitchen.

I pulled out a chair and sat at the island. The kettle wasn't boiling yet. So I could just sit here and not obsess about Bennett.

So much easier said than done.

With a sigh, I set my mug down and stood. I crossed to the pantry again and opened it. I had no snacks to offer. I needed to cross over to the mainland and do a big shop at the grocery store. Maybe even something like Costco or Sam's. The island market was fine for a lot of stuff, but even the locals who'd lived here all their lives didn't rely solely on it. So far, I'd loaded up on PB&J makings and some soup.

I guess I could offer soup.

It was long past suppertime, so he might not even need anything. But given the sheets of rain still whipping down out of the clouds, sprinkled liberally with flashes of lightning that seemed much too close for comfort, I wasn't offering to drive him back to his house any time soon.

"Only a moron would go out in this." I muttered as I closed the pantry door again.

The quiet chuckle behind me made me jump. My face burned and I closed my eyes. Were sinkholes a thing here? I could absolutely go for one that swallowed up the cottage right about now.

I cleared my throat and turned. "Sorry."

Amusement danced in his eyes. "No need. You're not wrong. Although, in my defense, I didn't realize it was going to do this when I started out for a walk."

The shrill whistle of the kettle saved me from making another snarky comment. I backed up two steps before turning and heading to the stove and turning off the heat to quiet the noise. "I thought you might like some tea."

"You drink tea now?" He moved to the island and leaned a hip against it.

"Well, no." I gestured toward my cocoa. "But I remembered —um, anyway, someone left a box of tea bags? Do they go bad?"

He shrugged and reached for the box. He flipped open the lid and sniffed. "They smell like tea. I'll risk it. Thanks."

"Sure." I smiled slightly and gestured toward the mug and sugar bowl. "I'll let you take it from here. Do you need milk? I didn't remem—" Ugh, I cut myself off. I needed to stop talking about remembering things about him. Bennet Thomas didn't need to know just how often I thought about him. "I didn't know if that was something you did."

"Depends. Do you have any?" He plucked a tea bag from the box and dropped it into the mug before pushing off the island and moving around to the stovetop. He grabbed the kettle and poured the steaming water in.

"I do."

His gaze flicked up and met mine for just a moment. The contact was brief. There was no way I'd seen the pain I imagined in it. That was just my overactive imagination bringing up the past. Right?

Refusing to dwell on that, I crossed to the fridge and opened it, suddenly self-conscious about its emptiness. I grabbed the quart of milk from the door and set it on the island. "I like cereal."

"Who doesn't?" Bennett didn't reach for the milk. He was poking at the tea bag with his spoon, bouncing it up and down in the mug.

"Can I get you anything else? Do you want soup or something?" I was perilously close to babbling. The quirk of his lips suggested he was well aware of that fact.

"I'm good. Why don't you sit and drink your cocoa before it's too cold?" He nodded toward my mug.

Good idea. Probably too late already, but I'd survive. I didn't like what the microwave did to the taste if I reheated it, so this wasn't the first mug of cold chocolate I'd consumed. It probably wouldn't be the last. I often got distracted and ended up forgetting about my beverage while I read. I sat on the stool by my mug and lifted it for a sip, only then noticing how short the arms of my sweatshirt were on him. I had to fight the urge to peek around the counter to check on the fit of the sweatpants. Even if the clothes were clownishly small, he'd look good in them.

I put my mug down and hopped out of my seat. "Your clothes! I'll go put them in the dryer."

"I'll get them. This has to steep anyway." He stopped plunking the tea bag up and down and pointed at me. "Don't let me disturb your evening plans more than I already have."

I swallowed a snicker. Evening plans? I'd been watching the storm and praying the electricity didn't go out. That was the sum total of my plans. Regardless, I resumed my seat and took another sip of the tepid liquid.

He was back in a matter of moments carrying not only his clothes but the towels. "You mind if I wash everything first?"

Honestly? Yes. It meant an extra hour of him in my space. Except the storm was supposed to last most of the night—so unless I wanted to change my mind and chance driving in this, he was going to be here a lot longer than the wash and dry cycle would take. "Go ahead."

He studied me before nodding slowly. "I'm sorry. Yours was the only porch light on."

Apparently, he'd noticed my hesitation. "Don't be sorry. I'm glad you were willing to knock."

I watched him cross the kitchen to the little mudroom door and go through. The sweatpants ended just north of the half-way point between his ankles and knees. I smothered a grin. At least he was still lanky, so they weren't stretched too tightly in all the other places.

I sighed and sipped the cocoa again, thinking through my last statement to him. Was glad really the right word there?

Actually, it might be.

Did that make me stupid, hopeless, or a combination of the two?

Bennett returned from the mud room, pulling the door closed behind him to close out the sound of the washing machine chugging away. "I really appreciate this."

"Stop." I gestured to the huge window in the living room. "Nobody would leave another person out in this. Not even me."

"I didn't mean it like that." He frowned as he fished the tea bag out of his mug and squeezed it against the spoon. Clearly at home, he crossed to the trash and dropped the tea bag in, then returned to doctor the drink with sugar and milk. He put the milk back in the fridge. "But since you mention it."

I winced.

I really, really didn't want to get into it.

But I definitely owed him whatever answers he needed.

I took a deep breath. "Okay?"

"What happened?" He lifted his mug, blew across the top, then drank.

Everything in me wanted to play dumb, but that would be an

insult to both of us. I looked away. "The short answer is that my parents' marriage fell apart. Or maybe it had never actually been held together with anything other than chewing gum and Scotch tape. I still don't know for sure. But I do know that they had embodied everything I thought I wanted in a relationship, and when it turned out to be smoke and mirrors, I didn't know what to do."

Bennett was silent long enough that I finally turned to look at him. He held his tea in both hands, his eyebrows drawn together.

"It didn't occur to you to talk to me about it."

He hadn't phrased it as a question, so I wasn't sure what to say. He was only partially right, though. It had occurred to me, but I hadn't been in the place where I had any idea how to do that. "I'm sorry."

He shook his head. "That's it?"

I shrugged. "I don't know what else to say, Bennett. I didn't know what to do. I had to be there for my sisters. Dad disappeared. Mom used me as her verbal punching bag, expecting me to somehow broker peace for her, furious when I couldn't. And, I'm sad to say, I tried. I turned myself inside out trying to be what everyone needed me to be, and I didn't have the ability to do that for you, too. It was all too much."

He stiffened. "I never asked or expected you to. But I would have treasured the chance to be there for you."

His words stabbed my already aching heart. There was a part of me—a big one—that wanted to rage at him about how easy it was for him to say that now. But the reality was that I hadn't given him the chance to do it then. So what else was he supposed to say?

Any hope of being done shedding tears for Bennett Thomas disappeared when the first hot, fat drop rolled down my cheek. I swiped it away and stood, then carried my mug to the sink and dumped it out. I set the empty dish down—I could deal with that tomorrow—and turned. I crossed my arms, suddenly so cold. Words choked together behind the lump in my throat.

"I don't know what to say besides I'm sorry." I swiped more tears off my cheeks and crossed the kitchen, aiming for the hallway. "Make yourself at home. Truly. Stay as long as you like. I'm going to bed."

He said something that I couldn't process as I nearly ran the short hall to my bedroom. I closed the door, punched the basically worthless lock, then turned and sagged back against the wood, slowly sinking to the floor.

I hugged my knees to my chest, rested my head on them, and let the tears flow.

11

BENNETT

I'd always loved the smell of the morning after a big storm. Today was no different, although it was odd to be walking on the beach well before the sun came up. On a Saturday. That was definitely not my norm—and I had big plans for a nap this afternoon to make up for it. I'd gotten just about three hours of fitful sleep on the couch at Heron Cottage. First, because I'd wanted to wait until the laundry was finished. And that included tossing the sweats she'd loaned me in to wash and dry when my clothes were done. And the rest? Because I'd been unable to get the memory of Jericho's face and the sound of her sobs out of my mind.

I hadn't been trying to be mean. Not like the first day I saw her at the bookstore when I'd let my hurt and anger control my tongue. But there had been some small part of me that wanted to make her understand just how deeply she'd wounded me.

"Mission accomplished." I muttered and kicked a glob of wet sand.

I sighed. Why had she come here, of all places? There were libraries literally everywhere. Sure, okay, they might not be hiring. But had ours really been her only option? Did she think I wouldn't still live here?

She knew better than that. She had to. All the dreams—the plans we'd made—centered on living right here. On building our dream house on the lot at the north end of the island that still waited for me.

My parents hadn't understood, not really, when I bought the house where I lived now. Mom, especially, had been unwilling to let it go, until I finally explained. She'd known Jericho and I were dating. But she'd thought it was just puppy love. Something I'd get over in college. The way most people did.

I'd tried.

Well. Sort of.

According to the girl I'd spent the most time dating, I wore the word "unavailable" like an invisible cloak. She'd enjoyed the dinners out and having a built-in date for dances or events, but she'd made a point of not letting herself feel. She'd ended up dumping me for a friend of a friend half-way through sophomore year. Pretty sure they were married now.

I trudged up the back stairs and unlocked my kitchen door. I stepped out of my shoes, leaving them on the deck to deal with when the sun was up. Flicking the light on, I glanced around. I should probably try to catch a few more hours of sleep. I didn't have anything planned today and there was no reason I couldn't sleep in. It was probably the saner choice. I never woke up well from naps.

I dragged a hand through my hair, then started toward the coffee machine. There was no way I was going to be able to sleep right now.

When the beans were ground and the coffee was brewing, I moved to the living room and flopped on the couch. I unlocked my phone and opened a browser. After sleeping on the couch in the cottage, it was probably time to consider replacing some of the furniture there. Renters—especially short-term renters—were apparently hard on things. No one had complained, but that had to be because no one tried to sleep on the thing.

At the same time, I didn't want to spend a ton on a couch that was going to be abused by vacationing families. The sheer amount of sand that got brought into the cottage—at least according to the cleaning crew—indicated that the renters weren't treating it like their home away from home. Either that, or they had seriously bad habits at home. Or maybe they figured they had to pay the cleaning deposit so they might as well get their money's worth.

Whatever the reason, it was one more thing in the "why I'm glad I don't have to deal with it this year" column. Maybe Jericho would decide she liked it enough to renew her lease next year. If the island came through and offered her a permanent position. Unless she ended up burning books in the middle of the library, I didn't see that not happening. Especially since she'd attained Mrs. Sanderson's seal of approval.

Ugh. Why was I sitting here thinking about Jericho? The whole point of leaving so early was to ensure that she didn't have to deal with me again. After last night, it seemed like the wiser course of action.

Dragging my thoughts away from Jericho—again—I put "couch" into the search engine. I made it nearly half-way down the first page of results before closing the browser and tossing my phone aside. Way too many options. And now I'd probably be getting ads for them for the rest of my life. I'd ask Mom to find something.

In fact...I grabbed my phone and shot her a quick text about it, then put it back on the cushion. The coffee machine beeped and I stood. Time to get that beautiful first hit of caffeine and then figure out what I was going to do with my day.

I was just tipping a splash of half and half into my mug when my phone rang. I frowned at the time on the coffee maker, then hurried back to the living room and grabbed it, answering after only briefly registering that it was my mom calling.

"What's wrong?" I clamped the phone to my ear with my shoulder and went back for my mug.

"Not a thing. Why would something be wrong?"

I took a deep breath and willed my heart to slow. "It's not quite five thirty?"

"You texted me."

I winced. "I thought you put your phone on silent at night."

"I do. Your father and I are up. We were just getting ready to put on an exercise program to start our day. Did you forget we're old?" Her cheerful laugh belied any hint of old age.

"Since it's not true, it's not something forgettable." I sipped my coffee and went back to the couch. "You could have waited to get in touch."

"Sure. But talking about furniture is better than sweating. And since I said I needed to call you, your father decided he'd make eggs benedict instead of working out. So really, we all win. Now. Why do you think Jericho needs a new couch?"

Oh. I had obviously not thought this through. I tried to organize my thoughts and figure out a way to keep from telling her the whole story.

"There's more of a story here than Jericho let Travis know and he passed it on to you. Why don't you come over? I'll tell Dad to throw another couple eggs in for you. Then you can fill us both in at the same time."

"I don't—"

"See you soon." Mom ended the call.

I scowled at my phone. Was it some kind of skill they taught mothers at the hospital after birth? How did she always know when I was putting together a story with enough elements of truth that wasn't exactly all of it? Maybe it's because she was a lawyer. Except I was a lawyer, too, and she still got the best of me that way every time.

Grumbling under my breath, I took my mug with me back to the bedroom. Mom and Dad had both been in the office yesterday, so I was absolutely not showing up at their house in the same clothes. Even if they were clean.

I took the time to hang everything up, then grabbed jeans and my college hoodie. I tugged on thicker socks, shoved my feet into my good pair of sneakers—the ones I didn't ever wear on the beach—and chugged the remainder of my coffee. I detoured to the kitchen to set my mug in the sink, then grabbed keys and headed out the front door. I considered the bike for about two seconds before unlocking my car instead and climbing in.

The problem with living on an island was that it never took long enough to get somewhere. I was still irritated when I pulled into Mom and Dad's driveway and parked outside their garage. I flexed my hands several times, breathing deeply the way my long-ago therapist had insisted would calm me down. It didn't actually seem to help, but maybe trying was the important thing.

I got out of the car, crossed the driveway, and climbed the stairs to the front door. I gave a perfunctory knock then walked in.

"It's me."

"Hi, me!" Dad yelled from the kitchen.

I smirked slightly even as my eyes rolled of their own volition. I made my way through the foyer that was bracketed by Dad's study on the left and their library on the right, then stepped into the sprawling open concept living space.

Dad grinned at me from behind the kitchen counter. "Heard you convinced Mom to let you wiggle in on our eggs Benedict."

I shook my head as I crossed to the kitchen space, pulled out a stool, and sat. "Is it really a matter of being allowed when it's a command performance?"

"I heard that." Mom poked her head around the door of their walk-in pantry. "You could have said no."

"Could I though? Really?"

"Try it sometime and see." Mom glared at me before she disappeared again.

I winced and looked at Dad. "That was a threat, right?"

He nodded. "You were always a smart boy."

That's what I figured. "Can I help?"

"Nope. Just sit there. We're almost ready." Dad gave the saucepan in front of him one more firm whisk before removing it from the stove and tipping the creamy, golden sauce into a serving bowl. He slid a spoon into the bowl and put it down in front of me just as a timer beeped. "That's the eggs done."

Mom came back into the kitchen. "I couldn't find any. Sorry, babe."

Dad shrugged. "That's fine. Add cinnamon to the list though, would you?"

"Cinnamon?" I wrinkled my nose. "On eggs Benedict?"

"No." Dad made a face like he was going to be sick. "I'd thought to make French toast, but couldn't find the cinnamon. Thus the eggs instead."

That made more sense. Dad's French toast was amazing, but cinnamon was a key ingredient. I nodded.

Mom fixed two mugs of coffee and carried them over to where I sat while Dad scooped poached eggs out of the pot and arranged them on the plates holding English muffins and Canadian bacon that were waiting nearby.

Dad put a plate in front of Mom and then another in front of me. He nodded toward the coffee. "Is one of those for me?"

"Sorry. I thought you had some already. I made this for Bennett." She kissed my cheek and nudged the mug toward me.

"I'll top mine off after we say grace." Dad glanced at me and I quickly bowed my head while he launched into a prayer. Dad wasn't one for short or perfunctory when it came to prayer, but he managed to wrap this one up before the food got cold. Then he moved to the coffee maker.

I waited for Mom to spoon sauce over her eggs before reaching for the bowl and doing the same.

"So." Mom cut one of the eggs on her plate open. "Oh, hon, these are perfect." She sliced off a bite then glanced at me. "What's the story on Jericho and a couch?"

I sighed and cut into my own food. Dad really had a good hand with poaching. Mine were always just slightly too runny or verging toward rubbery. "Have you talked to Aunt Deb about the situation with Travis at all?"

"Some." Mom reached for her coffee. "She's trying to let him take the lead, even though she's desperate to jump in and help. Travis...well, he's a Loring at heart, isn't he?"

Dad nearly choked as he started to laugh.

Mom elbowed him.

Dad held up a hand. "Sorry. Sorry. But I can never get past hearing how y'all pronounce the word stubborn."

"David Thomas." Mom glared at Dad, then laughed. "You're not wrong."

"I seem to recall being told that a strong will and firm convictions were good things." I took another bite. "That's just another way to pronounce stubborn."

"True enough." Dad spooned a bit more sauce onto his food. "But *I* seem to recall also driving home the idea that asking for and receiving help was also a good thing."

That was fair. Mom and Dad were big on asking for help. And giving it. I nodded.

"Deb's at a loss. Travis is a grown man, but he's still her son. It's hard to navigate." Mom shrugged. "And I don't see how this gets around to Jericho needing a new couch."

I sighed. "Travis has kept Grady home from school all week. He's struggling with the change in their routine without Caroline around. But Trav had some stuff he had to do for work yesterday afternoon and he couldn't drag Grady with this time, so we hung out. Then they stayed for dinner. I guess the situation with Grady has been getting worse and the school has been pushing since the start of the year for them to get him evaluated. But Caroline wouldn't hear it."

Mom stabbed her last bite of English muffin and used it to sop up the egg yolk and sauce on her plate. "That poor boy."

"Mom and I never said anything directly to Caroline, because it just isn't our place, but how could she not see that her little boy was struggling?" Dad scowled.

"Maybe she hoped if she ignored it long enough, it would go away?" I shrugged. "I don't really know. But Travis said she forbade him from talking to his folks about it—and anyone else in the family, I imagine—because I guess being a close family, living on top of each other like we do, was another pain point in their marriage."

"Deb wondered about that." Mom reached for her coffee. "But she didn't know how to approach it with them."

"There wouldn't have been a good way, I don't think." Dad frowned. "It's not like anyone in the family is high-handed about getting together. We just all happen to like it."

"Yeah. I never realized Caroline didn't." I pushed my plate away. "Anyway, after they left to go home, I went for a walk."

"You went out last night? With the storm coming?" Mom swiveled her seat to face me. "You know better than that."

I hunched my shoulders. "I didn't realize there was going to be a storm."

Dad shook his head.

"Oh, good grief. You have a phone. It has a weather app. Don't be an idiot." Mom made an exasperated noise.

"Yes'm." It was the only right response. Any sort of discussion about not liking being tied to a phone or whatever else I might try would have just gotten me The Look. And even at thirty-something, The Look was potent. I cleared my throat. "As I was saying, I went for a walk and was trying to figure out how we could help Travis, and the storm hit right about when I reached the lighthouse."

Dad hopped off his stool and started collecting the plates. "That's quite a walk."

Yes and no. I liked walking. Always had. Most of us in the family did. But I also understood what he was saying. "With the lightning and everything, I wasn't going to try to book it back home, and I didn't want to call someone and make them go out in it. I could see the porch light at Heron was on, so I took a chance."

"Hmm." Mom finished her coffee, then pointed at my mug. "You need more?"

"No, I'm good. Thanks." I hesitated. Did I need to finish the story, or could they figure it out from there? Well, obviously they could. The question was if they would. Mom and Dad often seemed to get a kick out of making me squirm.

"So she let you bunk on the couch." Dad rinsed plates and loaded them into the dishwasher. "Why not the other bedroom?"

"She probably expected me to use the other bedroom." I frowned and tried to dredge up any part of our conversation that might have touched on where I could sleep. Nothing. If she'd said, I'd already forgotten. "But we got to talking a little about what happened and..." I couldn't quite figure out how to finish that.

Mom laid her hand on mine. "It didn't go well?"

"Sure." I shrugged. "That's one way to put it. After she ran to her room and I heard her lock the door, then start to sob, it seemed like staying as far away as possible was a better idea than anything else. And if we're looking for a bright side, it made me realize that the couch in that cottage needs replacing."

Mom started to speak, but Dad gave the barest shake of his head. He probably didn't think I'd caught it—probably hoped I hadn't—but it wasn't like Mom to snap her mouth shut like that.

"Did it help?"

I could pretend that I didn't understand what Dad was asking, but what would be the point? "I don't know."

He nodded.

"I guess that's better than a flat no." Mom patted my hand, then stood. "I'll reach out to Jericho and ask if she has a couch she wants to use. If not, then I'll look around for something for you."

"She rented it furnished." Didn't that mean it was my obligation to fix this?

"Which is why I'll ask what she wants. She may say the couch is fine as it is. Maybe sitting on it isn't an issue. Not all couches are napping couches." Mom shrugged. "Saving some money is never a bad idea."

Money was the least of my problems, and Mom knew it. I had my trust that I hadn't really touched since school. I made enough from my job to more than cover my expenses—including the mortgage on my current place, which I hadn't bought outright because of tax liability. But if Mom wanted to make it about money when she talked to Jericho, she could try. Jericho would see through that, no question, but that wasn't my problem.

Dad dried his hands and crossed the kitchen to lean against

the counter next to me. "Do you think there's any chance the two of you can work things out now that she's back on the island?"

I pressed my lips together. Could we? Was she open to that? Even with all the heartache that lingered after all these years, I'd jump at the chance. But the rest of the questions had the same answer, "I don't know that, either."

12

JERICHO

I threw my leg over the bike I'd found at the thrift store after work yesterday and pedaled. My progress was wobbly, at first, but before long, I'd settled into a reasonable speed. I grinned. Maybe it really was just like riding a bike. I rode along the street, past the other cottages that fronted the public beach until I reached the corner that would take me out to the more main road. The plan, such as it was, was a ride down to the park-slash-nature preserve area and then around some of the trails I remembered being there.

Hopefully, those trails were still in existence.

Given that Loring Island advertised itself as a place to get away and spend time in nature, I had high hopes that they were.

The streets were empty. Most of the year-round residents were probably at church. I felt the tiniest twinge in my chest at that thought, but I ignored it. I was used to doing that when it came to church. I didn't need a building and a big group of hypocrites to worship God. In fact, that last bit tended to have the opposite effect.

I probably shouldn't paint everyone with the same brush. Bennett's family all went to church and actually lived what they believed. I'd seen that first hand in my teens and, so far, had no reason to suspect it had changed. Even if the horrible people were the exception to the rule, they'd made things hard enough when Mom and Dad split that I still wasn't willing to risk going back.

In the back of my mind, I heard Mom's voice chiding me, "Different church. Different people. You should give them a chance."

I shook my head to push that voice away. I was glad, truly, that Mom had found a new church when she'd moved from our hometown. The times I'd visited her, she'd seemed happy. Her church family, as she liked to call them, were definitely part of that. It didn't mean that I needed, or wanted, to do the same.

My music blinked out, replaced by a beep. My phone was in my pocket, so I couldn't check to see who was calling, but I tapped my earbud to accept the call anyway.

"Hello?"

"Heya." My sister Madeline's voice was loud in my ears. Did I know how to adjust the volume in these things?

"Are you getting psychic vibes again?" I chuckled, hoping it might cover the slight shortness of breath I was feeling. Either I was completely out of shape or the island wasn't as flat as I remembered it.

"Thinking about me, were you?"

"Sort of. Family, anyway. You're up early." I spotted the park entrance ahead and wanted to whoop for joy.

Madeline cleared her throat. "I was thinking I might check out a church. They have an early service. So I set an alarm."

My eyebrows lifted. Madeline was the sister who hadn't appreciated being made to go to church. Ever. For her to voluntarily seek it out suggested the world might literally be ending. "What brought this on?"

"You remember I mentioned the guy I matched with on a dating app just before Christmas?"

"Yeah. I thought you said there was no chemistry there." I turned into the park, then pulled to the side of the parking area and stopped. "You weren't going to see him again."

Madeline's voice was sheepish. "I know. But we kept chatting in the app. He's really nice. Sweet. And it's like he actually cares about more than scoring a hookup."

I winced. "Mads."

"I know, I know. I'm too loose for you. We don't all want to die virgins."

I ignored the barb and the defensive retort that wanted to escape. "So. The guy wants you to go to church with him?"

"Seth. Yeah." I could almost hear the shrug in her pause. "Is that bad?"

"No. It's good." I wrinkled my nose. Was I really telling my sister that going to church was good? Not that I was wrong, but given my own lack of attendance, did I have the right? "Just...be smart, okay?"

"What do you mean?"

I sighed. "If you're finally ready for a real relationship, something you want to last, then you need to be on the same page about things with the guy. You know?"

"I know that. I was there, too. Becca and I both heard more than you realize. It's not as if we were babies just because we were younger than you. Or..."

I waited several seconds, but she didn't continue. "Or what?"

"Are you worried about me? Or about him?"

I bit my lip. "Maybe a little bit of both."

"Wow."

"Am I wrong to have concerns?"

Her sigh was gusty in my ears. "Probably not. But I guess I hoped you'd be on my side."

"I am. Always. One hundred percent." That was never changing. She was my little sister and after Mom and Dad's divorce, she and Becca both ended up seeing me as a second mom. At least until Mom finally got her head screwed back on straight.

"Promise?"

"Absolutely. And I'm proud of you for being willing to give church a try. I hope you like it. You know how much my relationship with Jesus means to me."

"Ugh. Yes. Because you never stop working it into conversations."

I smiled slightly. "Looks like maybe that's finally paying off now, doesn't it?"

Madeline laughed. "I guess maybe. I really like this guy, Jericho."

"Then I'll be praying that the two of you can make things work."

"Thanks."

"Text me later and let me know how it goes."

"Okay. Love you."

"Love you too." The call ended and my music started back up. I took a moment to dig my phone out of my pocket to adjust the volume slightly and check the time. I put the phone away and re-mounted my bike, forcefully pushing away the usual annoyed thoughts that came after a call with either of my sisters.

It didn't matter who called who, the conversation was always about them. Neither even asked about me. Why did it never occur to either of them that I might have news to share or need their advice? Well, fine. I probably didn't need their advice, although it would still be nice to have a place to vent my frustration with things.

Or people.

People like Bennett who sneak out of the house at some ungodly hour in the morning after I was kind enough to rescue him from being struck by lightning. If that was dramatic, so be it. It was storming. He knocked. I didn't make him leave. And then? On top of all of that? He slept on the couch.

Who did that?

There was a perfectly good bedroom down the hall and he knew it. What sort of monster did he think I was that he slept on the world's most uncomfortable couch rather than what had to be a much comfier bed? Plus he washed my sweats. And the towels he used.

I blew out a breath, trying to calm my racing heart. I couldn't blame it all on being woefully out of shape and riding this bicycle like I was fleeing a tidal wave. Or trying to. It was hard to do with a bike that didn't have gears. I could almost hear my dad laughing and reminding me, "You get what you pay for."

Yeah, well, Dad, sometimes things that are discarded still have value.

Not that he'd know. Or care.

All he did was walk away when he decided things weren't as shiny and new as he seemed to think he deserved.

I should be over it.

I had years of therapy under my belt, and still sometimes the anger flared up. At both of them. Although it had felt like Mom tried. At least a little. Just not enough.

I slowed my pedaling and forced myself to look around. It really was beautiful here. Even in winter, the marshy grass hadn't completely died off. I spied the coast just ahead. The day was clear enough that I could see beyond that, across the inlet, to the mainland. In some ways, it seemed like another world. I'd always had that sense. It was part of why I'd loved coming here in the summer with my family.

Was that why I'd fallen for Bennett so thoroughly? Because he was removed from reality? Like a dream? Was that why I hadn't reached out when everything fell apart?

My mind flashed to the pain in his expression when I'd finally given him the answer to my disappearance. He probably wouldn't have known what to do, or say. How could he have? He came from the perfect family here on the perfect island with his perfect life. But he was also right: I hadn't given him the chance.

I hadn't trusted him.

I hadn't trusted us. Despite the plans we'd made, they'd just been part of the fantasy. Had I ever really believed that we'd stay together through college, get married, and live happily ever after?

Not deep down.

Not after seeing that happily ever after wasn't real.

And I hadn't been willing to risk my heart getting broken by another man who said he loved me.

So I'd broken his, instead.

I sighed and coasted to a stop beside a bench that faced the rugged shore. I hopped off the bike, fought the rusty kickstand down, and walked down to the water.

I probably owed Bennett something. But for the life of me, I couldn't figure out what.

I stood at the water's edge for a while before going back to my bike and completing the park's loop and heading home. There was more traffic—such as it was on the island in the offseason. Probably everyone leaving church. I kept my head down and stayed to the edge of the road so I wouldn't draw attention to myself. I almost made it.

I was waiting at the intersection that would let me cross the bigger road into the beach-side neighborhood when a sporty little two-seater convertible with its top up slowed, then pulled over. The window rolled down and I recognized the arm that waved out the window before Mrs. Thomas hollered my name.

"Jericho!"

I sighed. I could pretend I didn't hear her. My ear buds were in. The breeze was blowing. But I couldn't quite bring myself to be that overtly rude. And of course, now there was a break in the traffic.

I pedaled across the road and pulled up alongside the car. "Hello, Mrs. Thomas."

"Linda." She lifted her eyebrows.

My face heated. Hopefully, she'd simply attribute it to the exercise. "Right. It might take me a few reminders."

She laughed. "In that case, let's give you the opportunity to practice. Come for lunch."

"Oh. No, I couldn't. I've been riding." I gestured to my outfit, hoping she could draw her own conclusions.

"Pfft." Linda made a dismissive gesture. "David has to change and get the grill fired up. It's going to be at least forty-five minutes before we're even close to ready to sit down. That gives you plenty of time to get home and freshen up. You remember where our house is?"

I nodded.

She beamed. "Wonderful. Why don't we say an hour, just to make it a nice round number?"

A litany of arguments for why this was a terrible idea paraded through my mind, but I found myself saying, "All right. Thank you."

This time, Linda's smile could only be called approving. "See you soon!"

Mr. Thomas pulled back onto the road and I watched the car zip off toward their home. The Thomases—along with the rest of the extended family—all had homes on the far north end of the island. Occasionally, newcomers vacationing would grumble out in public about one family hogging all the good real estate. They'd very quickly get an education on the island's history. When we'd been dating, Bennett had told me of more than one family who found, after repeated attempts to push the subject, that they weren't able to find a vacation home on the island anymore.

His family did everything they could to discourage that behavior, but the island residents were fiercely loyal.

That realization sparked another fear deep in my heart. If everyone local was loyal to Bennett, and they found out about our past relationship...would I lose my job?

"Cross the bridge when you hit it." I muttered to myself and hopped back on my bike. If the town was holding a grudge, they wouldn't have hired me. Right?

Back home, I parked my bike beside my car and hurried inside to shower and put on clothing more appropriate than lazy Sunday bike ride wear. I cringed as I tossed the clothes into my hamper. They were not the sort of thing I expected to be seen in by people who knew me. They were decent—I had no worries there—they were just not the general impression I hoped to make when I had to interact with Bennett or his family.

I should have kept a better eye on the time and gotten home before the church crowd started to leave. Or held out longer until they were all eating.

Ugh.

Dressed in jeans and one of my nicer sweaters, I went into the kitchen. Mrs. Thom—Linda—hadn't said to bring anything. I hadn't asked, either. I bit my lip. I still didn't have a lot to offer in the "company food" category. I really needed to go over to the mainland and shop. It had, sort of, been in my plan for today. I should have gone yesterday. Or Friday. Those were my two half-days. Grocery shopping on Sunday didn't sit right. It flew in the face of the idea behind resting.

Regardless, the current state of my fridge and pantry meant I was showing up at the Thomas's house empty handed. And I probably had to head over the bridge tomorrow evening after the library closed at six.

I cringed. Driving over the bridge in broad daylight was bad enough. Was I really going to do it after sunset? My other option was to try to go earlier in the day, but I had to be ready to open the library by ten, so that would be a very early start.

I blew out a breath. Or I'd just make do with the island market until Friday. And then, no matter what excuses I tried to make, I would head out as soon as I closed up the library.

I checked the time and glanced around the cottage. If I worked at it, I could probably figure out a way to stall. Or talk myself out of going completely. And that wouldn't do. I crossed to the front door, shoved my feet into sneakers, and grabbed my purse. Before I could think better of it, I stepped out onto the porch and hurried down the steps to my car. What was the thing Dad always said? Something about soonest begun. He'd probably be appalled that I was thinking about it in terms of socializing, but he'd never know.

13

BENNETT

I leaned against the railing of the deck outside my parents' kitchen and watched Dad flip burgers. "You sure I can't help?"

Dad shook the spatula at me. "I've got it. I've been grilling since before you were born."

I held up my hands. "Just trying to be a good son."

"Keep it up." Dad winked. "Of course, since you're the only one of my sons who showed up on time, you're definitely winning today."

"Nice." I grinned. I was not "on time" as Dad said. I'd shown up about twenty minutes earlier than Mom told me. Because while Dad had never been military, he still firmly believed in the idea that early was on time and on time was late. I'd never heard him say what late was, but it was probably grounds for some sort of corporal punishment.

The kitchen door opened and I glanced over.

"Jericho's here. Can I send her out, or is this a men only space?"

I blinked at Mom trying to parse the words.

Dad closed the grill's lid. "Send that girl out, it's a lovely afternoon. I could use another glass of sweet tea."

"I'll get it." I snapped back from the temporary freeze my brain had gone into. I pushed off the railing and headed over toward Mom. "Does Jericho have a beverage?"

"Why don't you ask what she'd like?" Mom beamed at me and patted my arm.

Great. That wasn't what I'd had in mind, but manners were manners. I scooted past Mom and found Jericho hovering near the far wall of Mom and Dad's enormous kitchen. "Hi."

She twisted her hands together. "Hi. Is it okay that I'm here? Your Mom kind of took over when we ran into each other this morning, and I really did try to get out of it."

I shrugged and headed toward the fridge with Dad's glass. "It's fine with me. Drink?"

I got out the pitcher that was always there, full of Mom's homemade sweet tea and set it on the counter. I filled Dad's glass with ice, then poured in the tea. I glanced back at Jericho. "We have soda, if you'd rather."

"Water would be fine."

I smiled slightly. "Even that comes with options. Sparkling or regular?"

"Um. Sparkling, I guess?"

"Flavored or plain?" Mom had started on a flavored sparkling water kick maybe eight years ago, and it didn't look like it was going to end anytime soon. I opened the fridge and surveyed the options on her shelf. "Looks like there's lemon lime, grapefruit, some kind of berry, and I think watermelon. As well as plain."

"Have you had the berry one?" She edged closer, but still hadn't even made it to the center of the room.

"No. I tried the lemon lime. It's pretty decent. It's not Sprite or anything, but you can taste the flavoring." I'd been planning to have sweet tea, but maybe the lemon lime would be better. I grabbed a can off the shelf. "Live on the edge, try the berry."

"All right."

I took another can out and shut the fridge. "Glass with ice?"

"I can drink out of the can." Jericho held out her hand.

I gave her the drink. "I'll do the same, then. Mom can't fuss at me for being uncouth if we're both doing it."

She chuckled and popped the top, releasing the hiss of carbonation. She sniffed, then took a careful sip. Her head bobbed back and forth a couple times. "Not bad."

I put the tea pitcher back in the fridge and got Dad's glass. "Mom ran into you this morning? I didn't see you at church."

"No." She cleared her throat. "I was riding my bike."

"Ah." I gestured for her to go ahead of me. "We're going to eat outside. Dad's big on seizing the good days."

"It's a nice policy." It took her a moment, but Jericho finally started to cross to the door that would take her out to the deck. "I was thinking about eating outside myself."

I followed her out onto the deck.

Mom jumped up and reached for Dad's tea. "Oh, honey, you're not making her drink out of a can."

"I offered a glass. She said no." I opened my own can and sipped. "So I'm joining her."

Mom shook her head. "All right. Guests get to do what they want."

"I really appreciate you inviting me to lunch." Jericho glanced around before pulling out one of the chairs at the glass-topped table and sitting.

Dad laughed. "No, you don't. You were just too polite to say no. But we're glad you came, anyway."

Jericho's face blazed red and she ducked her head as if the can of sparkling water was the most interesting thing in the world.

"David." Mom frowned at Dad.

"What? Are we not glad?" Dad shot Mom an innocent look.

"Oh, honestly." Mom huffed out a breath. "I'm going to get the sides. The boys should be here soon."

"They should be here already." Dad's mutter wasn't quite loud enough for Mom to catch, but Jericho's lips twitched.

I stifled a snicker and waited for Mom to go inside before looking at Dad. "What do I get as your favorite of the day?"

"Hmm." Dad sipped his sweet tea. "Oh. I know. I'll let you be the managing partner of the family firm."

"Gee, Dad. Thanks." I shook my head and caught a moment out of the corner of my eye. I looked over at Jericho, who appeared confused. "I'm already the managing partner."

"Ah." She smiled. "Not so much of a prize, then."

"Seeing as how I'm also pretty much the only full-time employee these days, too. Not so much." I took a sip of my water. "But I'm still not going to complain. I don't need Dad coming back and expecting to run things again."

Dad laughed. "Fat chance. Your mother is pushing for us to be a little more than semi-retired."

"She always is. Then we get an interesting client and she's back with her nose to the grindstone." I shrugged. "I don't figure either of you will actually completely retire. You already live at the beach. Would you retire and move to the city?"

Dad made an exaggerated shudder. "Nope."

"The city's not all bad." Jericho looked surprised that she'd spoken.

"Maybe it depends on the city. Which one are you talking about?" It was a little underhanded, maybe, to try to get information about what she'd been up to for the last sixteen years this way, but I wasn't sure she'd answer me if I asked outright.

The look she gave me suggested she knew just what I was doing. "I spent time in Atlanta. It was nice. Friendly. Ish. Then I actually went to L.A. for a few years. There you can do city and beach at the same time. I liked it."

"Huh. I never pictured you as a California girl. But I guess having the beach right there would fit. Anywhere else?" The more I got out of her, the more I wanted to know. It wasn't smart. But I also couldn't talk myself out of it. I was still hurt, and frustrated, by how things between us ended. Even with that, my heart was hers for the taking. She just had to say the word.

Jericho wrinkled her nose. "Not for any length of time, really. Seattle. Austin. There was something to love in all of them. Then again, I think that's true in general. If you're willing to look."

"That is a fantastic attitude." Dad nodded approvingly at Jericho. "Applies to so many things, not just cities."

Jericho looked away.

I shot my dad a questioning glance, but he just shook his head slightly. I could let it go for now, but I wasn't letting him completely off the hook.

Mom stepped back out onto the porch. "Look who finally made it!"

My brothers, looking sheepish, followed in her wake.

"Sorry." Christian muttered. "I got called into the clinic for an overprotective mother who was convinced her son was going to die because he had a temperature of 99.2."

I snickered. "I can narrow that down to three families. You realize that?"

"I'm not breaking HIPAA if I don't give out personal information. So I will neither confirm nor deny." Christian pulled out the seat beside Jericho. "Hey, beautiful. If I'd known you were joining us, I would have hurried."

I couldn't control the scowl, though I neutralized my expression as quickly as I could when I realized what I was doing. I glanced at Evan. "What's your excuse? Science station emergency?"

"They can happen, you know." Evan glared at me. "But no. I got chatting with Aunt Deb about some ideas we're kicking around for nesting season. There are some grant opportunities that we should look into."

I pulled out the chair I'd been standing behind and sat across from Jericho, then glanced at Evan. "You need funding?"

He shrugged. "Who doesn't?"

Mom stepped back out with the last of the side dishes took a seat next to the one that Dad always claimed. "Generally speaking? Our family. We can make another investment in the station if it's not meeting its needs."

"No, Mom. It's not that. It's just...we want it to be self-sustaining. Not a little family project. There's a legitimacy concern in some quarters and neither Aunt Deb nor I want to have to fight to ensure that we can maintain control of it." Evan reached for the platter of cornbread and snagged the top square. He dropped it on his plate and blew on his fingers.

Dad brought the platter of burgers to the table and set it down, then took his seat. "Let's pray, then we can eat."

I smirked slightly at Dad's pointed glance at Evan, but hastily closed my eyes and bowed my head when Dad began to pray.

Jericho muttered, "Amen" along with the rest of us when Dad finished.

"Everyone grab what's in front of you and help yourself." Mom did as she instructed with the salad.

Surprised, I reached across Evan to snag cornbread then offered it to Jericho. "I guess you don't count as a guest."

She smiled. "I'm all right with that. This is very familiar."

Our eyes locked and held and for that moment, everything around me seemed to disappear. It was familiar. All of it. From Christian pretending to flirt and Evan fretting about the science station, to Mom and Dad bumping hands as they reached for the same food. The only difference was our age.

Evan's elbow dug into my side. "Pass the salad."

Mom shot him a look.

Evan sighed and tacked on, "Please."

Then, under his breath so I was the only one who heard it, added, "Romeo."

I grabbed the salad bowl and smacked it into Evan's chest with more force than necessary.

"Hey. Ouch." Evan rubbed his chest and glared at me before scooping some salad onto his plate.

I sent him a toothy, exaggerated smile. "Sorry."

"Boys." Humor filled Mom's voice. "Jericho might not need all our company manners, but maybe *some* manners would be appreciated."

Dad laughed. "You'd think we raised a pack of hooligans instead of three charming, handsome, well-educated men."

"Wow. Just men? Not young men?" Christian shook his head. "Thanks, Dad."

"What? You're all in your thirties. I believe the days of being considered 'young' have sailed." Dad flipped the top of his bun onto his burger and picked it up.

"I *just* turned thirty." Evan's protest was somewhat garbled from the mouthful of food he was trying to talk around. "I think I still get the qualifier."

I just shook my head, my gaze shifting over to Jericho again. Mirth filled her eyes. For the first time since she'd been back on the island, she seemed relaxed. She seemed just like the girl I remembered.

The girl I loved.

What was I going to do about that?

I mentally chewed on the problem as the meal progressed. I tried to keep part of my attention on the conversation and interact, but my family noticed I was distracted. I caught a few of their little verbal jabs and ignored them. Or jabbed back, if something came to mind without too much effort.

When Christian finished his burger, he checked his smart watch. "Are we watching the game here or should I head home?"

"Who's playing?" Evan scraped the last bit of his food onto his fork and put it in his mouth.

"Does it matter?" Christian frowned across the table. "It's football."

"It matters to me." Evan shrugged. "Especially if it means spending more time with you."

I snickered. "I'm going to pass."

"Yeah, big surprise." Christian turned to look at Dad. "How is it that your firstborn hates football again?"

"I was busy building the firm. Your mother had a lot more influence on him." Dad shook his head and shot me a sad look.

Mom slapped Dad's arm. "Please. I was just as involved in building the firm. It's not my fault that only my eldest son has taste and discernment."

I grinned and pushed my chair back, then stood. I picked up my plate, then glanced at Evan. "You finished?"

"Yeah, thanks." He nudged his plate toward me.

I stacked them together, then glanced at Jericho. "Can I get yours?"

"Oh. No, I've got it." Jericho stood and picked up her plate. "I'm going to head out as well. Thanks, again, for lunch."

"It was our pleasure. I hope it's the first of many Sunday afternoons together. Maybe next week we'll see you at church." Mom sent a guileless smile in Jericho's direction.

Jericho just smiled and headed toward the kitchen door.

I followed, hurrying my steps slightly so I could reach it before her and pull it open.

She looked at me. I couldn't identify the emotion that flickered in her gaze before disappearing. "Thanks."

"No problem." I glanced back at my family. They were all eyeing us with unconcealed interest. I frowned. "Thanks for lunch, Mom. And Dad."

I didn't wait for any response before stepping into the kitchen and tugging the door closed behind me.

Jericho glanced over as she rinsed her plate in the sink. "Is your mom going to let go of the church thing?"

I joined her at the sink. "Not without a good reason. Do you have one?"

"Maybe I want to go somewhere on the mainland."

I nodded and turned off the water. "That would be a good reason. Do you?"

Jericho groaned.

I slipped behind her and opened the dishwasher. I loaded my plate, then reached a hand for hers. "That's a no. Maybe you go online at your home church? Although, Mom isn't going to love that. She'll probably still keep pushing."

"No." She blew out a breath and held out the silverware for me to add to the basket. "It's a long story."

"I feel like I've mentioned I enjoy those." I flashed a smile, then closed the dishwasher. "But maybe you'd rather I didn't push."

She tipped her head to the side and studied me. "Is that actually a possibility?"

I laughed. "Me personally? Probably. Ish, at least. I can't vouch for the rest of my family."

Jericho blew out a breath. "I was afraid of that."

"So maybe you can just go to church next week and see if you remember how nice it is." I shrugged and pushed my hands into my pockets. "Can't hurt, can it?"

"Actually, yeah. It can."

I bit my lip. I wasn't sure what response might be appropriate in this situation. I didn't want to tell her she was wrong. Obviously, she'd had some bad experiences in there.

"So. I'll see you around." Jericho lifted a hand and started toward the front door.

"I'll head out with you. I'm not really in the mood to watch football." I fell into step beside her. "What will you do with the rest of your day?"

"It's my only full day off, so probably laundry. Housework. All the chores that don't do themselves, no matter how much I wish they would."

I nodded. "I forgot the library is only closed one full day a week. You know you could probably get them to change that, if you needed. I doubt it'd turn into a Saturday and Sunday combo, but maybe a day in the week?"

She tugged open the front door and stepped out onto my parents' sprawling front deck. "I don't mind. I have the two half-days. Honestly, it's better hours than I had at my last job. And really, it's never so busy that I can't do some personal stuff while I'm there."

"Yeah?" I pulled the door closed behind me when I exited and gestured toward the stairs leading down to Mom and Dad's driveway. "That's good."

I wanted to ask what kind of things she did, but given that she hadn't volunteered it, I didn't imagine she'd actually want to answer me.

Jericho just nodded and continued down the steps. She paused beside an older car that looked well cared for. "Thanks for not minding that I showed up for lunch."

"Why would I mind?" I frowned.

"Because..." Jericho trailed off. After a moment of silence, she sighed. "You weren't exactly welcoming when we bumped into each other at the bookstore."

"You're right. I'm sorry." I could offer explanations, but there was still never an excuse to be rude. So why try to make it seem like I was justified? I wasn't.

"And at the diner."

I chuckled. "I guess I gave you a pretty hard time that first week."

"You did."

"I'm sorry." I hunched my shoulders. "I know that doesn't make it better, but I don't know what else to say."

"It's okay. I kind of figured it was going to be awkward when I first decided to apply for the job. Honestly? It hasn't been as hard as I anticipated. So maybe I should say thanks."

"Nah. Not to me, at least. But I'm glad you came back. It's nice seeing you around again." Maybe that was too much. Given her expression, she wasn't sure how to react. Well, that was fine. She left me feeling that way a lot, too. "Anyway. Have a good rest of the afternoon."

I lifted a hand and started across the lawn toward the road. I'd been looking for some kind of exercise today, so I'd walked to lunch. That had been one of the reasons I was early. Sometimes I got distracted heading down to Mom and Dad's, so it ended up taking longer. Today, even though my mind wandered, I'd made good time.

I'd just reached the boundary with Aunt Deb's house, when Jericho pulled up beside me and lowered her window. "You want a ride?"

"Nah, I'm good. Thanks." I started walking.

Jericho drove slowly beside me. "Is one of these yours? I thought your lot was closer to the north point, next to your grandpa."

"It is. I haven't built yet. I bought a little cottage on the Atlantic side of the lighthouse."

"That's like two miles."

I nodded. "About that, yeah."

"And you walked to lunch."

"I did." I stopped and looked at her. "I like to walk. Always have."

Humor flirted with the corners of her lips. "I will allow you've always been a very good walker."

I laughed, even as the final vestiges of whatever protective wall I'd tried to build around my heart crumbled. "Jane always had a way with words."

"Get in the car, Bennett."

Everything about the way she said it filled me with warmth. Even still, I hesitated. If I got in the car, I wasn't sure I'd be able to let her get away again. Not if I was going to survive the experience emotionally.

Was it worth it?

Yeah.

Jericho was worth it.

I took a deep breath and crossed around the front of the hood.

Then I got in the car.

14

JERICHO

Why had I told him to get in the car?

The question had plagued me all week, and even now, five days later, I had no real explanation.

Well, no explanation I was willing to admit to myself. Just like I wasn't admitting that driving him home had felt like old times. As if the years between had never existed, and we were together. Had always been together.

Like we should have been.

I squeezed my eyes shut against the stab of pain in my heart.

I could look back and see all the little steps that got me from our end of summer plans to being able to walk away and not turn back. I couldn't honestly say I hadn't looked back, because I'd spent basically all my free time doing just that. But I'd held firm to my path—I hadn't believed there'd been another choice.

I glanced up as I caught movement from the corner of my eye, then stood, pasting on my friendly librarian smile. "Did you find everything you need?"

The older gentleman, Mr. Evans as he'd introduced himself to me the first time he'd come in, shrugged. "Mostly. Do you know if Bennett is going to have another recommendation for us soon? I'm all caught up."

"I'm not sure, but I can reach out to him and ask. Do you have a particular genre you enjoy reading?"

He eyed me a moment, a light frown creating a furrow in his forehead. "I don't like romance."

"Okay. Do you like science fiction? Mysteries? Hard-boiled detective stories? Spy thrillers?" I paused. Had I seen a flicker of interest from any of those suggestions?

"Haven't read a book with space battles in a while." Mr. Evans sniffed thoughtfully. "Don't suppose you could recommend something."

I fought a chuckle and nodded, schooling my expression. "Absolutely. Do you like Greek history?"

"Like the Trojan War? Sure. But I'm not following what that has to do with space."

This time I did chuckle. "Because I just finished reading a series that was somewhat inspired by the march of the ten thousand."

"Interesting." Mr. Evans pursed his lips, then nodded. "And there are battles?"

"Lots of space battles. And reasonably realistic physics, too. Honestly, I enjoyed the series so much it's on my list of books I'd be happy to read again."

"All right. Set me up." He tipped his head to the side. "I assume we have it here?"

"We do." I moved around the edge of the checkout desk. "Follow me."

I made my way through the stacks, slowing my pace when I noticed that Mr. Evans was lagging behind. I stopped when I reached the right shelf, and pulled out the paperback of the first in the series.

Mr. Evans took the book and studied the cover. "The Lost

Fleet, eh? Cover reminds me of the dime store novels from the sixties."

"It has that feel, for sure. But this isn't quite that vintage." I tapped the shelf. "And you can see we have all of them, so no getting through part of the series and being left high and dry."

Mr. Evans chuckled. "I think I'm going to like you, young lady."

"I'm glad to hear it." I grinned.

Mr. Evans took the next book in the series off the shelf. "Never could understand people who only needed one book waiting to be read. I like the library as much as anyone, but I don't think you want my ugly mug coming by every day."

"You're welcome here any time, Mr. Evans. Even if you don't need to check out another book."

He patted my arm. "I wasn't sure what to think when the council decided to hire someone so young to replace Mrs. Sanderson. Now, though, I guess they knew what they were up to. You have any objection to a couple of old farts playing chess at one of your study tables?"

"Not even one." I started back toward the front of the library.

"Mrs. Sanderson said we got too rowdy. Though I can own that might have been because Randall—have you met Randall Gentry?"

I shook my head.

Mr. Evans snorted. "Well, Randall cheats like a Tarheel."

My eyebrows lifted.

He chortled. "I come from a long line of Wolfpack members. Had a granddaughter change sides and go to UNC. Guess I can allow they have a good nursing program. She's doing well for herself, but I still think she would've been just fine at State. Anyway, don't play games with Randall Gentry less you watch him real close. That's all I'm sayin'. Got a little heated at him a time or two and Mrs. Sanderson decided we couldn't hang out in the library anymore."

"Well, I'm willing to risk it, even though I stay completely neutral when it comes to college rivalries. You let Mr. Gentry and your other friends know. And if you promise to be careful, I might even look the other way if you happened to have coffee and a snack with you." I took his library card and scanned it, then scanned the books. "Just don't spill on the reading material."

"Appreciate that." Mr. Evans tucked his books under his arm and nodded. "I'll be getting along. You re-think that neutral stance though. Nothing good ever came from avoiding choosing a side."

He saved me from having to respond by turning and ambling toward the exit. The door swung open before he reached it, and my gaze landed on Bennett as he held it open for the older man. The two of them chatted a moment, before Mr. Evans scooted through and Bennett entered the library.

I probably should have found a way to look busy, but instead I just watched him like an idiot. He crossed the room and came to stand in front of me.

"Hi. Can I help you?"

Bennett's eyebrows lifted. "Actually, I'm here to help you."

"How's that?" I had to play whack-a-mole with all the incredibly inappropriate ideas that flitted through my mind. It didn't matter that they were, essentially, a movie reel of memories from our time together as teenagers. Maybe it made things worse, because it brought back all the same feelings of love and longing. I'd buried those feelings. I'd thought they were dead. Turns out, they were hibernating and had just burst forth like flowers in the spring.

Laughter danced in Bennett's eyes and he leaned forward. "I realized I owed you a book recommendation. Mr. Evans seemed grateful that I was on my way in to deliver one. He seemed hesitant to accept that you'd follow through on your promise to ask me about one."

I frowned. "I was absolutely going to get in touch about that."

"That's what I told him. Although..."

I waited a moment before caving. "Although what?"

"I did wonder how you were going to do that without my number." He grinned like he'd scored the winning goal in a fiercely contested battle.

"Your law firm has a website. I planned to call during business hours and leave a message with the receptionist." I shot him a toothy smile. I hadn't planned that, but he didn't need to know it. I hadn't actually gotten as far as making a plan on how to reach out, but it wasn't as if the island was so huge I couldn't track him down. If nothing else, I could have biked over to his house, now that I knew where it was.

A low hum in his throat was his only response.

"So where is it?"

"Where's what?"

"The book recommendation. The one you said you brought by. Although, you know the library has a phone. And email. You didn't have to come by in person. Especially not at almost two on a Friday afternoon. We're closing. And shouldn't you be at work?" The words just kind of spilled out of my mouth and I regretted nearly all of them as they did. I wasn't trying to push him away. At least, I didn't think that's what I was trying to do. The problem was, of course, that I just didn't know where we stood.

"That was a lot." Bennett drummed his fingers on the checkout counter. "I guess I'll take them in reverse order. The joy of being my own boss is that I work the hours I need to work and I can leave early on Friday if I want to."

I nodded and prayed that the heat on my face wasn't visible as the blazing red beacon of mortification that I expected it was.

"I was hoping," Bennett stressed the last word, "that since it was closing time, I might be able to talk you into ice cream. Or a late lunch. Or early dinner."

"Like a date?" My hand flew up and covered my mouth. "Sorry. Please ignore me."

Bennett reached up and gently tugged my hand away from my face. His gaze held mine. "Yes. Like a date."

"Why?" I squeezed my eyes shut. "I'm sorry. I don't know what's wrong with me."

"If I had to guess, I'd say you were nervous. It's interesting."

I pried one eye open and squinted at him. "My nervousness is interesting to you?"

"Uh-huh."

I swallowed. "I'm pretty sure I'm going to regret asking, but why?"

"For one, I was reasonably certain that you had no interest in me. Not even as a potential friend. But your reaction means that maybe, just maybe, there's hope."

"It taught me to hope as I had scarcely allowed myself to hope before."

Bennett began to laugh. "Are you going to quote *Pride and Prejudice* every time we get together now?"

"No. Maybe. Probably not." I buried my face in my hands. "I hope not."

"Well now, that's too bad."

I uncovered my face and found him smiling at me. "Bennett."

"Jericho." He sighed. "You haven't answered me. Will you go out with me?"

I nodded, forcibly keeping back the words that wanted to escape. I'd blurted out entirely too much already, and another snarky question might just end up making him change his mind. I didn't want that.

"Excellent. Now, as for the book recommendation and my method of getting it to you, I am aware of both the email address and phone number of the library. In fact, that's generally how I'd send Mrs. Sanderson my recommendation. But then, I was never particularly interested in asking her out." He shrugged. "I think she would have said no. And Mr. Sanderson probably would have tried to beat me up, and I would have had to let him at least get in a few solid hits. It seemed like too much of a hassle."

"You're making fun of me."

Bennett held up his thumb and forefinger with a tiny bit of space between them.

I shook my head and reached over, pulling his fingers apart to widen the space.

"Since we're dating now, can I give you my phone number?"

My heart stuttered in my chest. "We're dating?"

"Am I moving too fast?"

I searched Bennett's face. He was serious. No trace of the humor that had seasoned the rest of our conversation. "No."

"Good." His smile flashed and he dug his phone out of his pocket, tapped the screen, then slid it across the counter. "Put your number in."

"I thought you were giving me your number? This is me giving you mine." I picked up his phone and added my name to the empty contact on the screen, then tapped in my number before handing it back to him.

Bennett took the phone and tapped. After a moment, a chime sounded from under the counter where I stored my things during working hours. "Now you have mine, too."

"Ah. And the book recommendation?"

He pulled a folded piece of lined yellow paper from his

pocket and set it down on the counter. "There are two. Both have a short explanation of what I liked."

I unfolded the paper, smiling when I saw his neat handwriting was just the same as it had been when he'd write notes and slip them under the mat at my parents' beach rental. "I see three books here."

"Only two are mine. Grady is hoping you'll include his choice, too, though. In fact, I told him I'd grab more from that series if I happened to be near the library."

I smoothed out the paper. "Of course I'll include his. I got the feeling that reading isn't his favorite thing."

"It's not even on the list of things he'll tolerate, usually." Bennett sighed. "Travis is starting the process of getting Grady evaluated. The school has been pushing for a while, but Caroline...well, anyway. It's happening now. Hopefully, it'll mean we can figure out what kind of help he needs."

"Maybe you can catch me up on the family over our ice cream." I moved around the counter and headed over to the shelves that held the easy readers. I grabbed the next three books in the dinosaur series and carried them back over to Bennett.

"Just ice cream?" His voice had a hint of plaintiveness.

I shook my head. "No. But it's where we'll start."

15

BENNETT

I was grinning like an idiot and didn't care.

It didn't take Jericho long to do her closing checks at the library, and before long, we were standing on the front step of the building in the winter sunlight.

"You really want ice cream?"

"Of course I do." Jericho bumped my shoulder with her own. "You don't dangle ice cream in front of a woman and then try to back out, buster."

I laughed. "Fair enough. Um. Offseason, that means Books & Bites. That okay?"

"Of course. I haven't had a chance to drop by and see Sara in a while." Jericho bit her lip.

"What?"

She shook her head. "It's nothing."

"It's not nothing. Tell me." I reached for her hand and squeezed it. I fully expected her to pull her hand away, but she didn't. Instead, she wove her fingers through mine.

Jericho sighed. "I just had a little list of errands to take care of after work today."

"Okay."

"What do you mean? I'd rather have ice cream and dinner with you."

I tugged her down the steps and started walking toward the bookstore. "And you will. But we have the rest of the day. We can run errands. Unless you have to do something you'd rather I wasn't along for."

She glanced over at me. "One of them is grocery shopping."

I wrinkled my nose. "Not my favorite, but it has to be done. In fact, if you're planning to drive over to Bennett, I could use a few things myself. I love our market, but it's not enough."

"It really isn't." She chuckled and stopped, turning so she faced me, and tipped her head to one side. "Since this is a date…"

"Should I be worried?"

"No." She shook her head. "Or at least, I don't think so. But if you're really running errands with me, maybe you can drive?"

I laughed. "You still hate the bridge."

"I really do. It's one of the reasons I've been making the market work."

"One day, you're going to have to explain to me why you moved here when you hate crossing that bridge. I'm not complaining, mind you." I glanced over at her. "I'm really glad you're back. But you can't survive here without going to the mainland every now and then."

"I know. I already figured out that I need Bennett."

Her words unlocked a longing in my heart that I didn't know how to process. She was talking about the town across the bridge. I wished she were talking about me.

Better not to dwell on it. "There's ice cream over there that's better. I'll deny it if you ever say I said so, though."

Jericho laughed. "My lips are sealed. And since you're the one driving, you get to choose."

The ice cream in Bennett really was better in the offseason.

We had several places that opened seasonally, and they had fantastic offerings for the visitors that I always took advantage of. Also? If we were calling this a date, I didn't feel like sharing it with another local. That would get the gossip mill churning faster than imaginable. And that would create pressure that I'd just as soon not put on Jericho until it was unavoidable.

I turned back toward the library. "Let's just head over. I need to grab a few things from home though, if we're shopping."

"Okay. I can drop you at your car if you want." Jericho dug in her bag as we walked and pulled out a set of keys as we approached the librarian parking spot.

I pointed across the street and up a few spots. "I planned ahead and drove over. Why don't I pick you up at the cottage in maybe twenty minutes?"

She nodded. "That'll work. Thanks, Bennett."

"My pleasure." I held her gaze a moment. Maybe I was imagining the warmth there, but if so, I wasn't going to complain. I'd deluded myself for too many years that I'd moved on. Now all I could do was pray she didn't break my heart a second time. Because I was already all in.

I strode quickly to my car and got in. There weren't exactly alternative options for driving through town, so I followed Jericho out to the main road, then gave her a friendly beep of the horn as I passed her when she slowed to turn into the neighborhood that ultimately led to her cottage and the public beach.

My own house wasn't much beyond that, so I was home quickly. I parked and hurried inside. If we'd stayed in town, I wouldn't have minded wearing the dress pants and button down that I habitually wore to the office. I didn't go full suit. I wasn't that kind of lawyer. But Mom and Dad had always insisted that jeans—even nice ones—weren't appropriate work attire.

They were absolutely date attire though.

I took the time to hang everything up neatly after changing

into dark jeans and a cream cable-knit sweater. I moved to the kitchen and grabbed the stack of reusable grocery bags I'd purchased when my favorite grocery store had started charging for paper bags last year.

I winced.

How had I gotten to the point in my life that I had a favorite grocery store? It might be possible to be more boring, but I wasn't sure how.

Shaking my head, I pulled open my freezer door and grabbed the stack of ice packs that I kept purely for grocery shopping trips. I pushed the door shut, tucked the ice into one of the grocery bags, and patted my pockets checking for all the essentials.

I blew out a breath. "Ready as I'm going to be."

Nerves jumped in my belly as I headed back out to the car. I popped the trunk, then opened the cooler I kept there and dropped in the ice blocks. I closed the cooler, then the trunk, and went back up front. I climbed behind the wheel, tucking the grocery bags into the footwell behind me, and started the engine.

The whole way to pick up Jericho, I prayed. It wasn't my most eloquent prayer. In fact, I was definitely relying on the Holy Spirit to make sense of it, because the only words that weren't a jumbled mess in my mind were, "Please, Jesus."

I turned into her driveway before my heart had a chance to settle down. She was standing on the porch and started down the stairs immediately. I shifted into "Park" and unfastened my seatbelt. I was just pushing open my door when she got to the car.

"Don't be dumb. I can open a car door." She was laughing as she said it.

I watched her round the front of the car and rehooked my seatbelt.

Jericho opened the door and slid into her seat. "I really appreciate you doing this. I know I have to get over the bridge thing, but I'm not really in a hurry to do so."

I chuckled, checked that she was buckled, and started backing out of her driveway. "I'm happy to do it."

"You always were."

Was I supposed to hear her say that? Since I had, I went ahead and answered. "I like spending time with you."

Her head tipped to the side. "That wasn't past tense."

I shrugged. It might have been a slip of the tongue, but that didn't make it false. "I've always been an upfront guy."

"You have."

"So, it's not going to surprise you, probably, if I just say flat out that I've missed you. And I never really got over you. Since it's been a long time, this probably counts as a first date, but I never stopped loving you. We can go as slow as you want, but you have to know I'm ready to pick up where we left off."

She didn't respond.

I waited, focusing on navigating through town. Finally, as we started onto the bridge, I glanced over. "Do you want me to turn around?"

"No." She shook her head emphatically. Jericho reached over and rested her hand on my arm for the briefest moment. "I just don't know what to say."

"Is that good or bad?" A gust of wind hit the car. I gripped the steering wheel to keep from drifting over the line into the next lane. There wasn't any traffic on the bridge—not unusual for January—but the wind was a constant, no matter the time of year.

"Good."

I glanced over. Jericho had her hands clasped in her lap. Her knuckles were white. Her eyes were squeezed shut. I fought a chuckle. That wasn't the way to get used to driving over the bridge, but she'd get there at some point. For now, I'd be grateful she didn't want to go home.

I switched on the satellite radio and turned down the volume on my usual choice of 80s music. Out of the corner of my eye, I spied one corner of her mouth twitch up and grinned in response. I'd always loved 80s music. My parents had played it all through my childhood. My aunt and uncle, too. It was, essentially, the musical soundtrack for our family.

In the time we spent together as teenagers, Jericho had come to love the music too.

Or at least, that's what she'd always told me.

Before long, we were over the bridge and making our way through town to the grocery store. The parking lot was reasonably full—I'd never seen it very empty, if I was honest—but there was a good space by one of the buggy returns, and that was always a good sign.

"We're shopping first?"

"Yeah. Knock it out and then we can figure out ice cream. And dinner. Maybe a movie?" I shrugged. "Whatever you'd like to do."

"Isn't that going to be a lot of back and forth across the bridge? I need refrigerated food, so we'd take it straight home. Right?"

"Ahhh. You're not yet wise in the way of island residency. Come see." I got out of the car and went back to the trunk.

Frowning, Jericho joined me.

I opened the trunk and gestured dramatically to the cooler. "Ta da!"

"Ooh. Smart. Everyone does this?"

I shrugged and closed the trunk. "I don't know about everyone, all the time, but in the summer? Probably, yeah."

"That actually makes sense. Mom and Dad," she stuttered over the words but kept going, "always worried about getting milk and other refrigerated things before we headed to our rental house. Sometimes traffic on the bridge meant we had to rely on windows instead of the air conditioner."

"Yeah. I try to schedule grocery trips in the middle of weekdays during the summer. That helps. Definitely not on rental turnover days though." I opened the car door and grabbed my grocery bags, then closed it again and hit lock on the key fob. "You'll get a rhythm going."

"I hope so." She glanced at my grocery bags. "I didn't realize I'd need those."

"I have extra." I rarely used every bag I brought, but I kept them all together. Today, I was mostly here for her, so I definitely wouldn't need more than one. Maybe two. "Ready?"

"Yeah."

After a moment's hesitation, I slipped my hand around Jericho's. She didn't pull away, and I walked into the grocery store with what I knew had to be a ridiculous grin on my face.

I'd never really spent time thinking about food shopping. It was something that had to be done, but I tended to put it off for as long as possible. Then, when it couldn't be avoided, I tried to zip through as quickly as I could.

Jericho, however, seemed to enjoy every moment of it. She touched all the produce, choosing tomatoes like the fate of the world depended on her getting just the right one. She read the labels. She sniffed the weird cheeses that I never even considered trying. The entire experience was different.

Because I was there with her.

When we finally wheeled the buggy out to the car and loaded everything into the cooler, I realized that I was going to be miserable if Jericho decided we needed to start our relationship over, like it was something new.

I'd respect her decision. Obviously. But that didn't mean I

wouldn't do everything in my power to get her to change her mind.

"I believe ice cream is the next thing on our agenda." I shut the trunk and skirted around her to open the passenger door. "Do you want a lot of options and slightly more commercial flavors, or creamy and homemade with only three or four flavor choices?"

"How is this a question? Creamy and homemade." Jericho slid into her seat.

I chuckled and closed the door, then rounded the car and climbed in. "Christian often prefers to have six cases of options stretched out in front of him, so he can taste all the strange offerings on tiny spoons."

"Does he ever choose them?"

I shook my head and started the car. "Nope. He always ends up with Rocky Road. Mom and Dad try to get him to acknowledge that he's never going to be adventurous, but he insists it's a possibility."

"At least Rocky Road is a good flavor. He could like something like pistachio."

"That would be a travesty." I chuckled as I backed out of the parking spot and headed across town. "You won't know this place. Jon and his family came here about ten years ago. His grandparents lived near Myrtle Beach, and his parents moved there to help care for them. He and his wife wanted to be close, but not too close, so they landed here."

"That...sounds really nice."

I glanced over, but her expression was unreadable, so I just kept talking. "Did you ever come over and go to the Dairy Bar?"

"Once or twice. Mom and Dad weren't big on leaving the island once we showed up. Sometimes we could talk them into stopping on the way over though. Why?"

"The family that had run it for, gosh, probably were open for a hundred years, ended up deciding to close. I guess none of the new generation wanted the business, and Mr. and Mrs. Kirk wanted to retire. Jon bought the building. I think the Kirks were kind of hoping he'd keep it as the Dairy Bar, but he totally rebranded. Honestly, I think it was the smart choice. MacLachlan's is its own thing." I slowed as a stop light switched from green to yellow, then stopped.

"I'll take your word for it. I don't think I remember the other well enough to say one way or another." Jericho was staring out the window. "Everything is so different. But also kind of the same."

I laughed. "That makes no sense."

"Hard to explain. It's familiar. There are still the old buildings that I recognize. The feel is the same. But the names on things are different. And there are all these new things, too." She shrugged.

"I guess that makes a little bit of sense." I couldn't say I'd experienced it. Maybe when I came home from college, but even then, there weren't the sweeping changes that a sixteen-year gap would have.

The light turned green, and I drove us the rest of the way to MacLachlan's. The parking lot was starting to fill up. It was a popular after-school spot for the high school crowd. Austin liked to come people watch here. He said he liked "the vibe." As the youngest of us, Austin was the only one who could possibly pull off trying out the modern-day slang. But the rest of us just teased him about it.

I found a spot and parked, then shut off the engine.

Jericho pushed open her door and got out. She looked across the hood at me. "It's busy."

"You'll see why."

This time, Jericho took my hand. "Is this going to spoil my dinner?"

"Maybe. We'll live on the edge."

She grinned at me.

We crossed the lot toward the patio that held maybe ten round tables with attached benches and red and white umbrellas. The line wasn't too long, so we slid into it. I squinted slightly to bring the menu board into focus. "Ooh. They have raspberry today."

"And cheesecake. Is that good?" Jericho looked up at me, stepping close enough that our bodies brushed.

My breath caught and I froze, not wanting to break the contact between us. "Yeah."

My voice was strained. If she noticed, she didn't comment on it. But she also didn't step away again to widen the distance.

I absolutely did not mind.

The line moved at a slow, but steady pace. Before too long, it was our turn at the ordering window.

"Hey there, Bennett. You're in Bennett." Jon MacLachlan laughed, a hearty, loud sound that never failed to make me grin.

"That I am. How's everything going? You've got a crowd today." I glanced over my shoulder at the mostly full tables.

"Not going to complain about that. What can I getcha?"

I gestured to Jericho to order.

"Um. Can I get the cheesecake and raspberry swirl?"

"Yes, ma'am." Jon tilted his head to the side. "Are you visiting Bennett? I don't think I've seen you around."

"Oh. Well, no." Jericho paused.

I stepped into the gap. "This is Jericho. She's the new librarian on Loring. But her family used to spend summers on the island, so she's not a complete outlander. Jericho, meet Jon."

"Hi."

"Pleasure." Jon grinned then looked at me. "For you?"

"You know what? That swirl sounds good. Make it two." I held up two fingers, even though it was completely unnecessary.

"Cups or cones?" Jon poked buttons on the cash register then gestured to the card reader at the edge of the window.

"Cone for me." I slipped my credit card out of my wallet and tapped it.

"A cone is good. Thanks." Jericho frowned slightly. "I could have gotten mine."

"Here you are." Jon held a receipt through the window. "It'll be a few. You know the drill."

"Sure do." I took the slip of paper and nudged Jericho toward the larger window a few steps down where a small crowd waited for their orders. "I thought we said this was a date."

"We did." Jericho looked at me, confused.

I let a little extra southern drawl into my voice. "You're in the South now. Date means I pay."

She pursed her lips a moment, then nodded. "All right. Thanks."

I met, then held her gaze. The noise and movement around us faded as I was swept away in her eyes. The only words I could think of said too little, but also too much. "It's my pleasure."

16

JERICHO

"Morning, Miss Jericho." Mr. Evans set his books down on the library counter with a nod.

"Good morning." I picked up the books. "Did you like them?"

"I did. I'll go ahead and grab the rest of the series today." He paused a moment and watched me as I scanned the books in and then set them on a cart for reshelving. "Heard you had a nice date, Friday."

My eyebrows lifted. "Did you?"

Mr. Evans chuckled. "You're in a small town now. Word gets around. Can't say I disapprove, though. Bennett's been pining for you since you left."

My mouth opened, but I honestly had no idea what to say in response, so I snapped it shut.

"Ha. Got you, didn't I?" He gave an emphatic nod. "See you treat him right this time. His family keeps a lot of the town going. We're all rather partial to them."

"I'll see what I can do." The smile I offered was tight. "Tell me something, Mr. Evans. Do you think everyone is going to ask me about our date today?"

"More than likely." He shrugged. "Cost of living around here. You get used to it."

I sighed quietly as he knocked on the counter and started to amble toward the science fiction shelves. He paused after a few steps and looked back. "You were serious about me playing chess in here, right?"

"Absolutely." I'd be happy with any signs of life during the day around here. There was a lot of downtime at this library. I had some ideas of how I could try to spice things up—story time a couple of times a week, maybe seeing if the science station wanted to offer some informational classes on the sea turtles that nested on the north end of the island. That kind of thing. I just didn't know if there was actually a large enough residential population to support that kind of thing. Or if people from the mainland would drive over for it.

Bennett had assured me that most people didn't hate the bridge like I did, but it was hard to believe. Still, maybe convincing people there was a reason to head over in the offseason would also boost some of the other year-round shops. If people came for story time, wouldn't they grab lunch? Maybe, down the line, I could even convince some of the shops to stay open offseason. I wouldn't mind having more shopping options that weren't online or across that bridge.

After a couple of minutes, Mr. Evans was back with a small stack of books. He plopped them down on the counter and dug out his library card. "I'm going to want more recommendations when I finish these up. You have different taste than Bennett. I like his, too, but variety is always a good thing. There's more to life than legal thrillers."

I chuckled as I checked out the books for him. "I'll see what I can come up with. You're firm on the no romance?"

He frowned slightly. "Guess I wouldn't mind something like you get on that Hallmark channel. Do they make books like that? I don't want none of that stuff where they're talking about body parts though. Seems like that's all I see people talking about on the TV or online. The missus reads romance she finds at the church book swap." He grinned. "She really likes the Regency ones. I act like I don't, but between you and me? I guess I don't mind them too much."

"Your secret's safe with me." I pushed the stack of books back to him as the library door opened again.

An older gentleman I didn't recognize stepped in and looked around. His voice filled the room when he spoke. "That you, Evans?"

"You got eyes, Randall, don't you?" Mr. Evans shook his head and picked up the books. "Go get the board set up. I'll be right there."

I leaned across the counter and lowered my voice. "I thought you said he cheats?"

Mr. Evans shrugged. "Sure he does. But calling him on it is half the fun. Keeps things interesting, anyway."

I chuckled. "Enjoy your game."

Mr. Evans tapped his forehead and turned. I watched him make his way slowly to one of the tables near the front windows where Randall was already setting up a chess board, before adding the last few books to a cart. I pushed the cart out from behind the checkout desk and started toward the stacks.

The door opened again and Grady came running in with a piercing scream. He tripped, sending the books in his arms flying. The scream turned to a wail.

"Grady. Hush." A woman who looked a lot like Bennett's mom hurried in behind Grady. She squatted beside him and took his hand. "Sit up, honey. It's okay."

I crossed the space and knelt down beside the boy. "Are you okay, Grady?"

Grady shrieked.

“I’m so sorry, Jericho.” The woman tugged on Grady’s arm. “Sit up, honey.”

“It’s fine. That was quite a spill.” I peered around, trying to decide if Grady had been injured. I didn’t see blood anywhere. If he was hurt, I would. Wouldn’t I? “I don’t—”

“I’m Deb. Bennett’s aunt? We met a few times, but I don’t expect you to remember.” Her smile didn’t quite reach her eyes. “I honestly hoped coming to the library would be a good distraction for him. Grady, hon, come on and sit up.”

Of course. That would explain why she looked a little like Linda. “It’s good to meet you again. Do you think he’s hurt?”

“No. That screeching is different.” Deb closed her eyes and winced. “That sounded awful.”

“It didn’t.” I pushed to my feet and went to collect the books. I took them back over to where Grady lay on the floor. He was, at least quieting some. “Look, Grady. The books are okay.”

He sniffled and turned his head.

I held up one of the books, smiling. “See? Good as new.”

He watched me a moment before slowly climbing to his hands and knees. He sat back, his legs fanning behind him in a W and reached for the books.

I handed them to him and smiled when he clutched them to his chest. “Did you like them?”

He nodded.

“I’m glad.” I glanced at Deb. “Did you come looking for more?”

“Yes. And just to pass some time.” Deb bit her lip. “Grady, do you want to go put those books in the return slot?”

Grady nodded and climbed to his feet before running across the rest of the room.

I lowered my voice. “Shouldn’t he be in school?”

Deb sighed. “In a perfect world, yes. He won’t go.”

My eyebrows shot up and I just barely managed to hold back

a comment that I hadn't realized that was an option. Obviously, there was more at play here. "How come? Not that it's my business. Sorry."

Deb waved the words away. "It's not a secret. Plus, you're basically family."

Family? Bennett and I had been on one date. No matter how much I wanted to believe his statement that he was still in love with me, it wasn't something I was banking on. I wanted us to find our footing again and see what we could do to make things work between us, but...there were complications.

Because life was always complicated.

Deb either didn't notice my shock, or she didn't care. She just kept talking. "I'm pretty sure Linda said she'd mentioned that Caroline walked out on Travis?"

I nodded.

"Ever since then, things with Grady have been getting worse. And they weren't amazing to start out. I'm reasonably sure he's on the autism spectrum. I had tried talking to Caroline and Travis about it. Caroline would never even listen. Travis...well he was stuck between listening to his mother and supporting his wife." Deb frowned. "It's not like I wanted him to choose me over her, but my grandson needed—needs—help. Regardless of whether or not his parents are too stubborn to admit it."

"Poor guy." I looked over at Grady who was carefully feeding one book at a time into the book return. "Can't school help him?"

"They've been pushing. And running into the great wall of Caroline." Deb shrugged. "And now that she's not an obstacle, Travis is getting the ball rolling, but Grady is struggling. Trying to get him to the bus is a meltdown. Driving him personally just moves the meltdown to school property. For now, I'm trying to help Travis choose his battles. Which means it's a Grandma Day."

"Well, I'm glad the library was on your list. Let's go see what we can find for Grady to read." I hesitated. It wasn't my business, and I'd really rather ask Bennett, but Deb was here. "Is he interested in books that would be closer to his grade level?"

Deb sighed. "I'm sure he'd be interested if there was any chance of him being able to read them. Right now, we aren't there. He's probably two grades behind. His behavior has always overshadowed his education at school. If they can keep him quiet and less disruptive, they call it a win. Teachers don't want to have him a second year, so he gets passed to the next grade. Although, to be fair, I think Caroline would have raised a ruckus if they'd suggested they hold him back."

"Okay." I bit my lip and considered options. The problem was going to be finding topics that weren't too babyish that were still at a reasonable reading level for him. Probably best to stick with dinosaurs. Because who didn't love dinos? I crossed to Grady and hunched down beside where he was squinting through the book return slot. "Ready to go see what books we can find?"

His shoulder slumped. "I guess."

"Maybe we can find more dinosaurs." I watched for any sign that that would be interesting, but his face remained stoic. "Or cars? Maybe space? What kind of things do you like?"

Grady shrugged.

I glanced back at Deb. She looked so defeated I couldn't help but hurt for her. At the same time, I was furious with Caroline, and I'd never met the woman.

I held out a hand to Grady. He eyed it suspiciously. I was just about to pull it back when he slid his hand into mine. I grinned and gave his hand a light squeeze. "C'mon kiddo. Let's go find books."

"Ha! Check!" The words were shouted and we all looked over.

"Randall." Mr. Evans looked pained. He raised his voice and glanced at me. "Sorry." Mr. Evans gave Randall a pointed look.

Randall sighed. "Sorry. Sorry. I'll keep it down."

"I appreciate that." I sent a smile their way, then turned my attention back to Grady. "Ready, bud?"

Grady pulled his hand free and zoomed across to where the older men were playing chess. Before anyone could intervene, he'd grabbed several pieces off the board and was looking at them intently.

"Oh, no." Deb moaned. Resigned, she stalked over toward her grandson.

I followed slowly behind.

"It's fine, just fine." Mr. Evans scooted his chair back some and patted his knee. "Hop on up here, young man, and we'll teach you the ins and outs of chess. Right, Randall?"

"Never too young to start learning the ways of the chessboard." Randall agreed. He reached for the pieces and began to reset the board. "I'd basically won."

"Now, Randall. You know I was about to get out of check and could have had your queen in two more moves."

"Coulda shoulda, Evans. Coulda shoulda."

Mr. Evans's cough sounded suspiciously like a smothered laugh. "We've got him, Ms. Debra. You go get yourself some books. Need to keep your science brain fed so you can make sure we're taking care of the island."

Grady had crawled onto Mr. Evans's spindly knee and was focused on the board, seemingly oblivious to the rest of the world.

Deb turned to me. "Maybe you could help me choose some books for him?"

"Absolutely. I think we might even have some books on chess for kids. Do you have a set at home?" I started toward the right section of the library.

"Not sure. But if we don't, it gives us something to do after this. We can drive across and get one at Walmart." Deb glanced back over her shoulder. "I haven't played chess in forever. Rob and I would play some in college, when we were dating. We learned pretty quickly that we had to choose between a relationship or chess. I think we chose well."

I laughed.

"It's true. He's a terrible winner. And he always beat me. Hm. Maybe Grandpa can teach Grady more about chess this evening."

"Travis is lucky to have you."

Deb blinked. "This is what family does."

Not every family.

I didn't say it aloud, but Deb seemed to understand anyway.

She patted my shoulder. "We have enough family to share. Like I said, you're already basically one of us."

"You know that Bennett and I aren't..." I trailed off, unsure of how to finish that statement.

"Not yet. But I firmly believe there's a reason God brought you back to Loring Island."

He had, hadn't He? I'd figured it was more because He knew I needed the peace I'd always felt here. Even though not every memory from our time on the island was positive, Loring was the only place I'd ever truly felt I belonged.

Deb smiled. "It's probably not my place to tell you this, but I'm going to anyway. All of us—Linda and Dave, Rob and me, all the boys—are praying you and Bennett get back to those plans you made years ago. There's never been anyone as perfect for him as you."

My throat closed and I had to look away and blink back tears. I took several deep breaths, then turned back. "Let's find you some books."

17

BENNETT

"Can I tempt you with dinner at the diner?"

Jericho looked up from the computer. I couldn't stop the smile that formed as our eyes met.

She tipped her head to the side. "Dinner with you? Or Monday Night Dinner with the Family?"

"Did you just capitalize all of those words? It sounded way more important than it actually is."

"So that's a yes to family dinner?" Her eyebrows lifted.

I shrugged. "It's Monday night. Mom said to tell you she was hoping to see you, though."

Jericho frowned down at the keyboard.

Had I misunderstood our date after all? We'd had fun grocery shopping and then ruining our dinner with ice cream at MacLachlan's. Not that it had stopped us from getting burgers and fries and talking for hours like we used to do as teenagers. I'd dropped her off at home, and it had taken everything in me not to try to kiss her goodnight.

I thought then—and still did—that she might have been open to it.

But even with our history, it was too fast.

So I'd invited her to church and Sunday lunch.

She hadn't showed up to either.

Which was why I was at the library, five minutes before closing, trying to talk her into dinner at the diner.

Well, that and, frankly? I missed seeing her. I'd tried giving her space over the weekend, just checking in with a couple of texts. But seriously, wasn't two days enough?

"Please?" How pathetic was I? "You know you love meatloaf."

She snorted out a laugh. "No. I do not know anything of the sort. Meatloaf is your most convincing argument?"

"It's been a while since I asked someone out." I shrugged. "I might have lost a little of my game."

She laughed again. "Well, for the record, meatloaf doesn't win the heart of women. Maybe it'd work on a guy."

"I can't say I see myself wanting to win the heart of a guy... ever. But I guess it's good to know?" I leaned closer until my face was close to hers. "C'mon, Jericho."

Her eyes closed and her head tipped back. "Fine."

I grinned and straightened. "Yay!"

"I'm going to be a few more minutes. I need to get these books shelved and run the end of day report." She gestured to a cart full of books.

"I can help." I nodded toward the cart and drawled, "I know how to Dewey Decimal."

"Ooh." Jericho fluttered her eyelashes. "Sexy."

I waggled my eyebrows. "Maybe I know how to woo a librarian after all."

She made a sweeping motion with one arm. "Be my guest. I'll come find you and help when I'm done here."

I grabbed hold of the cart and pushed. I fought to keep my face straight as the weight sank in. She pushed these around like they were weightless. I glanced over at her, trying to gauge her biceps, but she had on a sweater that completely hid her arms. Still. Who knew librarians had to be buff?

I managed to get the cart out from behind the desk and facing the shelves before I made a face. I glanced down at the top row of books to see what section to head for first, then looked up at the number ranges posted on neat cards on the edges of the shelves and angled the cart toward my first stop.

I'd finished the top shelf of the cart and was half-way through the middle when Jericho found me.

"You're fast. Should I be worried that it's all wrong?"

I frowned at her before noticing the laughter dancing in her eyes. "Ha. Ha."

Jericho patted my arm. "I really appreciate this. You sped up the closing process a lot. Mondays are a big book return day around here."

"Makes sense."

She reached down and grabbed two books off the middle shelf, then walked down a few paces to put them back. "Does it?"

"Sure. Weekends are when people have more time to read." I shrugged as I reached for the next book. I looked between the numbers on the spine and those on the shelves near me, then set it down on the empty top shelf and started pushing the cart down the aisle. "And it's when kids cram their research projects in. Or at least, it's when parents realize their kids have research projects."

She laughed and fell into step beside me. "True enough. Skip this row. That book's one more down."

I took her at her word and continued to the next aisle between shelves, then manhandled the cart around the corner. "These wheels need WD40."

"I keep meaning to do that." She shrugged and reached for the book on the top of the cart. "I'll get to it eventually."

I made a mental note to bring some over tomorrow. I had some in my garage—it was one of those things Dad insisted was mandatory for homeowners to have on hand. I reached down for another book and grabbed the final two. I had to walk down a bit to find their spots, but finally got them put back. I dusted my hands together. "Done."

Jericho grabbed the cart and pushed it ahead of herself. "So we are. Which means we can head out for that meatloaf. Yummy."

"I hear that sarcasm." I shook my head and reached for the cart before gently nudging her out of the way. "No one is insisting that you order the loaf of meat. Although, I have to say I don't understand the hate. It's basically a hamburger with the bun mixed in instead of on the outside."

"No." She stopped and propped her hands on her hips. "It is absolutely nothing like a hamburger. How did I not realize you were mental when we dated in high school?"

I chuckled. "It's a well-kept secret. Although, you knew I wanted to be a lawyer, so there were signs."

"This is true." She grinned at me.

It was like time stopped. I couldn't have named the feelings coursing through me if I'd been held at gunpoint, but they were all good. Amazing, even.

"What?" Her head tipped to the side.

I shook my head, as much to clear it as to answer her question.

She hummed quietly, but didn't push. Instead, she pointed to the wall in front of her office. "Park the cart there, if you would. I'll grab my things and we'll head out. Are we late?"

I did as she instructed. "Nah. I might have mentioned I was going to invite you. Everyone knows what time the library closes."

"True. But did they know we'd be," she paused and checked her smart watch, "about thirty minutes past that?"

"Probably. Mom's pretty good friends with Mrs. Sanderson. They used to get together every couple of weeks in the evening for dessert." I shrugged. "And if they get tired of waiting, they'll just order and let us catch up when we get there."

"Okay." She bit her lip.

I reached for her hand and squeezed it. "Don't stress. I'm serious. This isn't a big deal."

I barely heard her mutter, "Maybe not to you."

I wasn't sure what to say in response, so just stayed quiet as we crossed the library's foyer to the front door. She flipped off the lights and then turned the deadbolt to let us out. On the front stoop, she locked the library and dropped the keys into her purse. Then she took a deep breath.

"All right. I'm ready."

She hadn't pulled her hand away, so I squeezed it again. "Do you want to walk?"

"Would you mind terribly if I drove my car?" She glanced in its direction.

"Not at all. Especially not if you'll drop me back at my bike after. I left it at the office."

"I can just take you home." She started down the steps toward her car. "I don't think it's smart to bike when it's dark like this."

"Not bicycle. Motorcycle." I followed after her and beat her to the driver's door by a second. I waited for her to push the unlock button on her fob, then pulled it open. "It has a light. Perfectly safe."

She snorted and climbed into the car. "Safe and motorcycle aren't obvious companions."

"You sound like my mom." I shut the door, then went around and got in on the passenger side. "You can follow me home if you want. Mom did that for the first, oh, six weeks after I bought the thing."

"Seriously?" Jericho laughed and started the engine. "You know what? I can actually see her doing that. And strangely, it makes me feel a little better."

"She said something similar."

Jericho glanced over her shoulder before pulling out onto the street. "How old were you?"

"Almost twenty." I didn't expand on that. She could do the math. I couldn't lie and say that my mental state after she disappeared didn't factor into my lack of concern for safety. But even though I'd purchased the bike, I'd always used appropriate safety gear. I didn't—and never had—have a death wish.

"Do I owe your family an apology too?"

I hated how subdued she sounded. "No. Jericho—it's—it's okay. You did what you had to do. Or what you thought you needed to do. However it should be worded. That's the past, though. You're here now."

She was quiet as she signaled and then turned into the diner's parking lot. There were plenty of spaces, and she chose one she could pull through, then parked. She shut off the engine, but made no move to unhook her seatbelt or exit the car.

"I really am sorry." Finally, she turned to face me. Her eyes brimmed with tears. "If I could, I'd go back and do better."

"You were a kid." On our date, she'd explained a little more about the chaos of her parents' divorce and all the weight that fell on her as a result. I was honestly surprised she seemed as well adjusted now as she was. "Do I wish you'd let me know? Sure. But after all you've told me? I don't blame you."

She looked away and took a deep breath. "Thank you."

I reached over and with two fingers, gently turned her face back toward mine. "I'm serious when I say all that matters is that you're back. We have a second chance."

She swallowed, then nodded.

I had about six other things vying to be said, but I choked them back and instead infused as much light as I could into my voice. "Let's go eat."

Her smile was weak, but it was enough that she made the effort. She unbuckled her seatbelt and got out of the car. I followed suit. In the parking lot, I fell into step beside her and hooked my pinky with hers. She glanced up at me and smiled before intertwining the rest of our fingers.

Inside the diner, the hostess greeted us and pointed in the direction of the area our family usually occupied on Monday evenings.

I chuckled.

Jericho looked stricken. "We're late."

"Maybe they were early. It's all about perspective."

She glared at me and hurried her steps.

I followed at my usual pace, turning the corner a second after she did. I grinned. "Gramps!"

"Bennie, my boy. I heard a rumor that your young lady would be joining the meal and invited myself along. Hope that's all right." He was in the process of pushing himself unsteadily to his feet.

Jericho hurried over and took his arm. She leaned in and kissed his cheek. "Don't stand up for me."

He patted her hand and sank back into his chair. "Ingrained habit, honey. You're a sight for these old eyes."

Her eyes filled again and this time a tear dripped out.

"What's this?" Gramps frowned and reached up to brush away the tear with his thumb. "Don't you know we don't cry in the diner?"

Jericho gave a watery laugh, then sniffled. "I'll keep that in mind. It's really good to see you."

"You could have done that before now." There was a tiny hint of chiding in Gramps's voice. "I'm in the same place I've always been. You and Bennie spent enough time on my beach, I expect you know how to get there."

"I wasn't sure—"

"Don't you say it." Gramps frowned at her. "Don't you question your welcome. You know better."

"Yes, sir." She looked away.

"Maybe let her sit down before you scold her, Gramps?" I came over and pulled out the chair next to Gramps, giving Jericho's shoulder a quick rub as I did. "I did try to use seeing you as an enticement to join us at church. Just so you know."

Gramps nodded.

Jericho sat.

I took the seat on her other side. "I figured the rest of the family would be here already."

"Your mother called and said they were running a bit behind. I have their orders here somewhere." Gramps patted the pockets of his cardigan, finally pulling a folded piece of yellow lined paper from one. He opened it and smoothed it on the table.

"They could have just texted me." I dug out my phone to see if they'd done so and I just hadn't noticed. But there were no notifications. "How'd you get here?"

"I didn't drive, if that's what you're worried about." Gramps shook his head. "Though I don't see the problem with me driving my golf cart on the roads. It has lights. It doesn't go super-fast. And people know me."

"It's illegal, Gramps. You don't have a license anymore."

"Whose fault is that?" He scowled. "Your mother. That's who."

Jericho glanced at me, eyebrows lifted.

Gramps waved a hand. "Might as well tell her. Everyone but me thinks it's amusing."

"A few years after Grammie passed, Gramps started having some blood pressure troubles. He passed out behind the wheel. Twice. Mom was, obviously, concerned. Between her and the doctors, they agreed that it was time for him to stop driving. But he still lives on his own. At ninety, that's pretty good, don't you think, Gramps?"

"Eh." Gramps shrugged. "Your mother treats me like an old man."

"You are an old man." Mom came around the corner, shaking her head. "Just because Jericho is joining us, doesn't mean you need to take advantage of a new audience for your complaints."

I smiled as Mom went straight for Gramps and leaned down to pull him into a tight hug before kissing his cheek. When she pulled back, she turned to Jericho and I could see Mom struggle not to give her the same treatment.

Jericho stood up and hugged Mom.

I closed my eyes briefly and breathed a little prayer of thanks. When I opened my eyes, Mom met my gaze, her own full of understanding.

"Well." Mom stepped back and moved around to pull out the chair on the other side of Gramps, but Dad beat her to it and helped her before sitting himself. My brothers weren't far behind, each clattering into their spots.

Greetings and grumbles about the day flew across the table in a cacophony of sound. I watched Jericho from the corner of my eye. She didn't join in, but she didn't keep herself apart, either. She absorbed. And she relaxed.

The waitress finally came by and we probably overwhelmed her with our flurry of orders. She left with promises to bring drinks out quickly.

"So, Jericho. You're sticking around with this loser, huh?" Christian jerked his chin toward me. "I really feel like you're selling yourself short. I'm in the medical field, you know. He's just a lawyer."

Evan snickered. "You're a *nurse*, bro. Pretty sure lawyer trumps male nurse. And marine biologist trumps both of those. Of the three of us, I'm the only one who can be called doctor."

Jericho laughed.

"Bzzt. Sorry, Ev, that's incorrect." I leaned forward. "Law degree, here. JD. A.K.A juris *doctor*."

"Whatever." Evan waved it off. "No one calls you Doctor Bennett Thomas, whereas—and you lawyers do love your whereases—Doctor Evan Thomas is literally my professional title. Plus, I'm younger than both of these yahoos. Really, the all-around better choice."

"It's a compelling argument." Jericho tapped her lips with one finger. "If I could just get past the image of you with zinc oxide on your nose reading three-inch-thick biology books under an umbrella."

Evan's face flamed bright red as everyone around the table chuckled.

"He's always known what he wanted." Mom reached over and patted Evan's hand. "And my sister is glad that someone in the family wanted to keep up her work at the science station."

"It's a good thing." Gramps nodded. "The work they're doing matters. Our little island has done a lot for the sea turtle population."

"Among other things." Evan muttered. "And it's not like being smart is a bad thing."

"No one said it was. Also, I'm a nurse *practitioner*. Just feel like that's worth tacking on. In case it helps Jericho make the right choice." Christian grinned over at her.

I mock scowled at my brothers. "Do I need to ask the two of you out to the parking lot to settle this like men?"

"Please excuse my children, Jericho. Apparently, their

caveman tendencies come out when around a beautiful woman." Mom shook her head. "Boys. Settle down."

Jericho's cheeks pinked, but she glanced at me. "You don't have to worry. I've made my choice."

My grin was so wide, my cheeks hurt. It took all I could muster not to lean over and kiss her right then. It wouldn't have been appropriate. And I absolutely didn't want to share our first kiss since she returned in front of my family.

Besides all of that, my brothers, being the mature idiots that they were, were busy making retching noises while my father laughed, my mother tried to shush them, and Gramps just beamed.

I leaned closer to Jericho. "Even though they're part of the package?"

"*Especially* because they're part of the package." The look she gave me with those words tested my resolve to keep that first kiss private.

18

JERICHO

Somehow, I made it through dinner. It helped that conversation switched away from the topic of Bennett and me—and how adorable was it that Gramps still called him Bennie?—and on to more neutral topics.

I tried again, and failed again, to pay for my own meal. In this case, I didn't mind as much because Gramps insisted on picking up everyone's tab. Linda and Dave both seemed mildly put out by that, too, but you could only argue with a ninety-something-year-old for so long before it started feeling mean.

Back in my car, the air was charged. It was as if it was full of static electricity—like the beach when a storm was coming. My skin tingled. And where Bennett's fingers brushed against my fingers or arm? It burned.

I pulled into the empty parking spot behind Bennett's motorcycle and shifted into Park, then licked my lips.

Bennett unhooked his seatbelt and shifted in his seat. "Thanks for coming tonight. You'll come next week, right?"

I nodded. His parents had been firm that, as far as they were concerned, my attendance was expected and desired. "But I draw the line at ordering meatloaf."

He laughed and took my hand. "No meatloaf. Got it."

"Bennett—"

"Jericho—"

We both broke off, chuckling.

"You first." He stroked the back of my hand.

Darn. I was going to make him go first. His touch distracted me long enough that he got the words out before me.

I cleared my throat. "Friday night, on the bridge."

He tipped his head to the side, eyebrows lifted.

I shifted my gaze away from his. I was going to have to say it all aloud. I'd been holding on to the smallest hope that he'd let me off the hook. It wasn't as if he couldn't read my mind. Or at least, it sure seemed like he could.

My voice came out as a rasp. "When you said you still loved me. Did you mean it?"

"I did." He nodded. "I do."

I do. The words echoed through my brain, bringing back all the promises we'd made to one another all those years ago. The ones that would have culminated in both of us uttering those words before God and family.

Regret pierced my heart. Again. How many times would I have to experience the pain of my stupid choices? Would I ever be able to move past them?

Maybe this would be a tiny step in that direction. I looked back at him and held his gaze. "I still love you, too."

His lips slowly curved up. His gaze intensified and he leaned forward.

My breath caught.

I'd known this was coming since the start of dinner. Or at least, I'd hoped so. But the memory of his lips on mine paled in comparison to the actual experience. Was it just the fading that came with time, or was it more?

I'd have to think about that later.

Much. Later.

I slid my fingers along his jaw and into his hair. It was shorter now, in his professional lawyer hairstyle. But still silky smooth. His scent was the one that haunted my dreams. It was as though everything that had been off center for sixteen years clicked back into place now that I was in Bennett's arms.

I never wanted to leave.

Before I was ready, Bennett was easing back, his breathing heavy. He swallowed and rested his forehead on mine and closed his eyes. His voice was husky. "I should go."

I nodded. He should. I didn't want him to. And from his expression, he didn't want to, either. But we'd managed to avoid sexual sin when we were filled with teenage hormones and running around in bathing suits. Surely in our thirties, we could do the same.

Bennett pressed another kiss to my lips, pulling back before I could sink in.

"Can I see you tomorrow?" He pushed open the car door and slid one leg out.

"I hope you will." The rush of cold air from outside was what I needed to break the delightful haze kissing Bennett had fuzzed over my brain. "I'll be at the library."

He grinned. "Makes it easy to find you. Do you take a lunch break?"

I wiggled a hand from side to side. "Sort of? I eat in my office with a note to ring the bell if they need something. I don't lock up or anything though."

"Maybe I could eat with you?"

"I'd like that. I'll bring a picnic." As soon as the words left my mouth, my brain scrambled to recall if I had the ingredients for anything that would be special. I'd figure it out when I got home.

"That sounds nice. Eleven thirty?"

"Absolutely." I didn't usually eat until after twelve. Or one.

But I wasn't going to impose my schedule on him. I just wanted to see him again. As soon as possible. "I miss you already."

A grin flashed and he wagged a finger at me as he got completely out of the car. "Uh-uh. I'm leaving. For both our sakes." He rested an arm on the hood of my car and leaned down to look at me. "I love you."

"I love you back."

Bennett straightened and shut the car door.

I watched through the dissipating fog on the windshield as he unfastened the bungie cords that held a helmet to the motorcycle and put it on, then clipped the chin strap. He threw a leg over the bike and before long, the engine roared to life. I couldn't see his face through the visor when he glanced over his shoulder before pulling out into a tight turn, but he lifted a hand in a wave and, even though I knew he couldn't see it, I returned the gesture.

I put my car back into gear and managed a U-turn—much less graceful than the one he made—and followed his tail light toward home.

Bennett waved again when I flicked on my signal to turn into the neighborhood where my cottage sat. I idled in the turn lane until his tail light disappeared from view. Then, with a contented sigh, I headed home.

"READY TO GO?" Bennett leaned casually against the frame of my cottage's front door.

I turned to grab my stack of reusable grocery bags and patted my pocket to be sure I had my phone before slinging my purse over my shoulder and nodding. "Ready to go."

Over the last six weeks, Bennett and I had fallen into a steady routine. Mondays we had dinner at the diner with his family. More often than not these days, Gramps came out as well. Bennett spent his lunch break with me two or three times a week. Fridays, after the library closed at 2, he picked me up at home and we went across the bridge into town to get groceries and have a date. Saturdays and Sundays were more flexible. Sometimes we hung out. Sometimes I went to lunch at his parents' when they got back from church.

And every Saturday evening, he texted to ask me if I'd like him to pick me up for church in the morning. But he always took my "no thanks" well.

Even so, it was starting to worry me.

"You all right?" Bennett took my bags as we went down the steps to his waiting car.

"Yeah. Just thinking. Sorry."

"Never apologize for thinking. Thinking is always encouraged." He grinned as he opened the car door for me. "Care to share?"

I didn't have to answer right away, since he'd shut the door and was in the process of moving around to get behind the wheel. He shot me a curious look as he got in and buckled, then started the car.

I shook my head. "It's nothing big. Spring break starts tomorrow for UNC."

"Yeah. They're usually the first. Travis said the rentals are all pretty much booked up through mid-September now. It's a good thing."

"Are you sure you don't regret letting me rent Heron full time?"

"One hundred percent." He flashed a grin as he backed out of my driveway and started out of the neighborhood. "I promise. I only had it as a seasonal rental because Travis assured me it was easy. His definition of easy and mine aren't always in lockstep."

I chuckled. "Has he heard anything from Caroline?"

"No." Bennett sobered. "They finally have the results of Grady's evaluations though. I guess the school is working on putting together special plans to make sure he gets the support he needs."

"Deb mentioned that yesterday when they were in for more books." I hesitated. "Did you know she's considering home-schooling him permanently?"

"Is she?" Bennett frowned slightly. "I hadn't heard that. Wonder if Travis knows."

"Wouldn't he? I mean, he's Grady's dad. I assumed Deb was talking to him about it."

"Fifty-fifty on that." Bennett slowed as we neared the town limits. "Sometimes she makes up her mind and then just convinces you it was your idea in the first place."

I grinned. I could see that about Deb. And Bennett's mom, for that matter. "She does seem to think she knows best. Although, so far when it comes to pushing Grady about books, she also seems to have a point. He's moving up steadily in his ability to handle chapter books."

"Mom mentioned that. I guess Deb and she were discussing the evaluation report. Doesn't Grady want to go back to school? I always loved school."

I thought about the conversations I'd had with Grady at the library and also when I was visiting Bennett's parents. Since Deb lived next door and Travis was the house down, we tended to see a lot of the rest of the family whenever we were there. "I think school was a lot easier for you than it is for Grady."

Bennett sighed. "You're probably right. But Austin never really loved the academics and he still enjoyed the social aspect of school."

"I don't get the impression that Grady gets along with many —if any—of the kids in his class." There'd been a bully in one of the books he read a week ago. When he brought that book back, he told me all about it. And all about how horrible they were. And more. It had been obvious he had first-hand experience.

"That's probably true." Bennett checked over his shoulder before changing lanes and driving onto the bridge.

I shut my eyes. I was making progress—I didn't have to squeeze them shut anymore. And sometimes, I could even sneak peeks through my eyelashes as we crossed the span.

Bennett reached over and took my hand.

I curled my fingers around his and relaxed. I'd been expecting the sensations to end. But still, every touch, every kiss, was like coming home. "I love you."

"I love you, too." I could hear the smile in his voice, but I didn't open my eyes to look.

"One of these days, I'm going to conquer my fear of this bridge." It was a promise I made myself every Friday. But I had yet to force myself into my car to give it a try. I just waited for Fridays with Bennett.

"Maybe if we get Jon to add a mudslide flavor at MacLachalan's you'll cave." Bennett squeezed my hand before untangling his. "He'd have to make sure it wasn't available on Friday though."

"That's mean." My eyes snapped open and I glanced over at Bennett. He was laughing. The car tires bumped over the connection between the bridge and the mainland road. I let out a breath. "Don't you dare suggest it."

"We'll see." Bennett slowed as we approached a red light. "Groceries first?"

"That works." I looked around. "Why is it so busy?"

"Spring break." The light changed and Bennett eased the car into the intersection. "It only gets busier from here."

Right. Duh. We'd had that conversation at the start of this trip. "Oh. Speaking of that. Sort of. My sister Madeline and her boyfriend want to come out to visit. Maybe for Easter next month. Do you think he could stay with you? I know it's a lot to ask, but I only have the one guest room and—"

"Of course he can." Bennett cut me off. "It's not a lot to ask at all."

"Thanks. I guess the Inn is a little out of his price range. Plus, between you and me, I don't think Maddy wanted him that far away." I rolled my eyes.

"Are they living together?"

"No." I shook my head. "He actually got Maddy back to church when they started dating. The way she talks, I think she's on the cusp of giving her life to Jesus. If she hasn't already."

"Wouldn't she tell you?" He glanced over before turning into the grocery store lot. "That seems like something she'd share with a sister who has the same faith."

I sighed. "You'd think that. But she's pretty annoyed with me for not having jumped into a local church here. So now she's judging my faith. It's...ironic."

"I think you meant rude." Bennett parked the car and cut the engine, but didn't make any moves toward getting out. "It's one thing to ask. Or to encourage a change. But we aren't here to tell someone they don't love Jesus. Especially when it's obvious from the fruit in their life that they do."

"Thanks." I couldn't meet his gaze. "I know it disappoints you, too."

Bennett didn't reply for long enough that I was almost sure he wasn't going to. Then, he spoke. "I'm not sure disappointed is the right word. Although, I guess it's close enough. I just don't really understand. You've told me how badly the church treated your mom—your whole family, really—during the divorce. You've talked about how they gossiped and how hurt you were—are—by the lack of support you had. But it's been a long time. Don't you think it would help you to forgive them?"

I pressed my lips together, fighting back my immediate desire to retort defensively. "I've forgiven them."

"Okay." Bennett unhooked his seatbelt and pushed open his door.

"That's it? Just 'okay' like nothing happened?" I crossed my arms as acid burned in my gut. "You're not going to join the crowd who wants to tell me that I obviously haven't forgiven them if I'm still choosing to worship at home? Or point out how the people here aren't the ones who hurt me? Or, you could join my mom in reminding me that God commanded us not to avoid worshiping together."

"No." He looked over at me, compassion in his eyes.

I looked away.

"Jericho, I love you. I want you to have a rich and full spiritual life. I pray for that. I believe, firmly, that until you're ready to let go of the hurt they caused you that you're not going to experience the fullness of joy that we can have in Jesus. But I get it. People can—and do—do things that hurt us. Things we don't understand and that we may never understand or get an apology for. But it's our choice to let that interfere with how we view them. How we love them. And if we don't let go of the hurt, we only end up hurting ourselves." He stood and reached into the back seat for the grocery bags. "You already know that. You already know all the things you just spit out. So no. I'm not going to tell you any of them."

I heaved out a breath, anger still simmering in my gut. I wanted to argue with all the things he said. I wanted to explain why they were wrong and how he couldn't understand and throw his perfect, amazing life in his face.

But I couldn't.

Not after the words he said finally started to sink in. Really sink in.

People hurt us.

To Bennett, I was "people." Maybe not everyone. There were surely plenty of clients or islanders along the way who had hurt him. Heck, he had two brothers and three cousins who might as well be brothers. More than likely, they'd all hurt one another a lot over the course of their lives.

For the first time since I moved to the island, I wished I had driven to the store. Then I'd be in charge of when it was time to go home. I could insist we were leaving. Right now. I could drop him off and then...then what?

Go bury my head in the metaphorical sand? Hide out in my cottage for the night? It wasn't as if I could disappear for any length of time. The library opened tomorrow at ten. There were people counting on me. I couldn't let them down because I was irritated that someone told me the truth.

I unfastened my seatbelt and pushed open the car door. I grabbed my bags and stood. "Let's just go shop."

He tipped his head to the side and I had to force myself not to look away from the weight of his gaze. Then he nodded once and shut his car door. I did the same.

At the front of the car, Bennett paused and held out his hand, his gaze steady on me.

One corner of my mouth twitched up and I took it.

Bennett loved me in spite of my flaws. In spite of how I hurt him.

Maybe it was time for me to figure out how to do the same.

19

BENNETT

"Grady, my man." I squatted and held out my hand for a high five.

Grady smacked my palm and then darted into the living room where his ongoing Lego build waited for him.

I stood and grinned at Travis. "Hey, man. C'mon in."

"Your pizza, sir." Travis thrust the pizza box at me as he came in. "I went half plain cheese and half supreme."

I glanced at Grady and nodded. "Sounds perfect."

Travis shook his head, looked in the direction of his son, and then started toward the kitchen.

I followed, setting the pizza down on the island before heading to the fridge. "Soda?"

"Root beer?" Travis pulled out one of the chairs at the island and sat. "Or anything not caffeinated is fine."

"I happen to have root beer." I grabbed two bottles of the fancy root beer I splurged on sometimes, then frowned. "I have no idea if it has caffeine though."

Travis shrugged and reached for the bottle. "I guess I'll live dangerously. It's not like I sleep all that well anymore anyway."

"Sorry." I twisted the top off my bottle and took a drink. "What can I do?"

"Keep praying, I guess. Because I seriously have no other ideas. Mom is dead set on homeschooling. Grady is on board, because it would mean he doesn't have to go to school. I just—Caroline was so opposed to the idea." He sighed. "Maybe that doesn't matter. It's not like she's here."

"Still no word?"

"Nope. At this point, I'm beginning to think it would be better to go ahead and have you track her down and serve her. At least it would put an end to the limbo." Travis twisted off his bottle's cap. "What do I do, Bennett? How am I supposed to make all the decisions on my own?"

"First of all, you're not alone." I held up a finger. "You have a very big, very willing to be involved family."

Travis nodded once. "Fair point."

"Plus, you don't have to make permanent decisions all at once. Take school. Why not let your mom officially finish out the year? See how it goes for what, two, two and a half months? If it's a raging success, then maybe it's not such a bad idea to do next year. And if not, maybe the struggle will convince Aunt Deb that she needs to pivot." I didn't have a lot of hope that Aunt Deb would end up being willing to change her mind, but stranger things had happened. After the conversation in the car last Friday with Jericho, I was less inclined to consider homeschool a bad choice for Grady. I might worry about him making friends and that kind of thing, but there were other ways to accomplish that. Maybe in situations that were more welcoming than the public school was turning out to be.

"I guess that's true. I'm not sure I could get Grady back on the bus right now if I tried. Mom took him over to school with her this week, did I tell you that? They had a meeting about an

IEP and I wanted another set of ears. She brought Grady. He... did not respond well to being back in the building."

I winced. "I hadn't heard that."

"So, yeah. I didn't have that extra set of ears, and it was a definite tick in the 'don't send him back here' column." Travis set his bottle down and ran a hand over his face. "I hate this."

I reached out and squeezed his shoulder. "As for Caroline. What if I put the wheels in motion to at least find out where she is? Knowing that might help you decide on the steps that come after."

"How?" Travis frowned, then held up a hand. "Actually, don't tell me. I don't think I want to know."

"The possibilities aren't all bad." Most of them were. But I was trying to be a supportive cousin, not a buzzkill, so I left that unsaid.

"Yeah. Sure. Why not?" Travis's shoulders slumped. "Do it."

"All right. I'll get started on Monday."

"Let's talk about you. I'm tired of thinking about my life." Travis tapped the pizza box. "And can we eat this while it's hot?"

"Of course. Sorry." I chuckled and went to the cabinet to get plates. "Are we calling Grady or just letting him grab something when he's ready?"

"Let's just leave him happy. I've fought enough battles for today." Travis took a plate, flipped open the box, and took a slice of supreme.

I slid a slice of supreme on my plate, then picked up the box and moved it onto a different counter so I could take the seat next to Travis.

"What's new with you? Still in shiny happy world where birds sing and fart out hearts and rainbows?" Bitterness laced Travis's words.

I laughed. "That's a mental image. I can't say I've ever seen—or heard—a bird fart. Do they even do that?"

Travis gaped at me. "Why would you think I know the answer to that? Don't all animals fart?"

Curious, I dug my phone out of my pocket. "Let's ask Google."

"Let's not." Travis picked up his pizza.

"You started this, man." I opened a browser and tapped out my question. I scrolled the results, then tapped on a link from the Department of Fish and Wildlife. I turned the phone so Travis could see the screen. "Birds lack the bacteria necessary to cause farts. Also, they process food too quickly for gas to form."

"The more you know," Travis muttered, shaking his head.

"So apparently, the answer to your original question is no. Because it's not possible for a bird to fart a heart or a rainbow or anything else." I shot him an overly toothy grin and slid my phone back in my pocket, before picking up my pizza for a bite.

"Are you avoiding the real question, Counselor?"

I wrinkled my nose as I chewed. "Probably."

"Uh-oh. Trouble in paradise? Welcome to the club."

I hunched my shoulders. "I don't know that I'd call it trouble. Just...a bump in the road."

"Wanna talk about it?"

I did not. At the same time, if it would help Travis—even if it was only in the misery loves company type of way—I could. "You know we go grocery shopping on Fridays, right?"

"I do. Because she has bridge phobia."

"Right. Last week, we had this conversation about going to church—it's a big issue between her and one of her sisters right now—and it's been weird since. She still did dinner on Monday, but yesterday, she bailed on shopping. And our Friday night date. Maybe she really is under the weather, but she also didn't want me to bring her soup and NyQuil. So, yeah. I'm not sure what to do." I took another bite of pizza.

"Hmm. Anything else changed?"

"That's not enough?"

A smile flashed across Travis's face. "I meant more like are you doing anything different. Or weird. In response?"

"No." I dragged out the word, then frowned. "I didn't send her a text inviting her to church last Saturday. I wasn't planning on sending one tonight, either."

"Because?"

"I don't want her to feel pressured. It's very obviously a sore spot with her." I poked at the crust of my pizza. "She's a grownup and gets to do what she thinks is best."

Travis snickered. "That's not what being a grownup is, and you know it."

I sighed. He had a point. "I don't want to be the pushy boyfriend."

"Maybe that's what she needs you to be though." Travis took a sip of his root beer. "I can look back at my marriage and see places where I was not the spiritual leader I was supposed to be. Anyone who can do math knows why we got married as quickly as we did. So it's not as if I started things out at a high level of spirituality. But I thought we were growing together. So I didn't push. Even when I knew I needed to."

I blew out a breath and reached for my phone. "I don't want to lose her over this. I don't want to lose her again for any reason."

"I get that. I do. But I'm also starting to understand the idea of holding the things God gives us with an open hand."

The pastor mentioned that. A lot. It was something I could easily agree with and see the benefit of when I heard it preached from the pulpit. But implementing it in my life? Harder. I'd lost Jericho before. I'd survived. Thrived, even, after a while.

"Do you trust God with your relationship?" Travis's voice was quiet.

Oof. Not as much as I should, apparently. "I'll send the text."

~

I FILLED my travel mug with coffee from the urn in the foyer, dumped in sugar and cream, and gave it a quick stir before pushing the lid back on. The church offered insulated cups, but they were small. And they lacked lids. I'd learned, the hard way of course, that I really needed that lid if I was drinking coffee while also standing and sitting during the service.

"Morning." Christian reached past me for a cup.

I looked at my brother and swallowed the auto-pilot response. "You all right?"

"Not really. Late night. Or early morning, I guess." He shrugged and took several long swallows of coffee before holding his cup back under the spout to refill. "Emergency call in to the clinic."

I waited, but he didn't elaborate. Which was pretty standard. Christian was strict about patient privacy. As he should be. "Turn out okay?"

"Yeah. Just...a lot."

I patted my brother's shoulder. "You could have stayed home and slept. You know that, right?"

"I do. I'm probably bailing on lunch and grabbing a nap. I was still awake though, so I figured I might as well come." He turned and scanned the growing crowd in the foyer. He squinted. "Is that Jericho?"

"I doubt it." The words were out before I could stop them.

"Should have bet you. I would've won. She's talking to Mom. Over by the stairs."

My heart leapt. I worked to settle my thoughts and excitement, but it took effort. "Maybe I'll go say hi."

"Good plan." Christian shook his head.

I wove through the crowd toward Mom. And Jericho. She was wearing one of her librarian outfits—slacks and a nice shirt

—rather than the jeans and a sweater that I enjoyed seeing her in when we were out together. Not that she looked bad in her more formal clothes. She didn't. But she was clearly more comfortable when she was casual.

I shifted so Jericho would see me approach. I didn't want to surprise her or make her think I was sneaking up.

"Oh, there you are." Mom reached out her hand with a grin. "Look who I found."

"Morning." I raised my coffee in a brief salute. "You look really nice."

"I was just saying that." Mom grinned. "Oh. There's your father. I should go grab him. See you inside."

I watched Mom hurry off, then smiled at Jericho. "She's not subtle."

"No. She's not." Jericho chuckled. "I can't say I mind this time. Her enthusiasm because I showed up was a little much."

"I can see that. But I'm glad you did." *What changed?* I absolutely was not asking that. No matter how desperate for the answer I might be. I should just accept that she came and be glad. "We could sit by ourselves, if you wanted."

"You still sit with your family every week?" She looked surprised.

I shrugged. "It makes Mom happy. As far as I've ever been concerned, a seat is a seat. She won't mind if we don't though. Christian sometimes sits with friends. Evan too."

Was I the only weirdo who didn't really have a group of friends to hang with? I had my brothers and my cousins. I'd never really felt the need for more. Something to worry about later. Or never.

Jericho bit her lower lip and scanned the crowd, then turned back to me. "You really don't think she'd mind? I'd kind of like to sit in the back."

"She won't mind at all. But the back fills up fast. We should grab seats now." I turned toward the doors that led into the worship center, unsure of my move. I wanted to take her hand. I wanted to pretend that everything was perfect between us. I also wanted to know what changed. Why had she come today, after being invited so many times? Not that it mattered. It really didn't. But was this a new normal? Or was it a one-shot deal?

Jericho slid her fingers through mine. "Is that okay? At church, I mean?"

I squeezed her hand. "It's definitely okay."

We found seats in the back row. Mom and Dad smiled and waved as they walked past us on the way to their usual spot. Christian sat with them, but I didn't see where Evan ended up. Maybe he hadn't made it today. When the turtles hatched starting in July, he often missed because he was on a nest stakeout. But that was still months off.

I pulled my attention away from my brother and focused on the service that was about to begin. "I'm really glad you made it today."

"You said that." Jericho's smile was ever-so-slightly off. "I appreciate you inviting me."

"Any time." Of course, she already knew that. I'd been inviting her since the end of January. Had skipping one week made a difference? Weird. But I'd take it.

20

JERICHO

"Can you come to lunch?" Bennett stood facing me as the crowd of people milled around in the worship center and made their way out.

I nodded. "Would you want to pick me up at home? I'd like to change. Then we could take one car."

"That sounds perfect. Maybe we can walk Gramps home afterward. Mom doesn't want him going alone. He fell Friday morning. He's fine. Honestly, I think Mom and Aunt Deb are more traumatized by it than he was."

"Oh, boy." I put my hand on Bennett's arm. "I'm glad he's all right. Is he coming to eat?"

He nodded. "Mom said she was going to bring him over. She's keeping a close eye. She and Aunt Deb have been talking about making him move in with one of them for a couple of years. This might push them over the edge."

I nodded slowly. "It's a good idea. But it'll be hard on him."

"It will. Although, living alone in his nineties? He should be proud to have made it that far." He looked past me. "Crowd has thinned out. Ready to go?"

"Yeah. Of course." I turned and slid down the row to the

aisle, then headed for the doors. I could feel Bennett close behind me. It was a comforting warmth. One that made me feel safe. And loved.

He walked me to my car, even though he'd pointed out his own on the other side of the lot. He hadn't let me drive him over, either, saying it was a head start for me, since I needed to change. And all I could think was that it was one more example of the little, subtle things he did that showed me how much he cared.

Like texting and inviting me to church.

I waited in line to exit the parking lot. Last week, when I didn't get that text, I'd had to do a lot of soul searching to figure out why it bothered me so much. Maddy had had a lot to say on the subject—so much, in fact, that I'd almost showed up last week just to see how he'd react.

In the end I chickened out.

Like I almost had today.

It was finally my turn, and the traffic was clear, so I turned and started on my way back through town and then toward home. There was more foot traffic on the streets in town. More shops open. Not all of them—but more. Like things were waking up after a winter sleep now that the tourists were beginning to make their way to the island.

The library patronage hadn't changed. And it probably wouldn't. Mrs. Sanderson had been clear that mostly only locals came in, even though we offered visitor cards with a few extra steps to ensure we had a way to cover books that didn't get returned.

I'd been brainstorming ideas to see if I could bump that up some. We didn't necessarily need more people to come to the library than already did, but I could make the case to the council for bumping up our budget a little if that happened.

It didn't take long to get home. I loved that about living here.

I'd grown up in a medium-sized city where crossing town could take half an hour. On a good day. Traffic would pick up some as more and more of the summer people showed up, but I couldn't remember it ever being truly bad. Most people parked themselves on the beach and commuted on foot between the ocean and their rental. Folks who stayed at the Inn or the handful of B&Bs that opened up during high season in town had to drive to the lighthouse parking lot if they wanted to hit the public beach. But that traffic was limited by the capacity of the hotels in question. So it shouldn't be bad. At least, that's what I hoped.

I changed into jeans and a T-shirt and traded out my flats for sneakers, then went to wait for Bennett on the porch. I would have been happy to sit out there a lot more than the five minutes or so that it took for him to pull up. The weather was, finally, starting to be gorgeous. Not lie on the beach weather, but not the gloomy and windy winter weather either.

I hurried down the steps and got in on the passenger side. "Thanks."

"Not a problem. You look nice." He smiled over at me as he began backing out of the driveway.

"Should I have brought something? I always feel awkward not bringing something."

"Nope." Bennett pointed the car back toward the main road. "You know Mom always has way more food than we need. And today, I'm pretty sure Aunt Deb and the rest of the family's going to be there, too. So Aunt Deb will have added to the overabundance."

I pressed my lips together as my stomach sank. "They're all coming?"

"That's what Mom said. Why?" He shot a glance my way before returning his attention to the road. "Is that not okay?"

"Of course it's okay." It wasn't my place to say one way or the other. It wasn't as if I was family. Or in charge. I liked Deb and

Rob. And their sons. Or, well, I had before. I'd really only reconnected with Travis, and only then because they were the biggest real estate option on the island. Some of the agents in town on the mainland made it clear that they could work on Loring Island, too, but I never saw signs for anyone other than Travis or his dad.

"But?" Bennett reached over and took my hand. "I hear a but at the end of the sentence."

I sighed. "No. It's just..."

I wasn't sure how to explain.

"Mmhmm." Bennett slowed, then pulled the car off the road onto the shoulder. He shifted into Park and turned in his seat. "Tell me. Please? I can't help if I don't know the problem."

I squeezed my eyes shut for a moment, then met his gaze. "I'm embarrassed."

He frowned slightly. "Why?"

"I should have done things differently. I hurt you. You told me that. I probably hurt your family, too. Your parents and brothers have welcomed me with open arms, and I guess I keep waiting for someone to mention how awful I am."

Bennett shook his head. "Won't happen."

"You can't know that." I turned and looked out the window. My family always made a point of getting a little dig in about me coming back to the island and getting back together with Bennett. Oh, they were happy enough—as much as they cared—but poking at me was the one thing everyone agreed on. Wasn't that just how family was?

"Yeah, I can." He squeezed my hand. "Everyone—I mean that literally—is glad that you're back on the island. And, more, that we're together again. They know how much I love you. And how much you love me. You do, don't you?"

I whipped my gaze back to his. "I do. I do love you. You know it, right?"

He nodded, his lips curving. "And do you trust me?"

"Of course." I'd always trusted him. Well, I guess that wasn't entirely true. If I'd truly trusted him all those years ago, wouldn't I have gotten in touch instead of disappearing?

Thankfully, he let it slide.

"Good. Then trust me on this. My family loves you. They're all glad that you're here. That we've reconnected. And lunch today? It's just one in what we all want to be a lifetime of meals shared together." He squeezed my hand. "I promise."

Any words I thought of saying got stuck in my throat. I was fixated on the idea of "a lifetime." Had he meant it?

What was I thinking? Of course he did. This was Bennett. He didn't say things he didn't mean.

"I love you." I leaned over and kissed his cheek.

Bennett turned and stopped me from leaning back as his lips found mine. Time slowed, then seemed to stop as I got lost in the rightness of the contact.

In time, Bennett eased back, rubbing his lips together. His voice was husky. "We should get going. They're going to wonder where we are."

I nodded and took a deep, steadying breath.

After a glance over his shoulder, Bennett pulled back into the lane and minutes later we were at his parents' house. The driveway was full of cars. I winced.

"Looks like we're the last ones here." Bennett pulled up close to the bumper of one of the cars and turned off the engine.

I pushed open the door and got out. Bennett met me at the front of the car, took my hand, and we walked up the stairs and into the sprawling house together.

A wave of laughter and conversation rolled out from the kitchen. I smiled in spite of myself. Bennett's family was big on laughter. Teasing caused much of it, but I couldn't complain about that. It was good natured. And everyone took as well as they gave. No one crossed the line into mean-spirited.

"There you are. I was beginning to wonder if I should send out a search party." Linda set a large bowl on the counter and held open her arms.

Bennett crossed to hug his mom. I tried to hang back, but she grabbed my hand and pulled me in for a squeeze, too.

"I was going to volunteer, since I happened to see your car on the side of the road. Almost stopped to see if you were broken down, but things looked like they were under control." Austin, the youngest of the cousins, wiggled his eyebrows. "Good to see you again, Jericho."

"Thanks." My face was burning. Was that why they'd been laughing when we came in? And how both of us failed to hear the car go by?

"I'll be sure to return the favor sometime. If you ever get around to finding a woman." Bennett slung his arm across my shoulders, seeming completely unfazed by the teasing.

"I'm married to the ocean." Austin grinned.

"More like adrenaline." Christian shouldered Austin aside and reached for the bowl that Linda had set on the counter. "Or were you not mentioning that I had to give you eight stitches yesterday?"

"What?" Deb spun and sent a narrow-eyed glare at her youngest son. "I thought we had a deal that all injuries were reported immediately."

"It wasn't an injury." Austin glared at Christian. "Ever hear of HIPAA, man? Pretty sure I even had to sign something about that."

"Oh, please." Christian waved it off.

Aunt Deb crossed the kitchen and took Austin by his shoulders. She raised her chin so she was staring into his face. "Eight. Stitches."

Austin sighed and lifted the hem of his shirt, revealing a gauze bandage on his ribs. "I was cleaning out my garage. You know how you're always on my case about the extra gear that I don't use anymore?"

"Do not even attempt to make this somehow my fault." Deb poked a finger into his belly.

"Ow." Austin stepped back and rubbed his stomach. "Fine. Anyway, I forgot I had some fishing gear hanging up behind some of the surfboards. I moved the boards, the rods fell, lines got tangled." He shrugged.

Rob, Austin's dad, stopped mid-conversation with Dave and scowled at his son. "You left a hook on a rod that was being stored?"

"Oh my word." Austin threw his hands in the air. "Yes. Sue me. I'm an idiot, okay?"

Bennett covered a laugh by coughing.

I turned away to hide a smirk.

If nothing else, at least that interlude took the attention off Bennet and me. And our little pause by the side of the road.

Just thinking about it had my cheeks heating again.

"Food's ready. Let's pray." Linda spoke loudly enough that all the conversation quieted. She turned to where Gramps perched on a stool at the island. "Dad? You want to bless the food?"

"Of course." Gramps bowed his head. "Heavenly Father, thank You for this food and the hands that prepared it. More than that, thank You for family and for bringing back loved ones in Your time. Keep us in Your hands as we follow in Your footsteps. Amen."

I fought the urge to glance over at Bennett. Was Gramps talking about me? I let my gaze scan the room. Travis had Grady up on his hip—he looked as though he was struggling with the weight and awkwardness of long arms and legs, but Grady clung to his dad. Travis was pale.

Hmm. Maybe Gramps meant Caroline.

I fell into line behind Bennett as everyone rustled into place to load up plates from the spread arranged on the counters. He turned and handed me a plate and his fingers brushed mine. Would the thrill of his touch ever fade?

Hopefully not.

The clan was too large to all fit at one table, so Bennett and I found ourselves seated inside at the banquette in the kitchen. Grady and Travis approached just as we got settled.

Grady scooted onto the bench, getting as close to me as he could before grinning up at me. "Hi, Miss Jericho."

I returned the grin. "Hi, Grady. How are you liking the books you got with your grandma this week?"

He shrugged, then pointed at one of the plates Travis held.

"Do you mind?" Travis glanced over his shoulder toward the island.

"Of course not." Bennett gestured to the table. "Sit down."

"Thanks." Defeat hung on every letter of the word. Travis put a plate in front of Grady, then set down his own and pulled out one of the chairs from the side of the table opposite me. "If Grady makes things too crowded—"

"He's fine." I cut Travis off. "We're pals, right Grady?"

Grady shrugged again, intent on scooping mac and cheese into his mouth.

I couldn't see that there was much chewing happening. Grady's cheeks just kept getting fuller and fuller.

"Chew and swallow before you eat more, Grady." Travis reached across the table and touched Grady's hand.

Grady looked across at his dad, his brow furrowed.

"Chew." Travis reiterated.

Grady nodded and, still holding a forkful of noodles, began to chew noisily.

"How's it going?" Bennett seemed unfazed by Grady's eating.

If the two of them were okay, then I'd let it go, too. I started to eat.

"Eh. It's going." Travis sighed and poked at the food on his plate but didn't take a bite. "With some last-minute cancellations, rentals are down a tiny bit compared to last year, but it's been more overcast, so that's not surprising. In two weeks, we're back up to booked solid for the bulk of the summer. The manager at the inn mentioned she's full-up through July already."

"That's good. Not really what I meant, but still good." Bennett nodded toward Travis's plate. "You need to eat, or your mom's going to stage an intervention."

With another heavy sigh, Travis stabbed a forkful of salad and pushed it into his mouth. He chewed as if on autopilot.

"No news?"

"Postcard, actually. She's in Oregon." Travis set his fork down. "No mention of coming back. No questions about Grady. She needed money."

"Did you send it to her?" Bennett's tone was light, but I could see the tension in his jaw.

I reached under the table and rested my hand on his leg, squeezing lightly. Bennett glanced at me. I tried to send a subtle signal that he should let it go.

"She's my wife, Ben." Travis gave the plate in front of him a little push away from him.

I glanced at Grady. He seemed oblivious to the conversation as he single-mindedly stuffed mac and cheese into his mouth, pausing to chew only when no more would fit into his cheeks.

"That's fair. Are you content to leave it like that?"

I winced and glanced at Bennett.

Travis nodded. "I'm not going to be the one who ends this. But I'm pretty sure the money I sent her is a retainer for her own lawyer."

"Why? How much was it?"

"Sixty-five hundred." Everything about Travis seemed to sag.

"Trav."

"I know. Okay? I do."

"Let me know the minute you hear something. Promise me." Bennett waited until Travis looked up and met his gaze. "I'm serious."

Travis closed his eyes. "Fine. Yeah. I promise."

"I'm so sorry." Unable to take the pain radiating off Travis, I reached across the table and touched his hand.

"Thanks." With a visible effort, Travis straightened. "Thanks for your help with the books, Jericho."

"Not only my job, but my absolute pleasure." I smiled. "How's homeschooling going?"

"Mom says it's okay. I'm grateful she's willing to do it, because he and I just butt heads when I try to help. Given how things have gone the times I've tried to talk about going back to school in town, I think this may be what we have to do. At least for a little while." Travis shook his head. "Definitely not something I ever planned on. But I'll do whatever Grady needs."

I nodded. "I think that's all any parent can do."

"You're doing a great job, Trav. Seriously." Bennett scraped the last bite off his plate and turned a considering eye toward the area of the kitchen where the food sat out. "Do I want more, or do you think there's something amazing for dessert?"

"Mom made a chocolate cream pie."

"Really?" Bennett grinned. "It's in the fridge?"

"Probably. Bring some for me and Grady, would you?"

"Sure." Bennett turned to me. "You in?"

"Definitely. But...will there be any left for the rest of them?" As much as I wanted the pie—Aunt Deb's pies were a strong memory from my time here in my teens—I also didn't want to be the reason others missed out.

"Knowing Mom? She made three or four of them. She knows we're a crowd of pie hounds." Travis scooted his chair back. "You want a hand, Bennett?"

"I won't say no." Bennett slid out of the booth and stood. He picked up his plate and looked my way. "Are you finished with that?"

"Not yet." I held a hand over my plate. "But I still want the pie."

Travis laughed. He grabbed his plate and considered Grady's a moment, then left it alone.

I watched Bennett and his cousin cross over into the main area of the kitchen and smiled before returning my focus to my food. I liked Bennett's family. I always had. I couldn't quite believe how welcoming they'd been when I returned, but I also wasn't going to second-guess it.

Grady dropped his fork and leaned his head against my arm.

"You all right, bud?"

"Full."

"Too full for pie?" I felt his head shake against my arm and chuckled. "No such thing, right?"

A nod.

Before long, Travis and Bennett returned with pie and our conversation turned to lighter things. When the pie had been eaten, Travis and Grady made their excuses and headed out.

Bennett looked over at me. "Should we see if Gramps is ready to go? We could walk him home along the beach."

"I'd like that." I stacked my plates and started to slide out from behind the table.

Bennett grabbed my dishes and his, carrying them ahead of me into the kitchen and setting them in the sink.

"Don't leave them there." I crossed to the sink and turned on the tap. "Why don't you go find Gramps and ask about the walk, and I'll get these put in the dishwasher."

"You don't have—" At my stern look, Bennett stopped what he was going to say and nodded instead. "Yes, ma'am."

I laughed and continued rinsing dishes. There were a few more than just ours already piled up. I went ahead and loaded them since I was there. I was just closing the dishwasher and looking for a hand towel when the door opened from the deck and Linda stepped in.

"You didn't have to do that, but thank you."

"You're welcome." I finally spotted a towel hanging from the oven handle and crossed to it to dry my hands. "You always treat me like family. This is what family does."

"True enough." Linda came to stand in front of me. "I'm so glad you came back to the island. And to Bennett. You complete my son, the way Eve completed Adam. I hope you know that."

I couldn't speak around the lump in my throat, so I nodded.

Linda pulled me into a tight hug.

After a moment, I relaxed into her hug. How long had it been since I'd experienced a mother's comfort? With no strings attached? Probably before the divorce. I couldn't even say that was all Mom's fault though. Just like I'd been unwilling to give church another try, I'd also been holding back from my relationship with her.

Maybe it was time to change that.

Linda released me and stepped back. "I heard you and Bennett were going to walk Dad home. I appreciate it. I offered to drive him, but he had a lot to say about still being spry."

I laughed. "I imagine."

"I just wish I could convince him to move in here. Dave and I would be happy to move to the upstairs master so he could have the one on the main floor. It was always the plan. Or at Deb's, if he preferred. With her needing to pitch in more with Grady now, here makes more sense. Maybe you can see about slipping in a little nudge while you walk? He's always loved you."

"I can't promise it'll be a natural segue, but I'll see what I can do."

"That's all I ask." Linda turned as the door from outside opened and Gramps appeared, grasping both sides of the door-frame. "Dad, are you sure you want to walk home?"

"Stop fussing." Gramps's voice was teasing. He slowly crossed the room, occasionally reaching out to rest a hand on the counter.

Did he have good enough balance for that kind of walk?

"We'll go on the road, not the beach. He'll be okay, Mom. I'll make sure of it. Jericho will help." Bennett pointed at Gramps. "Don't *you* fuss about that. I seem to recall more than once you and Grammie lecturing me about the importance of compromise."

Gramps chuckled. "All right. All right. No need to throw my own words in my face. Since I get to walk with this lovely young woman, I'll just call it a win."

I crossed the handful of steps to Gramps's side and hooked my arm through his elbow before pressing a kiss to his papery cheek. "I consider it a win myself."

"Hear that, Bennie? Better watch out, or I might just scoop her up for myself."

Bennett crossed his arms, a mock scowl on his face. "Really, Gramps? Doesn't that just figure?"

Gramps just grinned and winked at me. "Let's get going. I think it'll be naptime by the time I get home. Tried and true Sunday tradition."

It took a while for us to get out of the house and down to the street. Gramps almost missed three steps on the stairs down to ground level, but between me and Bennett, we managed to avoid any spills. He got a lot steadier when we reached the pavement.

"Mom said she's trying to get you to move in with them."

Bennett took his grandfather's other arm. "How come you're not jumping on it?"

Gramps frowned. "Not one for subtle, are you, boy?"

"Didn't see the point. You're a grownup."

I laughed. "Linda asked me to slide in a nudge. She's really worried about you."

Gramps sighed. "I know it. Truth is, I'm a little worried myself. She told you I took a little tumble, I guess?"

Bennett nodded.

"Not as young as I used to be. Never thought I'd outlive your grandmother, honestly. Or stick around for so many years after she went home to Jesus. I miss her. It's hard to consider giving up the house where we made so many memories. Especially since we'd probably have to sell the place. It isn't as though any of you need a big place to live." Gramps continued his slow shuffle.

"Sell it?" Bennett appeared startled. He shook his head. "We couldn't sell it."

"Can't leave it empty, Bennie. Not good for houses. You know that." Gramps sighed. "But your mom is probably right that it's time. At least I know Rob—or more realistically, Travis—will find someone who will love it the way we did."

"What if I bought it?"

I glanced over at Bennett, my eyebrows lifted. "You have a house."

Bennett shrugged. "It was never supposed to be my permanent home. You know that. We all have lots that we were going to build on. I just hadn't gotten around to it yet."

Was that because of me? We'd sat on the beach up here on the north end of the island, on what Bennett had always said would be ours someday, and built a house in the air together. Bennett had said, more than once, that it was a lot like his grandparents' home.

"Well, now. I'd be fine with that. But you should talk to the family. Figure out what they think. What they expect you should pay. Not market price. I'm firm on that." Gramps shot a steely look at Bennett. "Don't try and tell me that'd be fair. Because we all know it wouldn't."

Bennett frowned, but he nodded. "I'll talk to everyone and let you know."

"Would you be all right with that, missy?" Gramps patted my arm. "You have to know we're all hoping you'll be the one building a future with Bennett here."

"Gramps." Bennett's mutter was barely audible.

I hid a grin. "Maybe I can take a look around when we get you home, just to refresh my memory."

"Good idea. Be nice for someone to walk through the upper stories. Been a while since I've been able to. Linda and Deb always say they will, but my daughters are busy women with families and lives. And that's as it should be. But I suspect there's no small amount of dust that we'll need to get rid of." Gramps tripped a little.

I tightened my hold on his arm. "You okay?"

"Course I am. Although I'm going to end up using that cane Linda bought me. Next thing it'll be one of those fancy, souped-up walkers that make so many old people into a menace."

"You could never be a menace, Gramps." I leaned my head briefly against his shoulder as we finally reached the entrance to his driveway.

"Maybe we could get Mom to let you skip the walker and go straight to a motorized scooter. Then you could zoom around like Grady on his bike." Bennett grinned.

Gramps laughed. "Wouldn't that be a sight?"

I could picture it. Unfortunately, I could also picture him deciding to take it for a spin into town. On the roads. That would be even more of a menace than the golf cart he still, at least according to Bennett, occasionally tried to take into town.

Thankfully, Linda had a good head on her shoulders and wouldn't allow it. And if she couldn't convince him? The family would unleash Deb.

Bennett and I got Gramps up the stairs into his house and settled in his recliner in the great room with a glass of water and a little bowl of pretzels at his side. I waved off his prodding to look around, and promised that I'd be back to do it soon.

When we stepped out on the front deck, Bennett took my hand. "You still up for that walk?"

"Absolutely."

21

BENNETT

I checked the time and started saving the estate documents I'd been working on. It was a slow day and about an hour ago, even though this wasn't one of the days we typically met for lunch, the idea of taking lunch over to the library to share with Jericho had wheedled its way into my mind. I hadn't been able to shake it.

Not that I'd tried all that hard.

I liked being with her. Obviously. Given that we ended up having supper together almost every night, she seemed to feel the same. We'd slid back into the comfortable relationship we'd had all those years ago.

Maybe comfortable was the wrong word. That made it sound boring. And being with Jericho was anything but boring. If I had to choose a word...I might end up at dangerous. If I'd thought being alone together and in love as teenagers had been a challenge, it was nothing compared to now, when there was no threat of someone checking up or barging in.

Was it time to take the next step, or was it too soon?

My office door flew open. Travis strode in and slapped a manila envelope on my desk. "She's doing it."

It didn't take long for me to figure out what my cousin meant. I glanced down at the return address on the package and nodded. "Shut the door and take a seat."

Travis raked a hand through his hair. "I know you said it was probably coming. I *knew* it was probably coming, but when last week went by with nothing, I started hoping maybe she'd needed the money for something else. Maybe there was some hope."

I mentally bade goodbye to a quiet lunch with the woman I loved and watched as my cousin finally closed the door and flopped into a chair. "Did you open it?"

"No. But it's from a lawyer's office. What else is it going to be?"

He had a point. And yet.

I flipped the envelope over and slid my letter opener across the crease of the flap. I set the letter opener aside and withdrew the documents. I took a few moments to scan the cover letter, then flipped through the accompanying pages. Then I set them down and looked at Travis. "She's not asking for a divorce."

Travis tipped his head to one side. "I hear a 'but'."

"It's more like a 'yet.' She wants to establish a legal separation. Reading between the lines, it looks like she's hoping to clarify spousal support so she can set up residency in Oregon. I'll have to do some digging into the laws there, but I'm guessing she thinks it'll be faster to file there than here."

"Can she do that?" Travis pinched the bridge of his nose. "Don't I get a say in this at all? I don't want a divorce."

I sighed. "Not really. We can make it harder, if that's what you want to do, but you can't force her to stay married."

"What about Grady?"

I flipped to the back of the packet and frowned. "She doesn't want him."

Travis blinked at me. "What?"

"They're clearly stating that you have and will maintain sole legal and physical custody, with visitation to be determined at a later date." I folded my hands on the papers. "I don't do a lot of divorces, you know that, but the times I've seen that—or heard about it? The visitation never gets exercised."

"She's abandoning him."

"She already did." I winced. "Sorry. That was unprofessional."

Travis waved it away. "You're right, of course. She did. It's been more than three months since she drove off without a backward glance. I just never thought...but that was naïve."

"No. It was just you being who you are. Optimistic. Willing to give people the benefit of the doubt. Compassionate. And firmly dedicated to your family. You never considered that she'd behave like this because it would never have occurred to you to do it."

Travis snorted. "That makes me sound like a sap."

"Trav."

"Sorry. I'm sorry. This is just—nothing prepares you." He sighed. "What do we do?"

"Couple of options. I think maybe the first, and perhaps best, is for me to reach out to her attorney in person and have a conversation. See if I can figure out what the endgame is. I'll look into Oregon's laws and see if it's worth fighting for jurisdiction. As far as the separation goes, you'd need that in place to divorce in North Carolina anyway." I shrugged. "It doesn't have to be legal, but it doesn't hurt if it is. So we might as well start that clock."

Travis shook his head. "Can't I insist on counseling?"

"I can try. I'm certainly not accepting their initial offer."

"What do you mean?" Travis leaned forward, clearly trying to see the papers. "What did she ask for?"

My stomach knotted. I didn't want to tell him, but he had a

right to know. "An immediate lump sum of six mil, plus a monthly stipend."

Travis's expression went stony. "How much?"

"Fifteen grand."

"A month?" Travis shot to his feet and paced across my office. "Are you serious?"

I picked up the papers and held them out. "You can read it yourself if you want. It's there in black and white."

He held up his hands like he was warding off evil. "I'm good."

"So, yeah. We won't be doing that."

Travis snickered and came back to his chair. "I couldn't if I wanted to."

"I know that. And you know that." I frowned. "Theoretically, she should also know that. But if she wants to try and figure out how to break the trusts Gramps set up, she's welcome to waste her money."

"What money is that, again?" Travis raked a hand through his hair. "Oh, right. My money."

I pointed at him. "And that's another thing I'll inform her attorney about. Now that she's started this process, we'll need to ensure the separation of finances. Her debts are her own. She's no longer a cardholder for any of your accounts. That sort of thing. I'll take care of it."

"Thanks. I don't know how you do this every day."

"If I handled divorces every day, I'd probably lose my mind. Thankfully, that's not the case. You're going to get through this, Travis. You and Grady both. You've got the family one hundred percent in your corner."

"Yeah, I know." He stood. "Is it crazy that I still want us to try to make it work?"

"No. And I'll see if I can work that into the separation. But even if I can make it required for her to show up to therapy, no one can make her participate."

Travis nodded. "Yeah. I know. But it's better than nothing. Isn't it?"

I paused before I answered. Was it? I didn't believe in just walking away from a marriage. It was a covenant between the couple and God, no matter how throw-away the culture today seemed to look at it. At the same time, I wasn't sure I could say that everyone should stay together at all costs. Was there a point when one party was so checked out that it was better all-around to call it quits? "I think you have to try. But keep in mind that it may not matter."

"Oh, I know." His shoulders slumped. "I guess I'll go see the pastor and see if he can recommend some marriage counselors who do telehealth. She won't agree to see him, so I'm not going to push that. But I'd like to at least try to have a say in who we see. Find someone who believes marriages are worth saving."

"All right." I checked the time. "I'm going to call this guy up and we'll go from there. Maybe you can come over tonight and we'll talk?"

"Can it be tomorrow during the day? I'd just as soon not dump this on Grady until I have to. He still asks where she is. Not as much as before, but he misses her."

I bit my lip. Poor kid. "All right. Maybe talk to the pastor about counseling for you and Grady separately."

"That's...not a bad idea. Thanks, Bennett."

I stood and moved around my desk so I could pull my cousin into a hard hug. "We'll get through this. I haven't stopped praying since she left. I'm not stopping now."

Travis stepped back. "Me, either."

When Travis had gone, I picked up the papers and read through them more carefully before swiveling to my computer to get at least a quick understanding of the Oregon divorce laws. It made more sense, to me at least, for this to be under North

Carolina's jurisdiction, but if Caroline had started the process in Oregon, there was probably a reason.

An hour or so later, I picked up the phone and called the other law firm.

By the end of the day, the headache that had started when I first opened the envelope from Caroline's lawyer had intensified. I wanted, more than anything, to go home and lie on the couch in silence. I should follow up with Travis. I should see if he'd found a marriage counselor—not that the attorney in Oregon thought Caroline would go for it. I should see if he'd gotten some ideas for helping Grady process the loss he is experiencing. I should talk to Mom and get her on board with rallying the family. Because we were all going to need to be there for Travis and Grady.

Not that we weren't already. But this felt like it would be long, drawn out, and very painful. Or "high conflict" as they said in the legal world.

Some days, I hated knowing anything about the legal world of divorce.

This was one of them.

I shut down my computer and gathered my things before heading out of the office. The to-do list ping-ponged around in my head, a nice counterpoint to the throbbing of the headache. I tried to shove it all aside. None of those "shoulds" had to be dealt with right now. I'd go home. Take another dose of pain killer. And then see where things stood.

I stopped outside the front door of the office and my shoulders sagged. I'd ridden the motorcycle today. Of course I had. Because it was a beautiful spring day and I hadn't had any plans that would involve needing the car. It wasn't as if I could have prepped for the possibility of a headache at the end of the day.

As I put on my helmet, I tried to come up with a positive spin and came up empty. I was out of optimism. At least for the time being.

Resigned to the inevitability of my headache worsening, I got on the bike, started it, and headed for home.

Even the short distance between my office and home took the headache from awful-but-bearable to curl-in-the-corner-and-whimper. Not that I was going to do that.

Probably.

When I was home, I parked the bike in the garage and headed up the steps to the front door. Inside, I dropped my bag on the floor, kicked off my shoes, and made a beeline for the kitchen cabinet that held my loose attempt at a first aid kit. I grabbed the bottle of painkiller, wrangled off the top with more effort than it should have taken, and shook the single, measly tablet into my hand.

Why was there only one?

I closed my eyes and let my head fall forward to rest on the open cabinet door.

After a moment, I forced myself to the sink to get water and wash down the pill. For all the good it was going to do. Then I crossed to the living room and stretched out on my sofa. I wasn't worried about drifting off—my head hurt too much for that—but maybe I could figure out how to will the pain away.

Across the room, from inside the bag I'd dropped by the door, my phone rang. I closed my eyes. The ringing stopped and, a minute later, the double-buzz sounded indicating a voice mail. I had enough time to let my eyes drift closed again before the ringing started back up.

"Leave me alone." I moaned.

It could be some kind of family emergency. Or it could be one of my brothers or cousins trying to figure out if I wanted to grab dinner. Or it could be Jericho.

I'd texted her to tell her it had been a rough day and I was just heading home, but maybe she was checking up on me? Was I supposed to let her know that I got home safely? I didn't even do that for Mom. Wouldn't she have told me she expected that of me?

Wondering about it wasn't helping my head.

With a sigh that morphed into a groan, I pushed myself up and off the couch so I could cross over and get the phone just as it started ringing a third time.

"Hi, Mom."

"You sound rough, honey. Are you okay?"

"Headache. I'm fine. What's up?" I hit the speaker button as I went back to the couch and swiped down to verify that the two previous calls were both Mom. They were.

"Travis talked to Deb. Deb called me. I think I'm probably caught up, but I wondered what you learned from the Oregon attorney."

"Basically that Caroline is likely to make this as awful as she possibly can because she wants money that she's not entitled to." That was a rough summary, but I didn't feel like getting into all the details right now.

"And Grady?"

I closed my eyes and tried to force my neck and shoulders to relax. "She's adamant that she doesn't want custody. The attorney said she brought up signing away her rights."

Mom made a rude noise.

Despite my headache, I smiled slightly. "Basically, yeah. At least the attorney seems to have explained how unlikely a judge would be to grant that request. And, if the judge did, how it would reflect badly on her in terms of all the other things she was trying to get."

"What a mess." Mom sighed. "How can Dad and I help?"

"Can we talk about it tomorrow? Maybe the two of you can

come in and we can strategize. Right now, my head is killing me and I just want to relax."

"Of course. Sorry. I told Deb I'd find out what I could. Try to get some sleep. Did you eat?"

"Not yet. I'll get to it. I'll see you tomorrow." I ended the call before Mom could respond, then dropped my phone on the coffee table, slung an arm over my eyes, and tried to clear my mind.

22

JERICHO

I pulled open the door to the bookstore and smiled slightly at the cheerful jingle of the bells. There was a homey buzz of chatter that filled the space from the patrons browsing the shelves and queuing up at the café. It was the busiest I'd seen the place since I moved to the island.

I didn't get here as often as I might have liked. I could blame Bennett for that.

Even the thought of him made my lips curve. I wasn't sad about having my free time filled up with him. After our rocky-ish start, we'd found our way back to that solid and happy place where we'd been sixteen years ago.

Sixteen years ago when I'd ruined things. Almost permanently. But for the grace of God.

"Heya, stranger."

I jolted slightly and turned to see Sara grinning at me.

"Sorry. People accuse me of sneaking up, but honestly, it's easy to do around here."

I chuckled. "No worries. Looks like business is booming."

"I never complain about the start of tourist season." Sara paused and tipped her head to the side. "I guess that's not completely true. But I try not to. Sales when we're slammed offset the locals-only months."

"I bet." I glanced over toward the café. "You have seasonal workers, too."

"Yeah. They're locals—high schoolers mostly, but a handful who aren't—and I couldn't do it without them. When it's not busy, I can do it all without anyone having to wait too long. But not when the tourists start. It's a good problem to have." Sara leaned against one of the bookshelves. "How have you been?"

I didn't miss the gleam in her eye that told me she knew all about me and Bennett. I wasn't surprised. The whole island knew—that was the joy of small-town living. It didn't help that Bennett was a Loring, regardless of his actual last name. Lorings on Loring Island were news. I smiled. "I'm good. Things are... really, really good."

Sara laughed and straightened. "So I hear. And I'm glad about it, for the record."

My eyebrows lifted. "Oookay? I mean, thanks, but..."

"Aha. You don't know."

"I don't know what?"

Sara rolled her eyes as she spoke. "Many of the old timers on the island—with the notable exception of Bennett and his family—have been pulling for him and me to get together."

"Oh." I frowned slightly. I couldn't think of any instances when Bennett had shown even the slightest interest in Sara. He was friendly with everyone.

"Hey." She touched my arm. "Totally not interested here. I'm pretty content being single. I have a fulfilling life and honestly? I'm reasonably convinced that marriage isn't what God has for me. Maybe ten years ago I wrestled with that more, but now? Nah. I like where I am in my life."

I nodded. The tension in my gut easing as I sensed the truth of her words. I wasn't generally a jealous or suspicious person, but for a moment, I'd wondered. Why was that?

"Content. I promise." Sara glanced over her shoulder as someone called her name. "Sorry, I—"

"Go. We're good." I smiled to emphasize that I got it. Conversations during working hours were never uninterrupted. And I hadn't come in here for that, anyway. Not that I minded chatting with her. I liked Sara. But mostly, since hanging out with Bennett wasn't on the table, I didn't want to go home and rattle around aimlessly.

I wove through the books until I reached the science fiction and fantasy shelves. There were a few new titles I wanted to get for the library, but I wanted to read them myself first. I liked to be able to offer recommendations. I'd also had a few patrons asking about sweet romance, so I needed to dig into that as well. I had a decent feel for Christian romance, but there were books out there without faith content that might be good to add in as well. A lot of it was from authors who self-published, but I didn't have a problem getting those books in. The days of big corporations gatekeeping fiction were, thankfully, on the decline. Sara stocked some of those indie books, too.

Were there ways she and I could do some cross promotion?

I'd have to ponder that.

I found the title I was looking for and pulled out a copy, then flipped it over to read the back.

"There you are."

I glanced up and grinned at Bennett's mom. "Here I am."

Linda chuckled. "I should have called, but I figured I could hunt you down just as easily."

I cocked my head to the side, a little niggle of worry starting to twist in my belly. "Is everything okay?"

"Oh. Yes. Or at least, it's nothing life threatening." She huffed out a breath. "Did you talk to Bennett today?"

"Not really. He texted to let me know he was busy and then again that he was going home with a headache. Why?"

"That child." Linda frowned. "I'm overstepping. I will one hundred percent admit that. So, if you ignore my suggestion I will absolutely understand. But I think, despite what he said, Bennett could really use your company this evening. Especially if you took him food. He promised he'd eat, but I don't think he will."

"I'm happy to take him some food. But..." I sighed. "I don't want him to think I can't respect his need for alone time. I don't want to be the clingy girlfriend who can't deal with time apart."

"You really are perfect for him."

"Thanks. He's pretty perfect for me, too."

Linda beamed at me. "I guess, since I'm already meddling, I'll go farther out on the limb and say this—don't let him stall too long. I know my son, and he's going to overthink things with you if you let him. Don't let him."

I scooted out of the way to let another book browser pass by us, then looked at Linda. "What do you mean?"

"The two of you were basically engaged the summer before your senior year. And while I don't have all of the details—nor do I need them, because that's for you and Bennett—I have enough of them to know that you didn't disappear because you stopped loving my son."

"No. That wasn't why."

She laid her hand on my arm. "He never stopped loving you, either. And now, you're back together. And you still love each other. It's like you picked right back up where you'd left off. So don't let him drag things out for too long before you start your lives together."

How was I supposed to respond to that? She meant well. That was obvious. Linda was a wonderful mother who, as a rule, didn't interfere in her children's lives. She had embraced them as adults. I'd seen the start of that process all those summers ago.

Bennett and I had talked about marriage. Family. All those things. We both agreed they were things we still wanted for us. I figured that was the end of that conversation. Now, it was just a matter of time for him to propose. Then we'd take that next step into the rest of our lives.

Would he really overthink so much that we'd end up wasting even more time than we already had?

"I flummoxed you." Linda winced. "I'm sorry. Start with some supper, then see where things go. You could talk to him about Gramps's house, if you needed a conversation opener."

"What about Gramps's house?" I was close to getting whiplash from this conversation.

"Hm. I was under the impression you'd been there when he talked about buying it."

"I was. He was going to talk to the family." What did that have to do with me? I wasn't part of the family—yet. "Oh. I'm on board with him moving there, if that was your question. It's a gorgeous home."

"I'm glad to hear that. Talk to Bennett. The soup here is good, if you haven't tried it. Probably just the thing for someone with a headache." Linda winked. "I'll let you get on with your evening."

"It was nice to see you." The response was more rote than something I truly felt. Not that it had been bad to see her, but now I had all these questions and no idea how to answer any of them. I looked down at the paperback in my hand and sighed. I put it back on the shelf and made my way to the café.

The line had grown while I was chatting with Linda, so I had to wait a few minutes to place a to-go order. Then it took another handful of minutes to pick up the order and pay. It was good. I liked seeing the town coming to life again as the beach-seekers came for their vacations and the seasonal residents moved back for the spring and summer.

Carrying a paper bag with dinner for two, I tossed a wave in Sara's direction as I left the bookstore and headed down to where I'd left my car. There were enough people out and about that I couldn't make my usual U-turn out of my parking spot, so I had to box around the block to get headed back toward the beach and Bennett's.

The sun was just setting and the glimpses of orange and yellow in my mirrors as I headed out of town almost convinced me to pull over and give it a proper look. But the soup and sandwiches were warm, and I'd just as soon they stayed that way. If only because it would be more convincing that this was a whim if I showed up with hot food.

It wasn't long before I pulled into the driveway of Bennett's cottage. I didn't see any lights on inside. I drummed my fingers on the steering wheel. Should I bother him? What if he'd already gone to bed? Maybe I should just go home and eat. I could have leftovers for lunch tomorrow.

Before I could make up my mind, the porch light turned on, and the door opened. Bennett stepped out on the deck. He leaned against the door frame with a slight smile.

At least he didn't look mad.

I turned off the engine and got out of the car with the bag of food. I closed the car door and paused, "Hey."

"Hey." He nodded toward the bag. "Whatcha got?"

"Italian wedding soup and caprese paninis." The combo had sounded really good to me when I saw it on the café menu.

"Enough for two?"

"Absolutely."

"Come on in." He straightened and went back inside.

Maybe not the most gracious invitation, but it was still an invitation. I climbed the steps and followed him in, taking a moment to close the door behind me and step out of my shoes. I nudged them toward the wall, where his shoes and work bag sat in a heap.

"How are you feeling?" I crossed to the kitchen and set the bag on the island.

Bennett got down two glasses and filled them with ice at the fridge. "A little better. Pain killer is kicking in, at least. Iced tea okay?"

"Sure. Thanks. I can get it."

"It's not a problem." But he didn't move to fill them.

I stepped closer and took the glasses out of his hands, then set them on the counter. I moved in, wrapping my arms around him and resting my head on his shoulder.

His arms came around me and tightened. After a moment, he rested his cheek on the top of my head and sighed.

I closed my eyes, enjoying the peace that always came with being close to Bennett. He was home.

"I'm glad you came by. I didn't realize how much I needed this." He kissed the top of my head and eased back. "And the headache has faded enough that I'm hungry."

I chuckled. "Then I'm just in time to save you from PB&J."

"You know me too well." He opened the fridge and got out the pitcher of iced tea.

"Your mom found me at the bookstore. She suggested that taking you at your word wasn't the right play. I guess I'm glad I listened. I was worried you'd be mad." I opened the paper bag and pulled out the tub of soup and the two wrapped sandwiches. Both were still plenty hot.

Bennett brought the tea over and set a glass next to each spot at the island. "Not mad. Grateful."

"I love you." I looked up and held his gaze for two heartbeats before I stepped around him to get plates and bowls out of the cupboards.

He reached up and around me to get to the bowls before I could. I turned and he nudged closer so I bumped against the counter and his body pressed against mine. He lowered his mouth to mine and the kiss left me breathless. He stepped away, one corner of his mouth poking up. "I love you, too."

I grabbed plates and followed him to the island, then went around to take a seat. I pried off the lid of the tub of soup and poured half into each bowl. Bennett retrieved spoons, then came to sit next to me. I unwrapped the sandwiches and put one on his plate and the other on mine.

"This smells incredible." Bennett leaned closer to the food and inhaled deeply. "I don't think I've seen paninis on the menu before."

"I hadn't either. The guy working the counter said they were new this month."

He took my hand and squeezed it. "I'll pray."

I closed my eyes and tried to focus on Bennett's words of thanks for the food instead of the mouth-watering smells and the little zips of electricity running between us. I mostly succeeded. I echoed his quiet "amen" and reached for my spoon.

"Did Mom give you the details?" Bennett picked up half of his sandwich and dipped a corner into his soup.

"No. She just said she thought you'd do better with company and food than alone. I know you can't talk about it, if it's work." I spooned up soup and blew across it before taking a bite.

"It's also family." Bennett bit off the dipped corner of his panini. "Mmm. This is good."

I tried to connect the dots in my mind. Family plus something that required an attorney plus a headache probably wasn't related to Bennett taking over Gramps's house or Gramps moving in with Linda. "Travis?"

"Travis." He sighed and picked up his spoon. "Caroline has a lawyer in Oregon. I talked to the guy and he seems to be exactly the kind of soulless shark I would imagine her hiring."

"I thought you liked her?" I reached for my sandwich and took a bite.

"I tried to. Because I love Travis and Grady. Most of the time, I managed it. But since she just took off at the start of the year? It's been a lot harder to keep up the pretense." He rubbed his forehead.

"We don't have to talk about it."

Bennett ate a few more bites. He set down his spoon. "It's all preliminary right now. I think she was testing the waters to see how much she can get away with. Because her attorney made it clear that Caroline was divorcing a billionaire, so obviously the billionaire should have to pay. A lot."

"Billionaire?" I'd always known Bennett had money. His family was the Loring family of Loring Island. And his parents were both lawyers. As was he. But I'd never made the jump from multi-millionaire to billions.

"Technically. Unfortunately for Caroline, most of it is tidily tied up in family trusts that she won't be able to touch. It's honestly a big deal for any of us to touch it. On purpose." He tipped his head to the side. "Does that matter?"

"Not to me." I reached for his hand. "I love you, not your wallet."

He leaned over and kissed my cheek.

"I'm sorry for Travis. And Grady. I'll keep praying for them."

"Pray for Caroline, too."

I winced. That was the right thing to do, obviously, but it wasn't one I'd been doing. I hadn't had the chance to meet her. That was the excuse I'd made, when I bothered to ask myself why she wasn't on my list. But in reality, I had a hard time praying for someone who could walk away from her child. Caroline. My dad. Even, to some extent, my mom. Though Mom hadn't physically left, she'd been mentally absent for a lot of years. "Right."

"She needs prayer too. God can save their marriage."

I raised my eyebrows. "Would Travis want her back after this?"

"Pretty sure he would. Wouldn't it be better for Grady?"

I shook my head. "Not if she doesn't want to be there."

"That's a point. But I also still believe God can heal the situation and make something wonderful out of it. He brought you back to me."

"He did. And it's wonderful." I finished the first half of my sandwich. I didn't need to eat the other half right now. Or the rest of my soup. I grabbed the paper and wrapped the sandwich back up. "While your mom was nudging me this way, she said I should talk to you about Gramps's house."

He laughed. "Wow. She's not usually a meddler, but I guess she was in a mood."

"You don't have to—"

"It's good. I was working my way around to it anyway." He lifted his bowl and drained the last bit of his soup, then glanced at my bowl. "Are you going to finish that?"

I nudged it toward him. "Help yourself."

"Thanks." He grinned and dipped his spoon in. "The family all agree that it's fine for me to take over the house and, since my lot that I haven't built on yet is right beside the house, I can just absorb the land into one parcel. I haven't decided if I'll sell this place or make it a rental."

That had been the best-case scenario he'd mentioned when we talked about it a week ago after walking Gramps home. "That's great!"

Bennett turned in his seat so he was facing me. He took both my hands and held my gaze. "It is. But only if you'll be happy living there with me. This isn't how I was thinking I'd do this. I hadn't actually gotten around to figuring that out, if we're honest. But I want to build a life with you, Jericho. Raise a family and add to the next generations of Lorings. And I guess, somewhere in the middle of wading through the mess of Travis's marriage, I realized it was dumb to wait. There's no perfect timing, and I don't want to waste another minute. Marry me?"

I stared at him for a moment torn between near-hysterical laughter and the urge to cry. His mother apparently hadn't needed to urge me to nudge him along on this point. Which was good, because I wasn't positive I could have pulled off being the one to propose. Then I smiled.

"I want all of that too. I'll marry you. I'll build that life and raise our family with you in our house by the sea." I leaned in to meet Bennett's lips with my own.

EPILOGUE

Christian

Easter Sunday, One Month Later

I stood on the deck and looked out over Mom and Dad's back yard where Grady was running around with a basket looking for eggs. His dog, Squirtle, was leaping and bouncing around as if it was the best game ever. Travis was giving hot and cold hints to help steer his son toward the various hidden goodies.

A flash of light caught my eye and I turned, then chuckled to myself. "That's some bling you've got on your finger there, Jericho."

Jericho laughed and held out her left hand to show off Grammie's engagement ring. "Isn't it the most gorgeous thing you've ever seen?"

"You're the most gorgeous thing I've ever seen." Bennett grabbed Jericho and swung her to his side, holding her close. He kissed her cheek. "Mom's talking about putting dessert out soon."

"Ugh." I patted my over-stuffed belly. "She's got to be kidding. There's no way any of us need dessert yet."

Bennett shrugged. "That's what she was telling Austin when I walked through the kitchen. If you want to change her mind, you should go tell her."

"I'm going to do that." I shook my head and turned to head inside. I paused to hug Gramps as I passed by where he was ensconced on a deck chair in the sun so he could be in the middle of everything without needing to move from one place to another. He patted my hand.

Dad and Aunt Deb and Uncle Rob sipped drinks at the big table. Mom's chair was scooted out at an angle beside Dad's. Water dripped down the side of her abandoned glass of iced tea.

I strode through the open door into the kitchen. Mom was putting out a stack of dessert plates.

"It's too soon for dessert, Mom." I came around the counter and slung my arm over her shoulder. "You should be out on the deck enjoying the afternoon still."

"Austin said he was snacky. And his brothers hollered from the game room that they could eat." Mom shrugged. "I can set things out. Nothing will get hurt from a little time on the counter. And this way, I can take Gramps his first choice before all the locust bellies of my sons and their cousins hoover it all up."

I grinned. "We're not that bad."

Mom snorted. "Tell me that when it's you doing the cooking."

My phone rang, cutting off my chance to reply. I dug it out of my pocket and answered, mouthing "Sorry" to mom before stepping away. "This is Christian."

"Oh. I thought...is this the Loring Clinic?" The woman on the other end of the line sounded like she was barely holding it together.

"It is. How can I help you?" I pushed past the sinking feeling in my gut. I'd hoped to spend one holiday this year without having to go into the clinic for something. Apparently, it wasn't going to be Easter. I reminded myself to be grateful we had a clinic on the island. People with minor injuries didn't have to truck across the bridge to get help. And I could triage major injuries as needed while the island's part-time emergency services got things moving.

"I...are you inside? I don't see lights on."

"No, ma'am. But I can be there in five minutes. Hang tight, all right? I'm on my way." I ended the call. "Sorry, Mom. I've gotta run."

"Never worry about that, honey. I'll be praying."

I shot mom a smile and rushed out to my car, grateful I'd ignored the desire to walk from home. It wasn't far, but it would have turned five minutes into at least ten. Even driving, I'd have to break the speed limit to make good on my time estimate. Thankfully, the police were pretty forgiving when they saw it was me. They'd check it out, which they should, but when they verified it was a clinic call, they gave me some leeway.

I zipped south and turned west at the lighthouse onto the road that would take me into town. I slowed as I entered the town proper, more out of necessity than desire. There were a lot of families out strolling. Church this morning had been packed to the walls with visitors. The tourist season was well under way.

I pulled into my reserved parking spot eight minutes after I ended the call. Oops. I got out of the car in a hurry, already digging into my pocket for the keys. I looked around, my gaze finally landing on a woman on the bench near our door. She was holding one hand over her eye.

"Ma'am? Did you call the clinic?"

She looked up at me. "Yes. I...maybe I shouldn't have. It's not a big deal."

I tipped my head to the side and offered a friendly smile. “Let’s go inside and I’ll take a look. Can’t hurt, right?”

She looked over her shoulder and seemed to hunch in on herself.

I fought to keep from frowning. “I’m Christian Thomas. I’m the nurse practitioner here. Will you tell me your name?”

“Teresa.” Her voice was a whisper.

I held out my hand. “Nice to meet you, Teresa.”

She eyed my hand for a moment, then stood and removed her hand from over her eye so she could shake mine. The deep gash over her eyebrow looked to have stopped bleeding, but it would need stitches, and if her nose wasn’t broken, I’d be amazed.

I didn’t comment on either though. Not yet. “Come on in. I’ll get you some ice.”

Teresa shot a furtive glance around, then finally nodded. “All right. Can...can you lock the door behind us?”

“Absolutely. I’m here to help.”

I unlocked the door and waited for her to go in, then I pulled it shut behind me and twisted the deadbolt. “Let’s head back to the exam room and you can tell me what happened.”

I picked up a clipboard from the front desk, then led the way to the door that opened into our main exam area. I flipped on the light.

“You can’t write anything down.” Teresa hovered near the door. “He can’t know I said anything.”

“Our records are confidential.” But I set the clipboard back down. “Let’s take care of that gash.”

Hesitantly, Teresa went into the exam room. When she passed close, I couldn’t help but notice that—under the swelling and bruises—she was a beautiful woman. My gaze flicked to her left hand. No ring. But that didn’t mean that someone hadn’t done this to her. Nurses weren’t supposed to make assumptions.

But we could—and should—still use our brains. An accident could have caused Teresa's injuries, but I didn't think so. Most people weren't skittish like this after an accident. And if I knew one thing right off the bat, it was that Teresa was scared.

And for whatever reason, every one of my protective instincts had just kicked in.

ACKNOWLEDGMENTS

This book has been a long time coming. Grief, y'all. It's hard. I feel like I owe every single one of you (and every single person in my real life) the biggest apology. Except they (and I imagine you) have been and continue to give me so much grace. Because they get it.

Still.

Thank you.

I'd be remiss if I didn't also publicly state how grateful I am to Jesus for carrying me through the loss of my sister. And the last 18 months of her being gone. And all that her death brought up again from the death of my mom. Because without Him? I couldn't have done it.

And I know it's not done. I know it's a foreverish kind of thing. But it's getting easier every day. And that's Jesus.

Thanks as ever to my beta readers and writer friends. And my editor (and bestie) Katie Hauquitz. Love y'all. So much.

And once again, thank you to you - my readers - whether you're new here or have been along with me on this journey since 2013 (!!) -- I couldn't do this without you.

WANT A FREE BOOK?

If you enjoyed this book and would like to read another of my books for free, you can get a free e-book simply by signing up for my newsletter on my website.

OTHER BOOKS BY ELIZABETH MADDREY

Beachfront Billionaires

Second Chance at the Seaside

Married at the Marina

Billionaire Next Door

The Billionaire's Nanny

The Billionaire's Best Friend

The Billionaire's Secret Crush

The Billionaire's Backup

The Billionaire's Teacher

The Billionaire's Wife

Postcards, A Novel

So You Want to Be a Billionaire

So You Want a Second Chance

So You Love to Hate Your Boss

So You Love Your Best Friend's Sister

So You Have My Secret Baby

So You Need a Fake Relationship

So You Forgot You Love Me

Hope Ranch Series

Hope for Christmas

Hope for Tomorrow

Hope for Love

Hope for Freedom

Hope for Family

Hope at Last

Peacock Hill Romance Series

A Heart Restored

A Heart Reclaimed

A Heart Realigned

A Heart Redirected

A Heart Rearranged

A Heart Reconsidered

Arcadia Valley Romance – Baxter Family Bakery Series

Loaves & Wishes

Muffins & Moonbeams

Cookies & Candlelight

Donuts & Daydreams

The 'Operation Romance' Series

Operation Mistletoe

Operation Valentine

Operation Fireworks

Operation Back-to-School

The 'Taste of Romance' Series

A Splash of Substance

A Pinch of Promise

A Dash of Daring

A Handful of Hope

A Tidbit of Trust

The 'Grant Us Grace' Series

Wisdom to Know

Courage to Change

Serenity to Accept

Pathway to Peace

Joint Venture

The 'Remnants' Series:

Faith Departed

Hope Deferred

Love Defined

Stand alones

Kinsale Kisses: An Irish Romance

Luna Rosa (part of A Tuscan Legacy)

Her Billionaire Benefactor (part of the Easter in Gilead series)

For the most recent listing of all my books, please visit my website.

ABOUT THE AUTHOR

USA Today bestselling author Elizabeth Maddrey is a semi-reformed computer geek and homeschooling mother of two who lives in the suburbs of Washington D.C. When she isn't writing, Elizabeth is a voracious consumer of books. She loves to write about Christians who struggle through their lives, dealing with sin and receiving God's grace on their way to their own romantic happily ever after.

facebook.com/ElizabethMaddrey
instagram.com/ElizabethMaddrey
amazon.com/Elizabeth-Maddrey/e/B00A11QGME
bookbub.com/authors/elizabeth-maddrey
youtube.com/@ElizabethMaddreyAuthor

www.ingramcontent.com/pod-product-compliance
Lightning Source LLC
Chambersburg PA
CBHW031613240626
47153CB00002B/747
9781947525207